ALSO BY MICHAEL McGARRITY

Serpent Gate
Tularosa
Mexican Hat

For information regarding special discounts for bulk purchases, please contact Simon & Schuster Special Sales at 1-800-456-6798 or business@simonandschuster.com

TULAROSA

MICHAEL McGARRITY

POCKET BOOKS

New York London Toronto Sydney Tokyo Singapore

This book is a work of fiction. Names, characters, places and
incidents are products of the author's imagination or are used
fictitiously. Any resemblance to actual events or locales or persons,
living or dead, is entirely coincidental.

 POCKET BOOKS, a division of Simon & Schuster Inc.
1230 Avenue of the Americas, New York, NY 10020

Copyright © 1996 by Michael McGarrity

Published by arrangement with W.W. Norton & Company, Inc.

ISBN: 0-671-00252-X

First Pocket Books printing April 1997

10 9 8 7 6 5 4 3

POCKET and colophon are registered trademarks of
Simon & Schuster Inc.

Cover art by Kazuhiko Sano

Printed in the U.S.A.

In memory of Maggie,
who taught me the meaning of perseverance,
and for Mimi and Sean, who always believed,
and HH, who helped me find the key.

Author's Note

Many of the historical events, people, and places described in this book are based on fact, while some are pure fiction or an elaboration of legend. *Tularosa* in Spanish means reddish reeds or willows.

TULAROSA

CHAPTER

1

Early-morning clouds, shreds of a heavy late-night rainstorm, masked the Ortiz Mountains. Wispy tendrils drifted over the foothills, turned into translucent streamers, and vanished in the sky. The cabin roof had leaked during the night, soaking a stack of unopened junk mail and the borrowed copy of a Winston Churchill biography left on the cushion of an easy chair. The chair smelled like wet cat piss, and Kerney didn't own a cat.

Kerney mopped up the floor, dragged the chair outside into the sun, and tipped it over. The junk mail and catalogs dribbled into a brown puddle in the driveway, floated momentarily, and sank out of sight. The cover model on the Victoria's Secret

1

catalog pouted up at him as the brown stain seeped into her eyes.

The saffron sun in the east, an extravagant eye, washed the mesa in soft light. Inside, Kerney popped the Tchaikovsky tape in the cassette desk and cranked up the volume. The music, pushed along by a slight breeze, followed him to the horse barn, where a gallon of roof asphalt sat next to the ladder, both conveniently at hand for the leaks that never failed to materialize after a soaking, wind-blown rain. He had patched the roof so many times it was now nothing more than a routine challenge. Given a few more storms, every seam, nail hole, and protrusion on the pitched roof would be coated with asphalt gook.

The old cabin wanted to sink into oblivion. Listing on a stone foundation, it was pretty to the eye, with a fresh coat of white paint and dark green trim around the windows and doors, but sadly in need of major renovation.

Kerney strapped on a tool belt, deciding he would pull up the whole strip of roofing paper and slop gook directly on the boards over the leak. He carried the ladder to the cabin, set it against the side of the house, and stripped off his shirt. With the asphalt can in one hand, Kerney hauled himself up the ladder, dragging his right leg slowly to each rung. The knee just didn't bend the way it used to, in spite of the best efforts of modern medicine.

He nailed a two-by-four to the roof to serve as a brace, crawled off the ladder, and planted his left foot against the brace to keep from sliding back-ward. In position, he stretched out on his stomach and got to work with the hammer pulling nails and stripping off the tar paper in the area of the leak. His reconstructed right knee, extended as far as it would go, protested.

The planks under the tar paper had separated, leaving an inch gap between the boards. He smeared asphalt into the crevices and on the boards, thinking it was time to ask his landlord to spring for the cost of materials for a new roof. Quinn would oblige, and Kerney would have another project to occupy his time.

The Tchaikovsky concerto recycled several times on the stereo before Kerney finished the patch job. He renailed the tar paper, coated the nail heads with gook, and looked out over the basin. There was a flash of reflected light on the dirt road that cut through the rock escarpment to the ranch. The road, still filled with runoff from the storm, glistened like a wire ribbon in the sharp morning light. He dropped the empty asphalt can to the ground and climbed down the ladder, using his left leg to hop from rung to rung. He walked to the gate and swung it open, leaving sticky black fingerprints on the railing, and watched the vehicle bounce in and out of the ruts of standing water, spewing mud as the tires dug through the puddles. There was no reason for a visitor. Quinn, his landlord, employer, and chief book lender, was presenting a paper at a medical convention in Seattle. After that, he was flying to Germany to attend another conference and take a long vacation. Kerney liked working for a wandering landlord. Most of the time he had the place to himself.

The car splattered through the mud and swerved through the slimy dirt in the roadbed, the tires throwing up a heavy spray of brown paste. Wind-shield wipers, operating at high speed, smeared the ooze over the glass, making it impossible for Kerney to see into the vehicle.

He walked to the porch, sat on the step, and started cleaning the asphalt gook from his hands with a rag drenched in paint thinner. The fumes of the solvent made him sneeze, and he covered his nose with sticky fingers. Before he could go in and clean his face, the car plowed through the last puddle by the gate and rolled to a stop on the packed gravel driveway. It was a new, slick-top police cruiser with emergency lights mounted on the front bumper. Even close up, with the wipers going full blast, the man behind the wheel was obscured by a grimy film of dirt. In Kerney's time at the ranch—well over a year—this was the first visit by a cop.

A stocky man in a white uniform shirt got out and stood behind the open door of the cruiser, with the engine still running. He wore a tribal police badge over the left pocket of the uniform shirt and a Sam Browne belt with a .357 pistol in a high-rise holster. From the waist down he wore blue jeans and cowboy boots.

The two men stared at each other across the ten yards that separated them.

"Goddamn mud," Terry Yazzi muttered, reaching in to turn off the engine.

Kerney stood up and said nothing as Terry left the car and walked toward him. In the cabin the tape deck recycled once again and the lyrical first move-ment of the concerto began anew.

Terry stopped three feet from Kerney, his eyes avoiding contact. Instead, he looked at the fore-

4

man's cabin, a white clapboard box with a small covered porch, then switched his gaze to the ranch house behind it, nestled at the base of a mesa. He took in the horse barn and corral off to one side across a small meadow, and the upended chair in front of the cabin porch.

He compressed his lips and finally looked at Kerney. As he opened his mouth to speak, Kerney hit him flush on the jaw, knocking him flat on his ass.

The blow made Terry's teeth ache. He got to his feet and brushed himself off. "Feel better?" he asked.

"No. I hurt my hand," Kerney replied. "What are you doing here, Terry?"

Terry's face had a healthy glow. His brown eyes were clear and serious. He had shed some weight and looked fit. Three years could bring changes.

"I asked you a question," Kerney said. God, he wanted to hit him again.

"I heard you," Terry answered.

He glanced at Kerney's naked stomach, turned away, and looked out at the expanse of the Galisteo Basin, trying hard to regain his composure. The land rolled down from the ranch through thickly studded stands of piñon and juniper trees. It gave way to rangeland that butted against an escarpment that looked almost like an enormous, ancient man-made fortification.

He took it in indifferently, and swallowed hard to keep down the bile that welled up in his mouth from the sight of the scar on Kerney's stomach. The ugly entry wound and the long surgical incision brought the memory smashing into his head like a freight

5

train. In spite of himself, he remembered the day three years ago at the stakeout. The image of Kerney curled into a ball clutching his gut as the blood came gushing out made Terry wince.

He turned around and glanced at the scar again. "You've got some tar on your face," he said finally, raising his eyes.

"Really?"

"Yeah. Around your nose and mouth."

"No shit?" Kerney rubbed his nose and inspected his fingertip. "You're right. Thanks for pointing it out. Now go away, Terry."

Terry stared back at him. His long, black hair, tied back at the nape of his neck, accentuated his Navajo features: a high forehead above dark brown eyes and round cheeks. His tense lips were pressed thin. Kerney wondered how long it would be before Terry stared at the scar again. It gave him a perverse sense of satisfaction.

"Did you get my letter?" Terry finally asked, shifting his gaze back to the scar.

"Letter? Let me check." Kerney walked to the puddle, retrieved the soggy envelopes, and pulled apart the coagulated mess until he found Terry's unopened letter. He held it up by the corner. "This must be it," he said, dropping it back in the puddle. "What did it say?"

"You're still really pissed, aren't you?"

"Not at all. I just don't give a damn."

Terry rubbed his jaw. "You punch pretty hard for somebody who doesn't care."

"I appreciated the opportunity to deck you. Why are you here?"

"It's Sammy. He's missing. He's AWOL from the Army."

Kerney took in the information, his anger at Terry dissipating as concern about Sammy rose to replace it. Terry's son was a person he cared about. "That's hard to believe."

"He's been stationed at White Sands for the past eight months. He disappeared six weeks ago. I've used up all my annual leave looking for him, *por nada.* Nothing. And the Army hasn't a clue why he's missing."

"Maria must be worried sick."

"Both of us are," Terry said. "We want you to find him for us."

Kerney's laugh was bitter. "I don't do that kind of work anymore."

"Listen, as far as the Army is concerned, Sammy is just another enlisted fuckup. All I got was a lot of bullshit about how I should go home and let them do their job. I was stonewalled at every turn."

"What makes you think I'd be treated any differently?"

"You won't be, but you're the best investigator I know. It's in your blood. You've got the right instincts."

"Is that so?"

Terry shook his head at the sarcasm in Kerney's voice. "I'm not trying to butter you up. I'm a street cop, not a detective. Sammy deserves better than what I can give."

Kerney said nothing for a minute. "I've never heard you sound so modest. Have you stopped drinking?"

"I've been sober for two years." Terry tried to force himself to keep his attention off Kerney's stomach. It didn't work. He looked one more time.

"Like it?" Kerney asked. "Wallace Stegner once wrote that the lessons of life amount to scar tissue."

Terry shifted his weight uneasily. "It makes me want to puke. You should have fired my ass."

"I would have," Kerney agreed, "if you had told me the truth."

Terry nodded in agreement. "That too."

"Don't start apologizing," Kerney retorted, "or *I'll* start to puke." He pointed at the badge on Terry's shirt and changed the subject. "I see you found another job after the department canned your ass."

"Maria pulled strings with the tribal council. I had to go through treatment before I could start the job. I'm on like a permanent probation. One drink or major fuckup and I'm fired."

Kerney weighed Terry's words. He sounded solid and straight. And it took some courage for him to show his face, Kerney thought. "I hope it works out for you," he said, with as much enthusiasm as he could muster.

"I'll make it work. Find Sammy for me," he insisted.

"I can't help you." Kerney turned and walked into the cabin, letting the screen door slam behind him.

"Can't or won't?" Terry called out over the concerto's cadenza.

In the bathroom Kerney scrubbed ferociously with a washcloth to get the asphalt off his face, cursing to himself under his breath. He heard the screen door slam shut again over the strains of the final coda, threw the cloth into the basin of the sink, and went back into the living room to kick Terry out of his house. One look at Terry, legs rooted to the floor, told him he'd have to drag him out inch by inch.

He walked to the tape deck and turned it off. Silence flooded the room. "You're a persistent son of a bitch," he said.

"Sammy's my only child. You're his godfather, for chrissake. Don't hold my fuckups against him." Terry squinted, looked away, and ground his teeth together to keep himself from begging. If it came to that, he'd do it. He took a breath and surveyed the room. It was sparsely furnished. Two old Navajo rugs, the sum total of Kerney's inheritance from his family, hung on the walls. A single bookshelf under a casement window held a television, radio, stereo, and some hardback books. A wrought-iron café table with a glass top and a matching chair stood to one side of the kitchen door, positioned for the view out a front window. It was as bleak as Terry's trailer; a far cry from the comfortable Santa Fe apartment Kerney had once shared with his girlfriend, now long gone.

"Get out of here, Terry," Kerney ordered.

Terry unbuttoned his uniform shirt, extracted an envelope, and held it out. "I'll pay for your time. Five thousand dollars."

Kerney didn't touch the envelope. "You don't have that kind of money."

"Banks do," Terry responded, thrusting the envelope closer. "I borrowed it."

Kerney plucked the envelope out of Terry's hand and opened the unsealed flap. It was stuffed with hundred-dollar bills. He felt the weight of the currency in his palm. Kerney waved the envelope at him. "Guilt money, Terry?"

Terry glared at him. "No way."

"I could spend it all and find nothing."

"I'll get more if you use it up."

Kerney stuffed the envelope into the pocket of his jeans. "Tell me everything you learned at the missile range."

Terry gestured at the door. "I've got a file in the squad car. It's slim pickings."

"Let's see it," Kerney said, following Terry outside. The New Mexico sky was piercing blue and the air felt humid with the promise of more rain. The volcanic escarpment that blocked the highway from view sat under a cloud, the jagged points of the rift vague in the distance. Terry moved quickly to his squad car, reached in through the open door, and retrieved a folder.

Kerney took it. "I'll get started right away."

"You don't know how much I appreciate this."

Kerney didn't respond. Head down, he leafed through the papers, scanning them quickly.

"Kevin?"

Kerney turned away. "I'll be in touch."

"When Sammy came to see you . . . before he went into the Army . . . I mean, what was that about?"

"He wanted to ask my opinion about enlisting. I told him to blow it off and go to college."

"Did he tell you what I said?"

"As a matter of fact he did. It seems you preached the gospel of Duty, Honor, and Country."

"Stupid," Terry muttered. "If anything happened

to him because of what I said . . ." He shook off the thought.

"Don't get ahead of yourself," Kerney cautioned. He closed the file and nestled it under his arm. "Did you develop any leads off the base?"

"No. Sammy stayed pretty close to the post. He spent some time in Las Cruces, but as far as I can tell he wasn't into the bar scene or doing a lot of skirt chasing."

"Was he having any personal problems?" Kerney asked.

"None that he talked about with me or his mother. Maria would have known if he was bummed out, or in a bind. She has a kind of radar about Sammy that way. His buddies I talked to drew a blank when I asked if he was in any trouble."

"Are you and Maria back together?"

"Not a chance."

"Still living in the same place?"

Terry nodded.

"Same phone number?"

Terry nodded again.

"I'll be in touch."

Terry handed him a business card. "Leave a message at the office if I'm not at home."

Kerney studied the card. "Okay, Chief," he said, slipping it into the folder.

The sarcasm stung. "Why didn't you finish kicking the shit out of me?"

Kerney laughed. "You'd let me do that?"

"No way," Terry replied. He got in the police car, closed the door, rolled down the window, and started the engine. The two men looked at each other.

"Thanks," Terry said.

"I'm doing this for Sammy, not for you."

"I know it."

Kerney watched the man responsible for his early retirement bounce the police cruiser down the ruts of the road. Three years ago he'd been chief of detectives for the Santa Fe Police Department. The first year after the shooting he'd been in and out of the hospital for reconstructive surgery on his knee and stomach, followed by a rehabilitation program that took every ounce of his willpower to complete, and put him in the best shape of his life, except for the patched-up gut and bum leg he had to live with.

Terry had it easy as far as Kerney could tell. Alcoholism was a reversible disease. Moreover, drunk or sober, Terry had managed to stay a cop; which was now something beyond Kerney's reach.

He touched the throbbing scar on his stomach. Too much stretching in the wrong direction on the roof, he decided. As the cruiser pulled slowly through the mud at the end of the road, Kerney halfway hoped Terry would get stuck and have to call for a tow. He wanted the pleasure of watching him sitting in mud over the hubcaps, just for the spite of it. No such luck. Terry passed around the escarpment where the dirt road met the highway and drove out of sight.

Back in the cabin, Kerney sat at the table and tried to read the file, but his mind kept wandering to the money in the envelope. He put the file down and counted the bills. The five thousand dollars matched what Kerney had in a bank account. His dream since coming to the ranch had been to lease acreage from

Quinn, buy some good cattle stock, and get into ranching in some small way. There were two thousand acres of prime rangeland, unused except as solitude for Quinn. To Kerney it was an unnatural waste. All the right ingredients for ranching existed on the property. Live streams cascaded down from Glorieta Mesa, native grass was abundant, and the water table was excellent.

He considered how many yearlings he could buy at auction after putting up the lease money for the land. Not many if he went with prime stock. But it sure would feel good to get started.

He stuffed the envelope into a pocket, shook off the daydream, retrieved the file, and read it again in greater detail.

The information consisted of notes from interviews Terry had conducted with members of Sammy's unit and a meeting with Sammy's commanding officer, a Captain James Meehan. The only official information supplied was a summary of Sammy's military service up to the point of his disappearance.

Specialist Fourth Class Samuel Yazzi had graduated at the top of his advanced training class, received an accelerated promotion, and been given the option of picking his permanent duty station. In his eight months at White Sands, his performance ratings had been excellent. With no blemishes on his record, Sammy was considered a prime candidate for continued advancement through the enlisted ranks.

Captain Meehan, the commanding officer, knew of no incident which might have prompted Sammy to go AWOL. There was no rumor of a budding romance with any of the local girls that might have contributed to his disappearance, and no evidence of dissatisfaction with military life. In fact, Sammy apparently liked his job and had adapted well to the military.

Terry's talks with the soldiers who knew Sammy confirmed that he wasn't using drugs, drinking heavily, or spending his money in the Juárez whorehouses or gambling dens. Nobody was riding his tail, and to the best of everybody's knowledge he had no enemies.

Everyone liked him, although he was characterized as quiet and something of a loner. He played on the post baseball team as a reserve right fielder. Sammy's coach was a master sergeant by the name of Wiliam Titus McVay. Terry hadn't spoken to the man. McVay had retired two weeks after Sammy vanished. A clerk in the personnel office reported McVay had turned in his papers months before Sammy disappeared from the base. There was no follow-up by Terry to find and talk to the coach.

Terry had made a few visits to some of the GI hangouts in Las Cruces, where Sammy was vaguely remembered, and had interviewed Sammy's closest buddy, Alonzo Tony, a full-blooded Navajo PFC who told him that for about a month Sammy had dated a girl who worked on the post. Tony hadn't been surprised when the girl lost interest in Sammy. She was a notorious husband-hunter who had moved on to greener pastures, and Sammy, according to his friend, hadn't been dating anyone else, as far as he knew.

Sammy's roommate had confirmed Tony's observations about the girl but had no clue why Sammy would have gone AWOL. A meeting with the officer in charge of the investigation, Captain S. J. Brannon, had turned into a question-and-answer session, with Brannon asking most of the questions. Terry hadn't gotten anything at all helpful out of the interview.

Kerney closed the file and looked through the front window. The clouds were gathering for another afternoon shower. A shaft of light cut through a small thunderhead, spotlighting the deep slash of a narrow canyon in the mountains. The view dissolved as the cloud covered the sun and shadows blunted the outline of the mountains. He decided to leave the Salvation Army easy chair outside and take it to the dump when he had the time. He would treat himself to something better when he got back.

Kerney walked up the driveway to the ranch house, wondering what in the hell had happened to Sammy. The border of privet bushes he had planted in the fall was thriving. The old mountain ash trees, slow to bud in spring, were finally putting out new growth. Shrubs and trees framed the driveway and drew the eye to the house, where the wide veranda offered shade and comfort. Usually the walk to the main house pleased him. Today it seemed much too artificial, like a movie set piece.

Quinn had been urging him to take a vacation. By choice, Kerney had worked for over a year with rarely a day off. He had rebuilt the horse barn and the corral and repaired fence lines. Once again water ran in the stock tanks as the windmills pumped them full, attracting deer, antelope, and coyotes. All done, Quinn pointed out, as he willingly paid for the improvements, for one domestic animal, a half-trained, nameless mustang Kerney had bought at a Bureau of Land Management auction.

The double-walled adobe house was a survivor of the days when the ranch ran two thousand head of cattle over thirty thousand acres. The veranda, with comfortable wicker chairs scattered about, provided tremendous views of the Galisteo Basin. Quinn's part-time housekeeper kept the terra-cotta pots filled with fresh petunias and geraniums. The porch, supported by hand-peeled logs dark with age, gave deep shade and welcomed the slightest breeze. Above the veranda the angle of the pitched roof was interrupted by a series of gabled windows. Kerney crossed the polished plank floor, entered the front door, and went directly to the library, his favorite room. Originally the living room, it was a long, rectangular space with a stone fireplace against the far wall, set off by two wide south-facing windows. The remaining walls, lined with bookshelves from floor to ceiling, contained Quinn's extensive library. A large Early Colonial desk in the center of the room was bracketed by soft leather reading chairs.

Quinn's library, Kerney's primary source of recreation, contained an excellent collection of biographies and histories. He would have to remember to replace the ruined Churchill book. Fortunately, it wasn't a prized first edition, and he knew a used book dealer in Santa Fe who probably had it in stock.

He walked across the flagstone floor to the desk,

wrote out a salary check for himself on one of the
signed bank drafts left behind for his use. He scribbled a note that he was taking some time off, just in
case Quinn decided to stop over before flying to
Germany, and taped it to the monitor of the computer so it wouldn't be overlooked. He left another
note on the refrigerator in the kitchen for the
housekeeper, locked all the windows and doors, and
returned to the foyer, where he switched on the
security system. The house was, as usual, too quiet.
Not used enough, Kerney thought.

The mustang ignored him when Kerney approached the corral. A bit too long in the back with a
thick muzzle and withers set too far forward, the
horse was no show animal, but his muscling was
good and he would be a sturdy ranch horse once he
was fully conditioned and trained. Kerney cleaned
out the stall, opened the barn doors for ventilation,
set out a new salt lick, and put out feed. Fresh water
was no problem; the stock tank in the corral filled
automatically.

At the cabin he packed a bag with enough clothes
to last several days, dug out his emergency cash, and
checked the time. If he got his tail in gear he could
bank the five thousand in Santa Fe, cash his pay-
check, pay a visit to Terry's ex-wife, and be on the
road to Las Cruces before much more of the day was
gone. He slung the bag over his arm, grabbed a
handful of cassette tapes, and started for his truck.
Ten steps away from the porch, Kerney realized he
was walking as fast as his bum leg would carry him.
It felt damn good to have an adrenaline rush again,
he thought.

* * *

Maria Littlebird Tafoya sat in the small studio where she created jewelry sold exclusively under her name at one of the best Santa Fe galleries. The room, both a studio and porch, had been added to the house by her mother, who had taught her the silversmith's craft. Now that the demand for Maria's jewelry stretched far beyond the boundaries of the pueblo, she could afford a more expensive home, but she had no intention of moving. One day she might build a place for herself when Sammy came back from the Army, finished school, married, and started a family, but that was a long way off.

The house, on the edge of the pueblo's plaza, had views of the Jemez Mountains beyond the Rio Grande. Ordinarily, the vista was comforting; she could look up from the workbench and rest her eyes on the scene that rolled earth and sky into a passionate steel-blue tapestry of constantly changing patterns.

Her home had been too quiet since Sammy went into the Army. During the last six weeks it had seemed more so. The pattern on the bracelet before her, a turquoise-and-coral inlay mosaic wrapped in silver, required a harmony and balance that were missing. Unhappy with the design, Maria debated removing the stones, putting the silver setting aside to salvage later, and starting another piece. Lately she simply couldn't seem to concentrate.

A muddy pickup truck with a dented fender halted in front of the porch. Maria sighed. She was constantly pestered by bargain hunters who wanted to buy directly from her at cut-rate prices. She would have none of it.

A man stepped out of the truck, walked with a limp to the porch door, and smiled at her through the screen. She got quickly to her feet, pulled Kerney inside by the hand, and hugged him tightly.

"It's you," Maria exclaimed, smiling up at him.

"And it's you," he replied, letting her go.

She stepped back and looked at his face. He smiled down at her, but his blue eyes didn't sparkle. His brown hair, slightly longer, covered the tips of his ears and showed a wisp of gray near the temples. His handsome uneven face, deeply tanned and older-looking, with the same square chin, broad forehead, and Celtic nose, was less expressive than Maria remembered it to be.

"It's been too long," Maria said.

"Much too long," Kerney agreed.

"Terry called and said you might stop by."

"Was it your idea to bring me in on this?"

"Terry suggested it, and I encouraged him to ask you."

"That's good to know." Kerney's smile brightened slightly. "So the two of you are talking to each other again, I take it."

"More than we did before the divorce. Isn't that strange?"

"Not necessarily."

"Come inside." Maria took his arm and led him into the living room. She wanted to ask Kerney a million questions about what he would do to find Sammy. She wanted him to assure her that he would bring Sammy home safe and sound. She held back, busying herself with getting Kerney settled, offering him food and something to drink.

He accepted her offer. She got him seated and went quickly to the kitchen. He waited patiently as she clattered about, asking chatty questions, her nervousness betrayed by quick appearances in the doorway as he responded. He sat in the Mission-style rocking chair next to the kiva fireplace and wondered when she would simply fall apart and start sobbing.

"How is Mary Beth?" Maria queried.

"Long gone," Kerney said. All sounds from the kitchen stopped. The original house, built by Maria's great-grandfather, was a hundred years old. The puddled adobe walls bulged at the bottom and flowed unevenly to the ceiling. The floor, packed dirt mixed with ox blood, had a deep red patina.

Maria stood in the kitchen door looking sadly at him. "What happened?"

"It doesn't matter."

"Yes, it does."

"She said I wasn't fun anymore. She was probably right."

Maria's expression was sympathetic. "Is that it?"

"Not really. I don't think she liked the idea of living with an invalid. It was taking me much too long to recover."

Maria made a face. "That stinks."

"I thought so."

Maria started to speak, changed her mind, shook her head disparagingly, and disappeared from sight. She brought a small tray of cheese and grapes along with a large glass of lemonade and placed it on the end table next to the rocking chair. Kerney's gut didn't react well to cheese, but he selected a small slice anyway and washed it down with the lemonade.

The grapes were sweet and chilled, just the way he liked them.

She sat across from him on a love seat covered with an antique Navajo rug. She was perfectly still, her hands folded stiffly in her lap. He could see the tension in her back and neck. Her long flowing skirt draped to the floor. Only the toes of her beaded moccasins showed under the fabric. Kerney got up, moved to the love seat, and sat next to her.

"Are you all right?"

"Oh, Kerney, I'm so sorry about Mary Beth."

"Don't worry. I'm over it."

"How can you be?"

"You're right. I'm almost over it. But in a strange way she helped me get over being so damn mad at Terry. She gave me someone else to be angry at besides him." He patted her hand. "How are you holding up?"

Maria gave him a brave smile. "I'm scared, Kerney."

"I know you are."

"It isn't like Sammy to vanish. He's such a responsible person." She shook her head vigorously to keep away the tears and looked at a framed picture of her son on the fireplace mantel. He wore his Army uniform and was photographed at an angle to display the insignia on his sleeve and a single row of ribbons on his jacket.

"I bet you talked him into sitting for that picture," Kerney ventured. He needed her to stay coherent.

Maria's smile returned. "I did. I admit it. I'm a proud mother."

"He's a handsome man. Why was he so determined to join the Army?"

"Oh, all the usual reasons. Said he wasn't ready to go to college and wanted to do something different." Exasperation crept into her voice. "I tried to talk him out of it, but he has a stubborn streak just like his father. That's why I sent him to see you. I thought maybe another man could talk some sense to him. Terry was no help whatsoever."

"I figured you had a hand in his visit."

Maria shrugged. "I'm your typical meddling mother. What's done is done. He plans to use the GI Bill after his discharge to attend the Art Institute in Chicago. He's already been accepted." Pride crept into her voice.

"He's still drawing and painting," Kerney ventured, trying to keep Maria upbeat and positive.

"Oh, yes. I think soon he'll be the best artist the pueblo ever produced. He has remarkable talent."

"You must be proud of him."

"Very." Maria fell silent. She was a striking woman, slender and fine-boned, with a symmetrical face and small nose. Her dark almond eyes, usually filled with vitality, were restless and tight. Her long black hair was thick and straight and spilled over her shoulders. There was a slight tic in the corner of one eye. "When will you start looking for him?" she asked.

"I already have," Kerney answered. "You're my first stop."

Some of Maria's stiffness dissipated. She turned and faced Kerney squarely. "How can I help? I want to do something. Anything."

"Answer some questions. Can you think of any reason why Sammy would go AWOL?"

"No. The Army investigator asked me the same question. It made me angry. He implied that Sammy had personal problems that made him go AWOL. He was looking for character flaws. I told him Sammy wasn't the kind of person to abandon his responsibilities."

"Sometimes people change," Kerney proposed.

"Not Sammy," Maria replied sharply, her eyes snapping. "I know him." She got up, walked to a small, standing cabinet, opened the door, removed a packet of letters, and thrust them at Kerney. "Read his letters. Go ahead. They're filled with his plans for the future. These are not the words of a young man in trouble." Her outstretched hand was shaking.

"I believe you, Maria," he said gently, taking the letters from her. "But sometimes hard questions have to be asked."

She sagged almost imperceptibly, and the anger drained from her voice. "I know. Forgive me. I feel so frustrated. He's been gone for so long."

"I understand. Did the investigator talk to anyone else?"

"Yes. Just about everybody. Former classmates, old friends, and most of the family. He wanted to know if Sammy had a girl in trouble or if he used drugs, or drank a lot when he was home on leave. He even checked with Terry to see if Sammy had an arrest record."

"I'm sure Terry liked that."

"It made him furious."

"Can I keep Sammy's letters for a while?" Kerney asked. "I'll return them when I'm done."

"Of course you can. Those are just the ones he wrote from the missile range," she explained. "I have more in my bedroom."

"These will do for now."

"Are you sure?"

Kerney nodded.

Maria smiled regretfully. "I'm sorry for snapping at you."

"Don't apologize. This is hard stuff. You're holding up beautifully."

"Am I?" She searched Kerney's face for any sign of false reassurance. "I feel powerless and ready to explode." Her voice broke with a little quiver.

"That's normal. Keep your chin up." She's about to lose it, Kerney thought. "When was the last time you spoke with Sammy?"

"About two weeks before he disappeared. I called him to ask if he was planning to come home to dance at a feast day. He said he wouldn't be able to get away."

"Did he talk about anything else?"

"No. It was a short conversation."

"How did he sound?"

"If you mean was Sammy upset, he wasn't."

Kerney stood up and put Sammy's letters in his shirt pocket. "Can I take a look at Sammy's bedroom?"

Maria hesitated. "Go ahead. I'll wait here, if you don't mind."

He could see the tears welling in Maria's eyes. She blinked them back. He walked through the narrow hallway that defined the end of the old part of the house into the addition Terry had built while the marriage was still intact. It was a suite of two bedrooms and baths that fanned out behind the original structure. He opened the door to Sammy's bedroom. The room had changed since Kerney's last visit. Gone were the high school treasures. The walls held a variety of Sammy's framed pen and pencil landscapes. They showed sensitivity, substance, and a keen eye for detail. On a writing table were a small electronic keyboard, some sheet music, and a desktop computer. Tacked to the bulletin board above the desk were a collage of snapshots and some unfinished watercolors. Kerney was surprised to see a picture of himself and Sammy in the collage. Both of them stood grinning at the camera while Sammy gripped the handlebars of the new bicycle Kerney had presented to him on his seventh birthday.

He closed the bedroom door and searched quietly, not wanting Maria to hear him rummaging through Sammy's possessions. She was feeling enough strain already. He opened every drawer, searched the closet, looked under and behind the furniture, and scanned the papers, books, and stacks of drawings. He turned out the pockets of Sammy's clothes and probed through the packing boxes on the floor of the closet that were filled with Sammy's childhood toys. When he finished, he put everything back in order. He had found nothing of interest.

Maria was standing in the living room when he returned. "That was hard for me to let you do," she said.

"I know," Kerney said.

"Sometimes I think I hear him in his room. I catch myself walking back there to talk to him."

"That happens."

"The mind plays such mean tricks." This time

Maria could not stop the tears. "I thought I was finished crying for the day."

He took her gently by the shoulders, pulled her close, and let her cry herself out.

Finished, she dried her eyes and wiped her nose. "Find Sammy for me."

"I'll do my best," Kerney replied.

CHAPTER

2

_ . _ . _ . _

South of the Albuquerque corridor, Kerney began to enjoy the drive. Santa Fe's unrelenting growth spurts were bad enough, but Albuquerque was pure, ugly clutter along the interstate highway. After the city, open desert country undulated in waves, broken by the Rio Grande valley and an endless parade of mountain ranges to the west and east. The small villages bordering the river were enclaves anchored against the expanse of open space, surrounded by green fields that dappled the stark landscape with color. The high country of northern New Mexico was beautiful, but it couldn't hold him the way the desert could. He had been away from it for far too long.

He gassed up on the main drag in Socorro, a

somewhat shoddy town that paralleled the interstate, found a self-service car wash, sprayed the crusted mud off the truck, and continued south toward Las Cruces with the music of Mozart filling the cab.

The office of the sheriff of Doña Ana County was in the old courthouse in downtown Las Cruces. He introduced himself to the secretary, who inquired as to the nature of his visit. He told her it was personal, and she gave him a quizzical look before announcing him on the phone. Still puzzled after she hung up, the secretary quickly ushered him into Andy Baca's office. Andy came out from behind a big walnut desk, grinning from ear to ear, and reached for Kerney's hand.

"I'll be damned," he said. "It's good to see you, Kevin."

"Hello, Sheriff," Kerney replied, grinning back at his old friend. "I thought you'd moved to Las Cruces to retire and play golf." He looked around the office. The walls were filled with the memorabilia of Andy's twenty-year career with the state police. Behind the desk, on a windowsill, miniature state and national flags stood in stanchions. "Seems you got bored," he added.

Andy laughed. "You've got the golf part right. I've got a ten stroke handicap, a wicked slice I can't seem to correct, and a standing offer to play every Friday afternoon with a bunch of guys who kick my butt and take my money."

Andy wore a conservative western suit that draped nicely over his sturdy frame. There was a slight hint of jowls under his jaw and a little less hair offset by longer sideburns. Aside from being a superior cop, Andy was one of the most warm-hearted men Kerney knew. He slipped into his executive chair behind the uncluttered walnut desk and gestured for Kerney to sit across from him. "And I did get bored," he added. "Started reading the newspaper with my morning coffee and wound up deciding that my predecessor was a political hack surrounded by uniformed cronies. It pissed me off, so I decided to do something about it. Ran for sheriff, and here I am."

"So here you are," Kerney said.

"And it makes Connie damned happy," Andy replied. "She was tired of having me underfoot. Complained that I was turning into a grouch. What brings you into my county?"

"I need a favor," Kerney replied.

In response, Andy raised a cautious eyebrow and nodded for Kerney to continue.

"I've been hired to find Terry Yazzi's son. He's AWOL from the missile range."

Andy's expression turned quizzical. "Is that why Terry stopped in to see me? I had no idea."

"I take it you didn't talk to him."

"No," Andy replied, getting up from his desk. "I was out improving my slice when he came by." He walked to the small conference table near the front of the office, sorted through a stack of papers, selected one, and held it up to read. "We're carrying a Specialist Sammy Yazzi on the daily report as an AWOL. Is that the kid?"

"It is. What information do you have on him?" Kerney asked as he joined him.

Andy slapped the paper with his free hand. "Nothing. Just date of birth, height, weight—that sort of stuff." He handed it to Kerney. "Who's paying your freight? Maria?"

"Terry's paying."

Andy walked back to his desk, perched on the corner, and waited for Kerney to join him. "How is Terry?"

"He's okay, I guess. He's chief of police at the pueblo. Says he's been off the sauce for two years. He looks sober. In fact, he looks good."

Andy studied his hands before speaking. "You can't be doing this for Terry."

"I'm not. Sammy's my godson. I've known him since the day he was born."

Andy nodded somberly. "That makes sense." The smile returned, and he slapped his leg with the palm of his hand. "Okay, how can I help?"

"The brass at the missile range stonewalled Terry. I was hoping you could grease some wheels for me."

"Sure, sure, but it won't amount to much. Army cops are no different from the rest of us—they think private investigators are a pain in the ass."

"I'm not licensed as an investigator," Kerney replied.

Andy frowned. "That's worse yet. You might as well turn around and go home for all the good I can do you."

"I can't do that."

Andy seemed amused. "Why am I not surprised?" He rubbed a hand over his chin and thought for a minute. "You'll need some juice if you want the military to cooperate. Why don't I put you on the payroll?"

The offer startled Kerney. "I'm medically retired. Not fit for active duty."

"So what? I can do it without bending any rules."

"You're serious?"

"You bet." Andy leaned over the desk, opened the top drawer, reached in, and tossed Kerney a badge. "Let's make you a lieutenant. That should be high enough on the pecking order to get the Army's attention."

Kerney held the badge in his hand, feeling slightly flabbergasted. "I wasn't expecting this."

"It's no big deal, but don't get too attached to that shield. Money is tight. You're on the payroll for thirty days. That's all I can afford." Andy shifted his weight against the edge of the desk. "Now it's your turn to pony up."

"Name it," Kerney replied, wondering what Andy wanted.

"Tell me what really happened with you and Terry. The shooting team report was a bunch of crap."

"It's not worth talking about."

"Indulge me."

Kerney swallowed hard, unwilling to start. The scene had played through his mind endlessly, but he'd never put it in words. Maybe it was time. He looked Andy directly in the eyes and started talking.

"We were on a stakeout waiting for an arrest warrant so we could pick up a cocaine dealer in the barrio. I covered the back door while Terry was inside the liquor store across the street, watching the front of the house. Just before the perp crawled out a front window, Terry decided he needed a beer chaser to go with the vodka he had been nipping at from a hip flask all morning. At the time, I had no idea he was hitting the sauce heavily. He was moody and sullen, but I passed it off as a reaction to his divorce.

"Anyway, while he's popping open a cold one at the cooler in the back of the store, the perp came out the front door and ran behind the house. He saw me and started shooting. I took the first round in the knee and the next one in the gut before I could drop him. By the time Terry got to me, it was over.

"While I was in surgery, Terry told the shooting team that the suspect came out a side window and that he never saw him. I believed his story. So did Internal Affairs."

"How did you learn the truth?"

"Three weeks later, Terry came to visit me when I was home from my second round of surgery. He was tanked up, suicidal, and guilt-ridden. I guess he felt a need to confess. That was the last time I saw him until this morning."

"You should have busted his ass," Andy counseled.

"At the time I was too doped up on painkillers to give a shit about anything. It really didn't sink in. Part of me didn't want to believe it. Anyway, Terry busted himself. After he left my place, he stayed drunk until he got fired." Kerney searched Andy's face. "How did you know Terry lied?"

Andy laughed and pushed himself upright. "I ran Internal Affairs for the state police, remember? It was my job to review the shooting team report for the DA. I interviewed Terry to confirm his story just before he got canned. For a man with nothing to hide—who had been cleared of any blame—he was in a cold sweat. It smelled fishy."

Andy leaned over the desk, scribbled a note, tore it from the pad, and handed it to Kerney. "Captain S. J. Brannon, *Sara* Brannon, is the officer-in-charge of the criminal investigation unit at the missile range." He checked his wristwatch. "She should still be in the office. I'll make an appointment for you. I'll tell her Terry's an old friend of mine who's asked me to look into his son's disappearance. My secretary will pull the active AWOL files for you to review. Check to see if Sammy went over the hill with a friend. Sometimes these kids run together to keep their courage up."

"I'll look into it. Thanks, Andy." Kerney held out his hand.

"No problem." Andy handshake was sincere. "Let's get you sworn in."

After the paperwork was completed and Kerney left the office, Andy absentmindedly drummed his fingers on the desktop. He'd acted impulsively, but it felt right. Putting a badge in Kerney's pocket might be the best thing he could do for the man.

He would gladly take ten officers like Kerney, gimpy leg and all, if he could find them. The man was one hell of a good cop.

He reached for the phone to call Captain Brannon. He not only wanted Sara to know she would soon have a visitor, he wanted her to know something about the new lieutenant he was sending her way.

Captain Sara Brannon inspected the man standing in front of her desk. His face was tan and his hands were calloused from physical work. He was built like an athlete, with big shoulders, a nicely formed chest, and a slim waist. He didn't look like a cop coming off a lengthy convalescence after being seriously wounded. If Andy hadn't told her, she would have guessed the limp was nothing more than an old football injury. Dressed in jeans that broke below the heels of his cowboy boots and a white starched western shirt that fit him nicely, he wore an oval belt buckle with a single turquoise stone in the center of a silver setting.

"Sit down, Lieutenant," she said as she shook his hand. He had the prettiest blue eyes she'd ever seen.

Kerney lowered himself into the straight-backed chair in front of the gray steel desk. "Thanks for seeing me."

"I hear that you're new to the sheriff's department," Sara replied. "I'm a bit surprised that Andy Baca would send a lieutenant to investigate this case."

He waited for the captain to be seated before replying. It gave him a brief chance to study her. Her fatigue uniform was crisp, with sharp creases in the sleeves. The shirt didn't hide the long, slender neck, offset by short strawberry-blond hair. Her eyes were sparkling green. The only jewlery she wore was a West Point ring. He'd seen a lot of academy rings during his tour of duty in Nam. "The sheriff and Chief Yazzi are old friends. He wants to give the case priority."

"So I understand. You are aware that Specialist Yazzi's case is purely a military matter?"

"Of course," Kerney answered cordially. "But I'd appreciate any information you can give me. Specialist Yazzi's parents are very worried, and Sheriff Baca would like to help as much as possible."

The captain nodded curtly. "Sheriff Baca made that clear. We take the disappearance of any soldier very seriously. Most of the personnel at White Sands work on highly secret projects. There are security implications to be considered in this situation."

"Do you have a motive you can share?" Kerney asked. Brannon's office was strictly functional: two metal chairs for visitors that matched the unpretentious desk, a filing cabinet within easy reach, a built-in bookcase along one wall, and a computer on a work station by a window that looked out at the distant Sacramento Mountains.

"Not presently," Sara responded. She rubbed the band of her ring with her thumb. Kerney kept looking at her hands. She folded them in front of her on the desk.

Kerney decided Captain Brannon had elegant hands. He looked at her face. "Your investigation is stalled," Kerney restated.

She bit her lip and scowled. "Dead in the water."

"Maybe a fresh perspective would help."

Sara bit her lip again. The close-cropped hairdo complimented her face. A small line of freckles ran across her nose. She considered the man in front of her. "I really don't see the need for your assistance."

Kerney countered quickly. "Give me twenty-four hours on the base. If I don't make any progress, I'll pack it in."

"What exactly do you propose to do?"

"Backtrack. Play up the fact that I'm not part of the military. Maybe something will shake loose."

Sara Brannon considered the idea. It was a long shot, but if Kerney could light a fire under the investigation it might help get another case off her desk. "You've got twenty-four hours," she finally said. "And tell Andy Baca he owes me one."

Kerney held back a smile of relief. "I'll pass along your message."

She nodded curtly. "You're restricted to the main post. I'll arrange a billet for you at the bachelor officer's quarters. The officer's club is nearby and the food is decent."

"Will I need an escort?" Kerney asked.

"If you make that necessary, Lieutenant, you'll be out of here before you can blink an eye."

"Fair enough," Kerney agreed, wondering how Brannon planned to have him watched.

She wrote a note on a pad, tore it off, and handed it to Kerney across the desk. "Give this to the duty sergeant at the front office. He'll take care of you."

She stood up. Kerney rose with her. She was tall enough to look him in the eye without difficulty.

"Thank you, Captain," he said.

"I expect to be kept informed. Call the post operator and ask for me by name. If I'm not available, I'll get back to you." She nodded in the direction of the door to indicate that he was dismissed. "Good luck."

Alone in her office, Sara rang for her second-in-command and asked what he had learned from the Armed Forces Record Center about Kevin Kerney. The officer came in bearing a packet, prepared to give an informal briefing. Sara stopped him short and had him sit quietly while she scanned the papers. Kerney, a Vietnam veteran, had served one tour in-country late in the war as an infantry platoon leader and had rotated stateside with an impressive array of citations and a recommendation for a

Regular Army commission, which he had turned down.

The personal information about Kerney intrigued her. His place of birth was listed as Tularosa, New Mexico, a small town on the eastern edge of the missile range. A native son. If his date of birth was correct, Kerney had been something of an over-achiever; he had received his ROTC commission at the age of twenty when he graduated from the state university in Las Cruces.

Sara looked at the young officer, who waited expectantly. "Query the FBI on Kerney and ask the post historian to see if he has information on the ranching families in the Tularosa Basin who pre-dated the missile range. Anything he has on the Kerney family I want to look at."

The officer wrote it down and waited for more.

"Put a tail on Kerney," Sara added. "Two men, full-time, and rotate the shifts starting at midnight. Run a background check on Specialist Yazzi's father. I want anything you can get on his work history in law enforcement. Look for a connection between the father and Kerney. Start with the Santa Fe Police Department. That's where Kerney was last employed."

"Anything else?" the officer inquired, getting to his feet.

"Tell the surveillance teams I want every move Kerney makes fully documented. They're to pull him in if he spits on the sidewalk."

"Problems?" the officer asked.

She closed the file, handed it to the lieutenant, and looked out the office window. Kerney was standing in the parking lot pasting a temporary vehicle pass

to the rear window of a pickup truck. She watched
him for a moment and turned back to the officer
with a smile. "That's what you're going to tell me.
But I find it strange that a sheriff's lieutenant, on
duty, drives his personal vehicle instead of a police
cruiser."

The late-afternoon sun burned through the fabric
of Kerney's shirt and the hot desert wind blew
against his neck. Behind him was the office of the
post provost marshal, where he'd left Captain Brannon. He was barely aware of the line of cars moving
slowly through the guard station as the civilians,
defense contractors, and off-post personnel began
their commutes home. His eyes were riveted on the
Sacramentos, sixty miles distant. He recalled the
trip to Frenchy's cabin in Dog Canyon, one of the
rare excursions of his childhood when his father
packed up the truck and took him camping in the
high, cool forest. It was a year when the cattle
brought a good price and the beef herd was sleek and
fat from a wet winter and spring. The year before the
drought.

His gaze moved down from the peaks to the sun-
drenched desert, chalky gray in a great sweep of
rolling space. Up the tube of the Tularosa Valley,
light danced on the fringe of the brilliant gypsum
dunes at the White Sands National Monument. To
the north the San Andres Mountains showed a
rugged, tortured countenance to the valley floor,
hiding the sinuous curves of narrow canyons that cut
deep into the mountain range.

He took a deep breath of the dry air and climbed

into the truck. To the west, the granite peaks of the Organ Mountains dominated the main post. He thought about Sara Brannon. She was damn pretty, with an oval face and high cheekbones that drew attention to her eyes. He wondered if she was involved with someone. Probably, he decided.

He attached the visitor's badge to his shirt pocket and drove down the street. The base, arranged with military precision, made finding your way fairly easy. There were directional signs everywhere, and all the buildings were numbered and named. The administrative offices were clustered on a main drive with shade trees marching in neat rows along the roadway. All the curbs were freshly painted, and there wasn't a piece of litter in sight. A large parade ground sat across the road from the headquarters. A permanent reviewing stand installed on the north side looked out over a grass field. He found the sign to the enlisted barracks and turned off. The quarters were a compound of two-story red-brick buildings with flat roofs, within walking distance of the dining hall and the post amenities. Kerney parked in the lot and walked into the empty compound between the buildings. Given the time of day, Kerney reckoned most of the people he wanted to see were in the chow line at the mess hall. A small, one-story building at the end of the compound was posted with a company headquarters sign. Kerney went in the open door and found a clerk at a desk finishing up reports for the day. He showed the soldier his badge and asked to see Captain Meehan, Sammy's commanding officer. He was told that Meehan was gone for the day and not due back until morning. Kerney asked to see the first sergeant. The private gave him directions to the sergeant's quarters at the opposite end of the compound.

Kerney walked to the two-room suite in the barracks that Master Sergeant Roy Enloe occupied and knocked on the door. It was jerked open by a hairy, naked man who was toweling dry his hair. He seemed unconcerned about his appearance or the stranger at his door.

"My company clerk just called from the office to say you were coming over. I don't have much time," Enloe said, leaving the door open and walking to the middle of his small sitting room. "What can I do for you?"

"What can you tell me about Sammy Yazzi?"

"He was a good soldier." Enloe picked up a fresh pair of boxer shorts from the arm of a chair, dropped the towel, and started dressing. "He pulled his duty without complaint and never gave me any trouble. I've been over this ground before, Lieutenant, with our own people. Ask me a question I haven't heard."

"Do you know how I can get a hold of William McVay?" Kerney asked.

"Bull McVay?" Enloe smiled as he pulled on an undershirt. "He's retired. Living up in a trailer park at Elephant Butte Lake. Why do you want to see Bull?"

"He was Sammy's baseball coach. Maybe he might know something about Sammy's disappearance."

Enloe shook his head in disagreement. "I doubt it."

"Why do you say that?"

40

"Bull likes to talk about three things. Baseball, religion, and the Army. He became a born-again Christian about three years ago. You can't get him to stop talking about Jesus Christ, the New York Mets, and the air cavalry, especially if he has a few beers in him. That's all he cares about. I don't think he'd have a clue about why Yazzi went AWOL." Enloe stepped into a pair of stretch denim jeans and sat down to put on his shoes and socks.

"Why did McVay retire?" Kerney inquired.

Enloe talked to the floor as he tied his shoelaces. "Bull was planning on being a thirty-year man until his mother got sick. Alzheimer's disease. It was real tough on him to put in his retirement papers, but he felt obligated to look after her. He got her admitted to the state veterans' home up in Truth or Consequences. She served in World War Two as a WAC ferry pilot, flying B-17 bombers."

"Have you seen him since he retired?"

"No." Enloe stood up and put on a clean shirt that had been draped over the back of the chair. "But he should be easy to find. Truth or Consequences isn't that big of a town."

"Why do you call him Bull?"

Enloe snorted as he buttoned his shirt. "Wait till you meet him. He's a foot shorter than me and built like a tank."

"Is he married?"

"Divorced. That's one reason he's working. The ex-wife gets a third of his retirement pay."

"Do you know where he works?"

"I haven't a clue. Somebody at the NCO club might be able to tell you."

"Thanks for your time."

Enloe smiled. "No sweat." He walked out the door behind Kerney and hurried across the compound to the parking lot.

Kerney went to locate PFC Alonzo Tony, who was nowhere to be found. His roommate, a slightly overweight boy with bony hands and a pug nose, arrived just as Kerney was about to leave. The soldier told Kerney that Tony worked swing shift at the post communication center, where he served as a cryptographer, and didn't get off until midnight. Kerney asked where Sammy Yazzi bunked, and the boy took him to a two-man room down the hall. Exactly half the room was empty, except for a bunk. The other half contained a precisely made bed with military corners, a foot-locker, and personal gear. The name on the closet door read PFC Robert Jaeger.

"Where is Sammy's gear?" Kerney asked.

"At the quartermaster's," the soldier answered. "They store your gear if you go AWOL."

Kerney could hear the sounds of the troops returning from dinner. A radio was cranked up to a rap music station. Someone shouted to turn down the noise. "What about his bunkmate?" Kerney asked.

"Bobby? He's on a pass."

"When is he due back?"

The soldier shrugged and looked down the hallway, anxious to be done with Kerney. "In a day or two, I guess. Anything else?"

"No. Thanks a lot."

The kid nodded and walked away. Kerney made a quick search of the room, checking the closets, the

built-in dressers and desks. The room was completely bare of any trace of Sammy. Outside, the
evening air was cooling quickly and the compound
was filled with young men, most of them in civilian
clothes, eager for diversion. The Organ Mountains
were tipped with a band of pink light as the final
shadows of dusk came on.

The post library, within walking distance of the
barracks, near the service club and the post movie
theater, was not the most popular attraction on the
post. Some housewives browsed through the new-
fiction display, and a few off-duty soldiers were in
the reading room. Kerney found the young woman
Sammy had briefly dated busily shelving books in
the stacks.

Carla Montoya was petite, bouncy, and talkative.
Long, curly hair framed her rather ordinary features
to advantage. She appeared to be in her early twen-
ties. She answered Kerney's questions willingly,
creating a sense of drama for herself in the process.

"I met him here at work," Carla said, responding
to Kerney's overture. "He spent a lot of time at the
library when he first came to the base. I thought he
was kinda cute. Real quiet-like and serious. He
didn't try to hustle me, but was real sincere-like. We
dated five or six times. The movies, a couple of
dances. Stuff like that."

"Who broke it off?"

Carla shook her head, the curls swirling over her
shoulder. She patted them down. "Nobody. It didn't
get that far. It was just dating, that's all. I like him
and everything, but . . ." She shrugged.

"Did Sammy talk about himself? His problems?"

Carla chewed on her lip. "Not really. It wasn't like he was unhappy or anything like that. He talked a lot about how much he wanted to go to art school when he got out. Some place back east. I forget exactly where."

"Nothing else?"

"He talked about cars," Carla answered. "He had an old Chevy sedan." She rolled her eyes in mock disgust and twirled her finger around a lock of hair. "It was really a piece of junk. I mean, embarrassing." She strung the word out. "He wanted to buy something better."

"Did he?"

Carla hesitated, her fingers toying with a strand of her hair. "I'm not sure. I saw him cruising in Las Cruces once after we stopped dating. He was driving a different car. Somebody was with him, but I couldn't tell who it was. I don't think he even saw me. I kinda figured he'd bought himself something better."

"When was that?"

"About two months ago. Just before he went AWOL."

"What kind of car was Sammy driving?"

"I think it was a Toyota. Not new. Maybe a couple of years old. Sort of a sandy beige two-door. An economy model." Carla's tone of voice suggested that the car was not at all cool.

"Have you talked to anyone about this?"

"Sure. Sammy's father. The Army investigator." She smiled brightly. "And now you. But I just remembered seeing him in a different car. I'd forgotten about that."

"Where did Sammy keep his car?" Kerney asked.

"I guess behind the barracks," Carla answered. "That's where the enlisted personnel have to park."

"Tell me about the Chevy," Kerney asked.

Cars meant a great deal to Carla. She described the junky Chevy in detail. Kerney left her to resume her book-stacking chores and walked back to the barracks. The parking lot was half empty. He looked for a beige Toyota and a beat-up Chevy. There was no Toyota that matched Carla's description, but there was a white Chevy sedan with a For Sale sign in the window parked at the back of the lot. He wiped away the film of dust from the window where the sign was taped. The sign had Sammy's name on it.

He circled the vehicle. There was enough light from the streetlamps to see hand and fingerprint smudges in the dust on the door near the handle. Someone had recently been in the vehicle. He found more smudges on the trunk lid. The car was locked. The interior was clean as a whistle. Kerney found that interesting. The Sammy he knew, on his best days, wasn't that neat.

He went to his truck and drove toward the BOQ. In the foothills that rose to meet the Organ Mountains, lights from the married officers' quarters dotted the landscape.

The orderly at the BOQ gave him the key to a room and said there was more than enough time left to get a meal at the officers' club. Kerney's stomach grumbled and his leg ached. The knee just didn't do too well on long trips in the truck. He carried his bag to the room, unpacked a fresh set of clothes, and sat

45

in the tub under the shower, letting the hot water
soak away the throbbing in his knee. While dressing,
he had an impulse to check in with Sara Brannon.
He rejected the notion. There was absolutely nothing to report. He closed the door and locked it.
There was no sense making it too easy for the room
to be searched.

CHAPTER

3

————————

Kerney entered the officers' club to find half a dozen men and women sitting at the far end of the bar away from the door. In the back dining area, separated by a waist-high partition, some junior officers and their wives were celebrating a young child's birthday. Laughter and chatter spilled over to the front of the room. Kerney sat at a small cocktail table in the barroom and received quick attention from a waiter. He ordered a light meal—his stomach, unable to digest any food in quantity, demanded it—and nursed a glass of iced tea while waiting for his food to arrive. The walls of the barroom, paneled in a rich walnut, were decorated with framed prints of nineteenth-century military scenes. Replicas of old regimental cavalry flags hung from the ceiling rafters.

His meal, a pasta salad with a cream dressing, was served quickly. He ate slowly, enjoying the food. Eating out was something of a treat, and the meal was well prepared. He was about to call for his check when Sara Brannon entered the club with a man. Both were dressed casually. Sara, in a loose ribbed pullover shirt, a denim skirt, and a soft pair of suede boots that accented her long legs, looked very classy. Her companion, a tall fellow, dressed in chinos, hiking boots, and a blue chambray shirt, with dark, sunbleached hair that curled up at the nape of his neck, had a studious, intelligent face. Eyeglasses highlighted his scholarly appearance. Sara didn't see Kerney as she passed by; her attention was diverted by something the man was saying as he led her by the arm to the bar.

Hoping to leave undetected, Kerney watched Sara as he waited for the waiter to bring the check. She talked with her hands and seemed much more relaxed and animated than when Kerney had met her in her office. The tendency to fidget with her class ring was a habit, Kerney decided. She unconsciously toyed with it, rubbing her thumb along the band.

The waiter came with the check, and Kerney settled up immediately, hoping for a discreet exit. Sara saw his reflection in the bar mirror and waved him over.

"Lieutenant Kerney," she called.

Forcing a smile, Kerney veered toward the bar. The man turned and eyed him with interest.

"I'd like you to meet Fred Utley," she said.

Utley got off the bar stool. "Nice to meet you," he said with a grin, extending his hand.

Utley was in his mid-thirties, about Kerney's height. His hand was calloused and his grip firm. "Likewise," Kerney replied.

"You must be new on the post," Utley said, reclaiming his seat at the bar.

"Lieutenant Kerney is with the Doña Ana Sheriff's Department," Sara clarified. Her eyes, guarded and unsmiling, never left Kerney's face. "Join us for a drink, Lieutenant." She patted an empty stool next to her.

In spite of her relaxed veneer, it was an order, not a request. Instead of sitting next to Sara, Kerney slid onto the stool beside Utley, using the man as a buffer, and ordered a glass of white wine.

Utley didn't notice the unspoken exchange. "Are you here on official business or just visiting?" he asked.

Sara didn't give Kerney a chance to answer. She touched Utley lightly on the arm. "The lieutenant is working on a case with us." With Utley placated, she gave Kerney a sharp, quick look, while her voice remained unruffled. "Fred is the chief archaeologist at the missile range."

Kerney hesitated. The lady is pissed, he thought, without a clue as to why. He smiled at Utley. "Your job must be very interesting."

Utley nodded with satisfaction. "It is. White Sands is an anthropologist's dream. There are over five thousand square miles on the base that were hardly touched by modern civilization before the Army took it over. The Apaches traversed the area, mostly to hunt or camp, and Hispanic settlers farmed on the fringes of the basin, but that was about it until cattlemen moved in from Texas, looking for free range. It was really one of the last western frontiers.

"It's a vast area that's been protected for almost half a century. That means no destruction of historical sites, no pot hunters digging for artifacts, no massive public use of the land. Some of the old ranches are still standing, with everything in them that the previous owners didn't carry away."

Utley paused while the bartender served Kerney his wine. "You may not be interested in all this," he said, with an apologetic wave of his hand.

"But I am," Kerney replied.

Utley gave him an appreciative smile. Kerney leaned back, glanced at Sara, and decided she was really pissed off. The smile on her face didn't hide the antagonistic gleam in her eyes.

Utley continued talking, unaware. "I've been here seven years and we've barely begun to touch all the historical sites on the range. I'm excavating right now at a place called Indian Hills, north of here in the San Andres. It was part of the old Pat Garrett ranch. He was the sheriff that killed Billy the Kid. In fact, Garrett himself was murdered at the San Andrews Pass. His killer was never caught."

"Interesting," Kerney said, taking a sip of wine. He put the glass down, pushed it to one side, looked at Sara in the mirror behind the bar, and inclined his head toward the exit.

She caught the cue, interceded by touching Utley lightly on the shoulder, and gave Kerney a charming smile. "I should have warned you not to get Fred started."

"I enjoyed it," Kerney announced as he stood up. "Thanks for the drink and the conversation."

"Let me walk you out, Lieutenant," Sara said, touching Utley again to keep him in place. "I'll be back in a few minutes, Fred."

"Shoptalk?" he asked her with a grin. "Or should I say cop talk?"

"A bit of both."

After another staunch handshake from Utley, Kerney walked outside with Sara. In silence they waited as the birthday party celebrants trailing behind them passed by, loaded themselves into cars, and drove away.

"You wanted to speak to me, Captain?"

"Your little deception didn't work," Sara snapped. "I know that Sammy's father once worked for you, and he's hired you to find his son. For some weird reason, Andy Baca decided to give you a badge and make you legitimate."

"You work fast," Kerney replied.

"Don't try to butter me up, Lieutenant. I don't like being lied to. I want an explanation and I want it now."

The irritation in Sara's eyes made Kerney break contact. The full moon was high, projecting a glow that created hushed charcoal shadows in the basin. The distant Sacramento Mountains, blurred shapes, glistened with a satin polish.

He turned back to her, looked her square in the eyes, and spoke carefully, admitting the truth to himself for the first time. "For a long time, Sammy and his parents were like family to me. I guess I can't shake that off as easily as I thought."

"So, you're saying this is strictly a matter of an old

family friendship." Sara's lips were two thin lines of reproach. "I find that hard to believe, if you're being paid."

"It's not just the money. Sammy is one of the few people I really care about."

Sara waited for more, and nothing came. "Is that it?"

"Pretty much. I assume you've learned enough to fill in some of the blanks."

Sara sighed in exasperation. She knew Terry Yazzi had been with Kerney the day he got shot, and that the friendship between the two men had ended soon after, but there were blank pages that needed filling in. "I'd like to hear more," she prompted.

Kerney shook his head. "It's not relevant. Regardless of what you decide, I'm going to keep working on the case."

Sara bit her lip. Confronted by the facts, Kerney, to his credit, didn't sulk or cave in. And Andy Baca, after getting an earful from her on the telephone, had stood his ground about Kerney's skills as an investigator. "You don't make it easy on yourself," she said.

"I know. It's your call, Captain. I'd like our agreement to stand."

"All right," she finally said, "but the clock is ticking, and when the twenty-four hours are up, you leave."

Kerney smiled in relief. "Thanks."

Sara nodded, her green eyes searching his face for the slightest sign of gloating. Satisfied there was none, she switched gears. "What have you learned so far?"

"Nothing. Does Sammy's disappearance fit a victim pattern? Are there any similarities to other AWOL cases?"

Sara shook her head. "We looked at that. There are two open AWOL cases involving young single males. Neither of them has surfaced, but we can find absolutely no connection between them and Specialist Yazzi."

"How old are the cases?"

"Recent. One involves a civilian employee and the other is a Navy seaman."

"Can you arrange for me to speak to Sammy's supervisor?" Kerney asked.

"I'll set it up and call you at the BOQ in the morning. His name is Sergeant Steiner." She turned to leave.

"Captain Brannon."

Sara looked over her shoulder. "What is it?"

"Bobby Jaeger. Sammy's roommate."

"What about him?"

"When is he due back on base?"

"Check with his first sergeant. Good night, Lieutenant."

"Good night." He watched her walk through the door to the club, thinking that Sara Brannon was one sharp lady.

A visit to the NCO club, a more crowded, louder, and livelier establishment than the officers' club, with a honky-tonk atmosphere, yielded no information on Bull McVay. Kerney hung around asking questions until he ran out of people to quiz. He spent the next hour in the empty dayroom at the enlisted barracks waiting for PFC Alonzo Tony to get off duty. It was after midnight when, half asleep, he heard the barracks door open and footsteps on the tile floor. He called out PFC Tony's name, and a young man detached himself from a small group of soldiers who were quietly scattering down the hallway to their rooms. Kerney introduced himself and asked Tony to talk to him in the dayroom. Tony eyed Kerney uneasily and only agreed to join him after Kerney explained his purpose.

"I don't believe Sammy went AWOL," Tony said, fishing out a cigarette. "No way, man." Tony had a full upper lip, prominent cheekbones, and a symmetrical nose. He was about five feet eight with a long trunk and no waist; just a straight line from chest to hips.

"Not his style?"

"You got that right," Tony agreed, lighting his smoke.

"Do you think something bad happened to Sammy?" Kerney inquired.

"That's the only thing that makes any sense. Sammy is just about my best friend. I know him pretty well. He's not the kind to go off half-cocked."

"Do you have any ideas about what happened to him?"

Tony shook his head. "Nope."

"I understand he was spending some time in town after he stopped dating Carla."

"He was, but I don't know if he was seeing anybody. We didn't talk about girls all that much. He'd bail out of here for Las Cruces, just like the rest of us, but I didn't get the feeling he was chasing some skirt."

"Did you go with him?"

"Sometimes. We'd hang together now and then,

like if we had the same day off. He has wheels and I don't."

"Did you hang at any particular place?"

"Not really. We'd take in a movie or cruise—things like that."

"Did he buy a new car?"

"He was going to. The Chevy died on him. He's been saving money for a down payment. He doesn't like riding the shuttle bus to town. Can't say that I blame him; it's embarrassing."

"Did he keep anything personal in his car?"

"His art stuff. He likes to draw."

"Did Sammy say anything about buying a Toyota?"

"Nope."

"Where does he work?"

"Uprange. He's got a wacky schedule: pulls four days on and three off. He was trying to work a deal to change his duty so he could take some art courses at the university."

Kerney cut off his questioning. "Thanks. I may want to talk to you again."

"That's cool."

Back in his room at the BOQ, Kerney checked the zipper on his carryall bag. He'd left it open a fraction of an inch and now it was completely closed. He undressed and got into bed, exhausted from the twenty-hour day. He reread Sammy's letters to Maria. She was absolutely right about his attitude. The letters were upbeat and filled with plans for the future. Kerney mulled over the information he'd gathered since his arrival. It was both inconclusive and unpromising. He was almost asleep when he started thinking about Sara Brannon and the muddle he'd made with her. He groaned at the memory, stuffed a pillow over his head, and went to sleep.

PFC Bobby Jaeger drove his Camaro up the back road from Fort Bliss toward the missile range. He was a little drunk from all the beers that guy had bought him in a Juárez nightclub. What was his name? Greg, or something like that. Jesus, what a build! He looked like he could bench-press three hundred pounds easy, maybe more. A real nice guy.

The Camaro started to weave. Bobby brought it to the center line and concentrated on the white stripe. He could ride the middle of the two-lane road straight to Orogrande. There weren't any other cars on the road. He gave the Camaro a nudge up to eighty-five and listened to the sound of the pipes. Sweet.

Greg—that was his name. He knew Sammy. Couldn't believe Sammy went AWOL. Shit! Who could believe it? Asked a lot of questions about Sammy.

Bobby's eyes started to close. He snapped his head up and shook off the cobwebs. No problem, he thought, blinking rapidly to get things in focus. He was still in the middle of the road. Pick up the pace a little bit, he counseled himself. Need to get home and get some rack time.

PFC Bobby Jaeger was fast asleep as the Camaro sped toward the ninety-degree turn at the Orogrande curve. When the right tires left the pavement, Bobby woke up. He turned the wheel and stood on the brakes, and the Camaro slowed to a hundred miles an hour before crashing through the barrier. It flipped on the hood and ground a deep furrow through the desert.

The phone rang at two-thirty in the morning, waking Kerney from a deep sleep.

"Get dressed and meet me outside," Sara Brannon ordered when Kerney answered.

Kerney grunted, got up, and dressed. Outside Captain Brannon waited in a marked patrol car.

"What's up?" Kerney asked, as he climbed into the front seat.

Sara hit the overhead emergency lights and pulled away from the curb before Kerney had the door closed. "PFC Jaeger is dead."

Kerney was wide awake. "What happened?"

"He rolled his car and put his face through the windshield."

They drove through the main post to the Oro-grande turnoff, where Sara floored the unit. In the distance Kerney could see the flashing lights of emergency vehicles.

There were four military police and a medical team at the scene when Sara and Kerney arrived. Two units blocked the road and two more were positioned to spotlight a length of the highway. The sergeant in charge approached at a run as Sara jumped out of the unit and slammed the door.

"What have you got, Sergeant?" she demanded.

"Skid marks and yaw marks, ma'am," the sergeant replied. He was an Asian-American about thirty, with the frame of a distance runner. "He went off the pavement with the right tires, tried to adjust, and hit the brakes. Looks like he fell asleep at the wheel. Probably alcohol-induced."

"Walk me through it."

Kerney watched Sara put the sergeant through his paces as he reviewed the skid marks and physical evidence on the roadway. She asked all the right questions. Then, with Kerney in tow, they walked to the Camaro, which was upside down a good hundred feet from the pavement. A portable generator and light illuminated the overturned vehicle. Bobby Jaeger's face, his expression frozen in surprise, features mangled and bloody, protruded halfway through the shattered glass.

"No seat belt," the sergeant noted.

Sara nodded. "I want a forensic team out here on the double. Nobody touches the body or the car until they're finished. I want to know the mechanical condition of that car before Jaeger rolled it. Arrange for an immediate autopsy when forensics releases the body. Understood?"

"Yes, ma'am," the sergeant answered.

"Also get me full background information on Jaeger before you go off duty. Everything you can dig up about him—drug-screening results, rap sheet, his personnel jacket. You know the drill."

The sergeant nodded glumly. That meant a good three hours of extra work. "Yes, Captain."

"Carry on," Sara said, turning to Kerney. "Are you ready, Lieutenant?"

"Sure."

Sara Brannon said little on the drive back to the base.

"Mind telling me why you brought me along for the ride?" Kerney finally asked.

"Two men room together. Within weeks one goes AWOL and the second dies in an auto accident." She glanced over at Kerney. "Are you good at math? What's the statistical probability?"

"I understand that. What else?"

"You wanted to meet Bobby Jaeger."

"Paybacks are a bitch," Kerney commented.

"Isn't that the truth," Sara replied, with a charming smile.

Captain Brannon called again at six in the morning, rousing Kerney out of a stupor. She gave him instructions on when and where to meet Sergeant Steiner, Sammy's NCOIC, and granted permission for Kerney to search Sammy's gear stored with the quartermaster. Groggy, he shaved in the bathroom mirror, trying not to look too closely at his haggard face. It wasn't a pretty sight.

Finished, he strapped on the ankle weight, sat on the end of the bed, and exercised the knee, working the few remaining ligaments that held the leg together until the pain forced him to quit. He stretched and soaked the leg before getting dressed.

The beefy sergeant in the supply room watched him carefully as he pawed through Sammy's belongings. There were some framed family snapshots, letters from Maria—but none from Terry—civilian clothing, uniforms, and standard-issue military equipment. Sammy had a small desktop stereo system, a fairly eclectic collection of cassette tapes and compact disks, and a small library of paperback novels and art books. There were several unused sketchbooks still wrapped in protective cellophane and an assortment of pens, acrylic paints, and watercolors, but not a single example of Sammy's art work.

Kerney dumped all the clothing on the floor and went through each piece systematically, turning everything inside out. He took the case off the stereo, the covers off the speakers, and the pictures out of the frames. He shook each book by the binding and inspected each cassette tape. Each time he added something to the pile, the sergeant snorted with displeasure. Satisfied that there was nothing, Kerney thanked the sergeant, who grumbled openly about the mess on the floor and damn civilians. Kerney smiled benignly and left.

Staff Sergeant Steiner was waiting for Kerney outside the headquarters building, looking preoccupied. Steiner had a long, angular frame topped off by an owl-like, bookish face. He stiffened as Kerney approached, hands clasped behind his back in an at-ease position. Kerney introduced himself.

"How can I help you, Lieutenant?" Steiner's formal tone indicated he was not a happy volunteer.

"I understand Specialist Yazzi worked for you."

"That's correct."

"What test facility do you work at?" Kerney added.

"It's an uprange site," Steiner replied brusquely.

"Can you tell me about Sammy's work?"

"Not specifically."

"Can you give me a thumbnail sketch without revealing any secrets?"

"In general terms, I can. We work with a new ordnance designed for armored units. We study the products under laboratory and simulated field conditions. I can't say any more than that."

"That's good enough," Kerney said. "How large is your contingent at the test site?"

"Thirty-two, including civilians. We operate twenty-four hours a day, seven days a week. The Gulf War bumped the project to the top of the priority list."

"I was told that Yazzi wanted to change his schedule so he could take some art courses. Did he talk to you about it?"

"He certainly did," Steiner replied emphatically. "I had no problem with the request if it added to his technical skills. I didn't think art courses qualified. I turned him down."

"Was he disappointed?"

"Maybe a little bit," Steiner responded, "but he knew that the job came first. Is that all, Lieutenant?"

"Did you ever have any reason to informally discipline Sammy?"

"Sammy never gave me any problems."

"When did you notice him absent from duty?"

"He failed to report back to work after his rest period."

"He wasn't missed until then?"

"The facility covers a lot of territory. Think of it like an outpost. We have full dining, sleeping, and recreational accommodations, supply and support buildings, plus a number of secure structures."

"What did Sammy like to do on his downtime?"

Steiner ran his finger over the brim of his fatigue cap and hesitated before answering. "He liked to draw."

"And that was okay for him to do?"

He rubbed the back of his neck with his hand and didn't answer.

"You liked Sammy, didn't you?" Kerney said with an understanding smile.

Steiner relaxed a bit. "Sure I did. He was damn good at his job and easy to get along with."

"And you couldn't change the schedule for one man," Kerney added sympathetically. "I understand that. I bet Sammy did, too. Police work is the same way. You just can't afford to play favorites."

"That's right," Steiner agreed.

"But somebody like Sammy," Kerney continued, "a good worker, a team player—if it was me, I'd try to keep him happy, keep him productive."

Steiner nodded in agreement. "That's what being a good supervisor is all about. Is this conversation off the record?"

"Absolutely. I don't work for the Army, Sergeant. I'll make sure it doesn't get back to anybody on the post."

Steiner thought about that for a minute, removed his fatigue hat, and wiped his brow with the back of his hand. "Okay. Technically, any kind of drawing or photography isn't allowed uprange. He knew I wasn't going to change my mind about the duty roster, and I knew he wasn't going to draw pictures that jeopardized national security. Sometimes the regulations just don't match the individual circumstance. So when he asked if he could do his artwork on his free time, I said I would allow it, as long as he turned the drawings over to me when he returned."

"Returned from where?"

"I told him he could only sketch away from the compound. He'd hike into the desert and come back in a couple of hours with some drawings. It was all harmless stuff."

"What did you do with pictures?"

"I destroyed them. That was part of the deal."

Steiner put his fatigue cap back on his head and looked at his wristwatch. "I've got a long drive ahead of me. Is that all, Lieutenant?"

"Was Sammy on a hike the day he turned up missing?"

"Yeah. He always checked in with me before he took off. He was real good about it."

"Who went looking for him when he didn't return?"

"Half the MPs on the post, plus myself and all the off-duty people at the facility."

"How long was he gone before you started looking?"

"Almost the full twelve hours."

Kerney didn't hold Steiner back from leaving. He ran the information through his mind, his spirits sinking. From what Steiner told him, the probability that Sammy had gone AWOL, no matter what the Army believed, was highly unlikely.

Kerney cooled his heels in the company orderly room outside Captain James Meehan's office. Master Sergeant Roy Enloe was at his desk, reading reports and ignoring him. Finally, the phone on Enloe's desk rang. After answering it, Enloe sent Kerney into the captain's office.

The captain, young and engaging, had a thin nose, a dimpled chin, and sandy hair cut short. His uniform was sharply tailored, with airborne jump wings pinned above two rows of service ribbons. Like Sara Brannon, he wore a West Point ring.

Meehan leaned back in his chair and studied Kerney, his expression somewhat perplexed. "I'm a little confused here, Lieutenant. Is Specialist Yazzi wanted by the civilian authorities?"

"No. Sammy's parents are worried about their son. They asked Sheriff Baca to make inquiries. He sent me."

Meehan shook his head and smiled. "I don't see how I can help you. You've talked with my first sergeant. I share his opinion that Sammy was a good soldier. Right now he faces company punishment: loss of rank, confinement to barracks. He can still salvage an honorable discharge if he gets his butt back here soon and doesn't fuck up again." Meehan smiled. "Let the Army sort it out, Lieutenant."

"That's good advice," Kerney replied. "Have you been informed that Sammy's roommate died in an auto accident early this morning?"

Meehan nodded, a grave look crossing his face. "Yes, I have. Tragic."

"Did Jaeger have a drinking problem?"

Meehan bent forward, arms resting on the desk, his expression filled with candor. "Look, Lieutenant, I can bend the rules a bit and talk to you about Specialist Yazzi, but I'm really in no position to talk about PFC Jaeger. I wish I could be more helpful, but you'll have to speak with Captain Brannon about the matter."

Meehan's telephone rang, and Kerney used the interruption as his cue to leave. At the main gate he turned in his visitor's badge and headed for Las Cruces, hoping for better luck in the city. So far, he had fragments of information that added up to a big fat zero.

James Meehan sat in Sara's office, looking at her eyes, which, at the moment, were filled with indignation.

"I don't work for you, Jim," Sara said in response to his comment that letting a civilian cop conduct an investigation on the base wasn't very wise. "It was my call to make."

"All I'm saying is I wish you had told me about it before he showed up in my office. Do you have any background on this Lieutenant Kerney?"

Sara pushed a thin file to the far edge of her desk. Meehan collected it and started reading.

Aside from his regular duties as a company commander, Meehan ran a covert intelligence operation that was completely separate from Army intelligence. Meehan and his people—whoever they were, Sara thought sullenly—watched everything and everybody, and reported directly to the Pentagon. Sara was one of a few officers at the missile range who knew what Meehan really did. When necessary, he used her resources. It might consist of detaining a suspect, conducting a search, or arranging for a traffic stop. Most of the time, Sara had no idea why, but she had standing orders from the highest authority to cooperate. With AWOL cases, however, the cooperation was supposed to be mutual, up to a point.

Meehan laughed when he finished reading Kerney's biography. "This is ludicrous," he said, replacing the folder on the desk. "It serves no purpose to have him on the base. He's just a loose cannon."

"He may well be," Sara replied, "but it was my decision to make."

"I thought we were cooperating on the AWOL cases, Sara."

"Are we? As far as I can tell, it's a pretty one-sided

arrangement. My team does all the grunt work while you stonewall me with need-to-know bullshit. Is Yazzi a security risk or isn't he? Do you have anything to suggest he may have compromised national security?"

"That's not fair, Sara. You know the conditions I have to work under. I'll answer those questions if and when I can. If your people could find Yazzi, things would go a lot faster."

Sara wrinkled her nose. "Right."

"I'm not criticizing. I realize it's a tough case." Meehan stood up. "I do have some good news for you. You can close the Benton file."

Sara arched an eyebrow. Benton was the missing civilian employee. "Really? Tell me about it."

"That's all you get," Meehan responded.

"That stinks."

"All right, I'll tell you this. We have Benton in custody, but the situation involves a possible security breach at another research installation. It should be cleared up in a week."

Sara gave Meehan a sour look. "That's better than nothing, I suppose." She walked to the door and held it open. "Jim, don't ever come into my office again and try to tell me how to do my job. Understood?"

"Feeling a little testy?" Meehan asked with a chuckle.

"Just setting the ground rules, Captain."

Meehan smirked. "You really can be a bitch, Sara."

"You bring it out in me," she answered sweetly, closing the door behind him. She hoped Meehan's assessment of Kerney was wrong. It would give her great pleasure if Kerney turned up something she could stuff it down Jim Meehan's throat, bit by bit.

"You're not walking with your tail between your legs," Andy observed, as Kerney came into his office. "I thought for sure Sara would rough you up a bit."

"She did," he said, sinking into the chair in front of the desk. "The lady is an expert butt-chewer."

Andy nodded sympathetically. "Don't feel bad. She jumped down my throat with both feet." He shrugged philosophically. "Trying to finesse the captain wasn't such a good idea. I think I underestimated her. After living with Connie for twenty-two years, I should know better. Did she send you packing?"

"No."

"Amazing."

"I need your help, Andy. I have one slim lead that may go nowhere and not much time to run it down."

"Tell me what you've got."

Kerney filled him in on everything he knew before getting to his request. The most disquieting fact, Sammy's disappearance in the middle of the desert from a highly secret test site, raised the chances that the boy was dead. Unhappy with the thought, Andy got out of his chair and walked to the window, wondering what pressures Sara Brannon was facing. It was a standing joke in the community that the missile range had more garden-variety spooks, spies, and intelligence operatives than the Pentagon had two-star generals.

He turned to Kerney, who was making his pitch.

"I want to find the Toyota Sammy was driving and talk to the man who was with him the night Carla Montoya saw them together."

"That's a long shot," Andy noted.

"I know it."

Andy decided swiftly. "It's worth a try. I'll give you two deputies for the remainder of the day. Both are fresh out of the academy. That's the best I can do." He picked up the phone and asked for two officers to report to his office.

Kerney's temporary detail arrived quickly. Both of the boys, one with peach fuzz on his chin and the other with the gangly look of an awkward adolescent, looked much too young to hold commissions. Andy filled the deputies in on their assignment and told Kerney to use a small office near the radio room.

Kerney put himself and the team to work immediately, reviewing computerized motor vehicle records on the off chance that Sammy had bought and registered another car, and calling all the dealers in the city to see if anyone remembered Sammy as a customer. It was boring, repetitive work, and after hours on the phone with no success the initial enthusiasm of the deputies had waned.

He looked at the wall clock. The lunch hour had come and gone. Maybe his guys were simply running out of fuel. He ordered pizza to be delivered and got appreciative smiles. When the food arrived, they kept at it, chasing down car salesmen who were at home on days off.

Kerney hung up on his last call and rubbed his ear. His team was back to looking wilted. "Let's try insurance agents," Kerney suggested, as he flipped through a phone book and reached for the telephone. "Hit the ones that cater to military personnel. Call the national offices if you have to. Ask if Sammy inquired about car insurance or got a rate quote."

The deputies nodded dully and got back to work. Kerney was in the middle of his list when the gangly deputy put the mouthpiece against his chest.

"I've got something," he said.

Kerney waited impatiently as the deputy asked questions, scribbled some notes, and finally hung up. He almost yanked the piece of paper out of the officer's hand. At the door, he stopped and remembered his manners. "Thanks. I'll let the sheriff know that you both did good work."

"Any time, Lieutenant," the gangly kid replied, his face breaking into a big smile.

The officers watched the door slam shut behind Kerney, looked at each other, and went to find the incoming shift. The troops would definitely want to hear about the new lieutenant with the bad leg, searching for a missing soldier, who seemed to be the sheriff's friend.

According to the insurance agent, Sammy had asked for a rate quote for a Toyota he planned to buy from D&B Auto Sales. Kerney found the used-car dealership along a four-lane highway on the outskirts of the city. The business, situated on a long, narrow lot, consisted of an old residence converted to an office, a detached single-car garage that served as a repair shop, and fifty or so cars parked under pennants strung between light poles. On top of the office a billboard announced that the dealer would finance any car with a low down payment.

Kerney parked on the street and walked between tightly packed rows of cars to the office. It was unoccupied. At the far corner of the lot, a portly older man was talking to a young Hispanic couple and gesturing at a black Pontiac Firebird with a customized paint job. He spied Kerney and waved. Kerney waved back and waited, his attention drawn to the angry yellow sky.

The evening winds were kicking up a dust storm on the desert beyond the river valley. Billowing plumes of sand diffused the sunlight, creating a false sense of coolness. It was still hot as hell and dry as a bone, but the clouds told of a big blow and the promise of rain sometime soon. As a boy Kerney had stretched his imagination in those clouds, even as he learned to read them from his father, who ranched with one eye on the stock and the other on the weather.

The salesman walked the young couple to their car, talking vigorously and pointing back at the Firebird. The man shook his hand, got the girl in the car, and drove away.

Kerney met the salesman halfway across the lot. He was a roly-poly fellow with a chubby face burned bright pink by the sun.

"How you doing today?" The man asked, extending his hand. "I'm Dewey Boursard."

Kerney identified himself and showed Boursard his badge.

"My lot boy said the police had called here a while ago. I was picking up a new battery at the time. He doesn't speak very good English, so he didn't tell me very much."

"Do you remember a soldier by the name of Sammy Yazzi who wanted to buy a Toyota?"

Dewey smiled. "Almost closed the deal. He was interested in a nice little Toyota subcompact. Came in twice to look at it. Second time I knocked the price down a little and he gave me a hundred dollars in earnest money to hold it until he could arrange financing.

"I sure thought I had a sale. Those Army boys don't get paid enough to give up a hundred dollars that easy. I held that car way past the delivery date. Cherry little vehicle. Low mileage. One owner. I even tried to call him at the base to let him know I'd finance the contract myself if he was having trouble getting a loan."

"Did you get through to him?"

"No. I left a message. He never called back."

"Do you still have the car?"

Dewey smiled and shook his head. "That puppy sold real fast. A college kid from the university bought it. I advertise in the student newspaper. Get a lot of my business from the kids out there."

"Did he ever drive the vehicle?"

"Both times he was here," Dewey replied. "The second time he came in, he brought a buddy along with him."

"Tell me about the buddy," Kerney invited.

Dewey pursed his lips. "I didn't catch his name. He was a black man. A little shorter than you. Maybe six feet tall. He looked to be twenty-five or so, I'd guess. Had an East Coast accent. A mechanic."

"Why do you say that?"

"He drove a '68 Ford Mustang he restored himself. I offered to buy it. Mint condition. Real collector's car."

"That doesn't make him a mechanic."

"He knew cars. Went over that Toyota real careful-like. I think he tagged along to check the Toyota out for his friend. I'll bet you a dollar to a doughnut he's a wrench jockey at the missile range."

"What makes you think so?"

Dewey held out both hands, palms down. His nails were dull and dingy. "Grease," he explained. "I do all the minor work on my inventory. Saves a few dollars. You never get that gunk completely cleaned off. His hands looked worse than mine. Stuff's like dye almost."

"Anything else?"

"He had a base vehicle sticker on the Mustang."

"Do you remember what kind?"

"Enlisted personnel. I see a lot of those on trade-ins."

"Did Sammy talk to you about anything besides the Toyota?"

"Not that I recall," Dewey answered. He changed his mind quickly. "As a matter of fact, he did. I thought he wanted to use an old Chevy for part of his down payment. We'd talked about it the first time he came in. Wasn't worth much, but I could wholesale it and make a few bucks. When I asked, he said the black guy was gonna buy it."

"Thanks for your time."

Dewey smiled and glanced at Kerney's truck. "No problem. If you want to sell that truck, bring it by for an appraisal. If it runs good, I can sell it in a week. Lot of people can't afford the new ones. I could move a dozen late-model trucks a month if I had them. They go like hotcakes."

"I'll keep that in mind," Kerney said.

The dust storm intensified near the mountains that separated the missile range from the rest of the world. An updraft blew sand against the rear window with a faint hissing sound. Kerney topped out at the San Andres Pass. The Tularosa Basin was hidden from view by a grimy sky. He turned off the highway onto the access road to the missile range and checked the time. His twenty-four hours had expired. Captain Sara Brannon wouldn't be any too pleased at his checking in late, but maybe new information just might cut him some slack.

CHAPTER

4

Sara found an MP buttoned up in his patrol vehicle in front of her house. The dust storm whipped sand at her face that felt like so many hot pinpricks. She took a packet from him, hurried into the house, and went immediately to the bedroom, trailing sand along the way. She dropped the envelope on the bed, stripped off her uniform, and stood under a hot shower, letting the water soak away the dryness. If she stayed in the desert much longer, she thought, she would shrivel up and blow away. If not that, she'd have skin like shoe leather. Naked in front of the bathroom mirror, she worked body lotion into her skin, rubbed on some face cream, and brushed her hair dry.

Dressed in a tank top, cutoff jeans, and a pair of

flats, she took the envelope into the living room and checked for messages on the answering machine. Fred Utley had called to invite her to a movie at the post theater. He continued to show romantic interest in her, and she wished he would just chill out. In a way, it was her own damn fault for sleeping with him once when she couldn't think of a good reason not to. She'd call him back and decline.

A second message, from one of the investigators assigned to follow Kerney, got her full attention. Kerney was back on base asking to speak to her after spending hours at the sheriff's department in Las Cruces, and then interviewing a salesman at a used-car dealership. The investigator's partner was talking to the salesman and would report as soon as he returned.

She reached for the phone, hesitated, and took her hand off the receiver. Fred could wait, and Kerney could cool his heels for a while. Curling up on the couch, she opened the envelope. It contained an FBI report on Kerney and a memorandum to her from the post historian. Setting the memorandum aside, she read the FBI report.

Kerney had been born at home on the 7-Bar-K Ranch east of Tularosa, New Mexico, on land now part of the missile range. A year younger than his high school classmates, he had graduated as valedictorian and won the state high school rodeo championship in his senior year. Taking a heavy load in college, he had earned his degree in three years, finishing in the top 10 percent of his class.

His parents, Matthew and Mary, had been killed in a head-on automobile accident while driving to

Albuquerque to meet Kerney upon his return from duty in Vietnam.

Sara skimmed his military service record, pausing to read the Silver Star citation. Kerney had led an extraction team into VC territory, encountered heavy enemy resistance, and successfully brought out a downed fighter pilot.

After returning home, Kerney had enrolled in graduate school at the university in Albuquerque and married a woman who was a first-year law school student. In less than a year, the marriage had ended, and Kerney had quit school to join the Santa Fe Police Department. Sara wondered what had happened to precipitate so much change so quickly in Kerney's life.

The report finished with a summary of Kerney's law enforcement experience. Rising rapidly through the ranks, Kerney had been a prime candidate to become the next police chief until he was badly wounded and forced to retire.

Sara dropped the report on the cushion, rummaged through the bookcase for a map of the missile range, and spread it out on the carpet. The location of the old 7-Bar-K Ranch, identified clearly on the map, was almost within shouting distance of Sammy Yazzi's duty station.

Sara's eyes wandered over the topographical symbols. Where in hell had Sammy Yazzi gone? Through Seep Canyon? Tip Top Canyon? He had stayed on the restricted road that crossed the basin to the small ranching settlement at Engle, but trackers had lost all sign of him at the entrance to Rhodes Canyon, still deep in the missile range.

Sara knew Yazzi hadn't used Rhodes Canyon as

an escape route. He would have been spotted by personnel stationed at the secret observation post that guarded the pass. And most probably he had not traveled through Engle. Every inhabitant, including the area ranchers, had been interviewed, with no reported sightings. So Sammy had skirted the canyon, but none of the intrusion sensors on the base perimeter had picked him up. The search and rescue teams she'd sent in had scoured the immediate area for his body with no luck.

As her eyes drifted back to the 7-Bar-K Ranch symbol on the map, the telephone rang. Not wanting to talk to Fred, she let the answering machine click on and didn't pick up until she recognized the watch commander's voice. "What is it?"

"That sheriff's lieutenant is still waiting to see you," the voice replied.

"Send him over," she said.

She put the report in her briefcase—she would finish it later—walked to the patio door that led to the backyard, and watched the wind spatter sand against the glass. The branches of a lone willow tree bent and jerked in the force of the gale. She caught a glimpse of her reflection in the glass door, made a face, and went to change into something less informal.

Kerney slipped inside as Sara Brannon closed the door behind him, blinking his eyes and rubbing sand from his face. The short walk from his truck to the front porch made him feel as if he had been sandblasted. The weather had turned ferocious. Sara said nothing as she ushered him to the living room through the hall that divided a galley kitchen and dining nook from the main part of the house. In the living room another small corridor took a left turn to the bedrooms and bath.

The house, a utilitarian cement-block structure, would have been depressing if not for Sara's good taste. A wicker chair with a matching ottoman served as a reading niche next to an oak bookcase. The chair faced the patio door to the backyard. On the top shelf of the bookcase were framed family photographs. Sara gestured for Kerney to sit in a second easy chair that matched an expensive tan couch. She arranged herself at the corner of the couch by an end table that held a lamp, telephone, and answering machine. On the floor in front of a low coffee table was an open map.

"I expected to hear from you before now," she said. She wore jeans, a red short-sleeved turtleneck top, and sandals, and sat with one leg tucked under the other.

"I wanted to have something to say first," Kerney countered.

"Fair enough. What have you got?"

Kerney started talking, and Sara listened for anything that would contradict the reports she'd received from the surveillance teams. He gave it to her straight, including his curiosity about Bull McVay and the surprising fact, unknown to Sara before Kerney's arrival, that Sergeant Steiner had let Sammy do pencil sketches on his free time without getting proper authorization.

She paid even closer attention when Kerney briefed her on his conversation with Dewey Boursard—that was fresh information that had yet to come to her from the team.

He concluded with a smile and added: "I'm sure none of this is news to you. Your people have been with me every step of the way."

"What tipped you?"

"The cars. Same make and model. Plus your men are sloppy on the shift changeovers. They like to chit-chat with each other before they make the switch," He got up, stepped around the coffee table, and bent over the map. "Show me where you searched for Sammy."

She joined him, sat on the floor, and gave him a rundown, watching for a reaction as she traced her finger past the 7-Bar-K Ranch location. There was none.

"Were there any visitors uprange at the time of his disappearance?" he inquired when she stopped.

"Nobody who wasn't authorized and cleared."

"Any ideas where he went to do his sketching?"

"None at all."

"What did the Jaeger autopsy reveal?" Kerney asked, moving the map aside.

"Jaeger's blood alcohol level was twice the legal limit," Sara replied. "He had a clean record—no disciplinary action, no history of substance abuse, and no DWI arrests."

"And the Camaro?"

"Clean as a whistle. The only mechanical damage was caused during the accident."

"So much for statistical probabilities."

The phone rang, and Sara went to answer it. With her back to him, she listened without comment for several minutes, thanked the caller, hung up, and swiveled her head in his direction. "We've found your man," she said. "The Mustang is owned by

Specialist Fifth Class Weldon Robinson. He supervises the post auto shop."

Kerney smiled broadly. "Your people work fast."

Sara wrinkled her nose at him. "Come on," she said, getting to her feet. "Let's go talk to Robinson."

The Post Auto Shop, in an old Quonset hut near the motor pool, served as a do-it-yourself center for shade-tree mechanics. The building was locked, but the inside lights were on, and through a window Kerney saw a Mustang parked over a service bay. He pounded on the door while Sara huddled for cover from the strong gusts of wind that made the outside light above the door flap precariously.

Kerney kept pounding until a surly-looking black man climbed out of the service bay, came to the window, and pointed at a closed sign. Robinson's name was stitched over the right pocket of his fatigue shirt. Kerney put his badge against the glass and pointed at the door. The surly look cleared, and Robinson nodded in agreement. He let them in and slammed the door shut fast to keep out the storm.

"Sorry about that," Robinson said, "but if I don't stick to my schedule, I'd have guys in here twenty-four hours a day."

"That's okay," Kerney replied.

Robinson gave Sara a cautious look. "Captain," he said politely, "is there a problem?"

"Relax, Specialist," Sara said easily. "We're here to talk about Sammy Yazzi. Do you know him?"

Robinson pulled at the tail of his greasy fatigue shirt. "I sure do," he answered. "Me and him had an agreement. I was gonna buy his old Chevy. The fuel pump is busted and the carburetor needs to be rebuilt. I was gonna give him the money on payday, but then he went AWOL. It's still parked up by the barracks."

"Did you take anything out of the car?" Kerney asked.

Robinson nodded. "Right before Sammy split he said I could start working on it anytime and gave me the keys. There was a bunch of stuff inside that I cleaned out."

"What stuff?" Sara demanded.

"Just the usual junk people leave in cars, and a big leather case to keep art stuff in."

"A portfolio," Sara clarified.

"That's it."

"Do you still have it?"

Robinson inclined his head toward the small office next to the service bay. "Yes, ma'am. I kept everything."

They followed Robinson to the office and waited while he pulled the portfolio out from behind a filing cabinet and located a small box mixed in with some cartons on the floor. "That's all of it," he said.

Sara took the portfolio, Kerney grabbed the box, and Robinson walked them to the door. "Is that all you need, Captain?" he asked.

"Yes."

"Don't you drive a Jeep Cherokee?" Robinson inquired.

"I do."

"Bring it down and I'll give it a tune-up. Cost you for the parts only."

"I may do that, Specialist."

Outside she told Kerney to take her back to her house. Protocol called for them to log the items as evidence immediately, and Kerney had assumed they would do it at Sara's office. He said nothing, and they drove in silence, the box on the floorboard and the portfolio in Sara's lap. The storm had blown itself out quickly, and the sky had cleared enough for a moonlight haze to pour over the basin. The top of the post water tower emerged on the side of a hill above the residential area, and streetlights illuminated the precise rows of military housing units with neat lawns and carefully trimmed shrubbery. A soft breeze pushed lines of sand across the pavement in lacy waves.

In the living room, Sara put away the map to make space on the carpet for the evidence. They sat opposite one another and went through the contents of the box first, like children saving the best present for last. It contained a pair of sunglasses, cassette tapes for the car stereo, a class catalog from the university, a small car repair kit in a plastic case, and several wrinkled road maps.

Sara unzipped the portfolio and spread it open on the carpet, revealing a series of watercolors and pencil drawings, each separated by a sheet of clear plastic. She laid them out in order, fingers touching only the tips of the paper. Kerney scooted next to her on the rug, his bad leg protesting the movement.

"Marvelous," she said, almost to herself, switching her attention from one painting to another. "Sergeant Steiner said nothing about a portfolio of watercolors."

"Did you have Steiner picked up after I talked to him?"

Sara smiled sweetly. "Of course I did."

"I promised him he wouldn't get in trouble."

"He's not, although I did chew him out for not leveling with us."

"Did you find any other artwork?"

Sara nodded. "We have Sammy's sketchbooks that were in his quarters. All very harmless: anatomy studies of animals, pencil sketches of plant life, caricatures of some of his buddies. Until you talked to Steiner we had no knowledge that Sammy was sketching in restricted areas."

"What Steiner said amounts to nothing more than the reason Sammy went hiking on his free time," Kerney replied.

"I agree, but until now, we operated on the assumption that Specialist Yazzi left with the intent to go AWOL. That no longer seems to be the case."

She dropped her gaze to the watercolors, a series of wildlife studies. Each consisted of three separate panels: a landscape field sketch, a pencil drawing of a wildlife subject, and the final watercolor version, combining both elements. The landscape pencil drawings showed the locations of Sammy's field trips—the rickety windmill at Windy Well, the dilapidated corral at old John Prather's ranch, the mesa above the 7-Bar-K Ranch. Sammy had traversed a large chunk of real estate on the missile range.

"I wish we'd had these when we were looking for him," Sara reflected. "He's been all over the damn base, at places we didn't even think to search."

"Maybe we should search again," Kerney suggested.

"Maybe we should."

"He's been to some remote back country, from the looks of it," Kerney added. "Not places you can hike into in less than a day. Any ideas on how he got there?"

Sara watched carefully to see what drawing Kerney looked at as he spoke. A bobcat seemed to command his attention. She had no idea what the locale for the painting might be. "The service club operates a jeep excursion program for post personnel. They can sign out for a vehicle for day trips into the wilderness areas. Use is limited to specific roads and locations on the range."

"A jeep would do it," Kerney said, getting up stiffly from the carpet. "I'll check the service club records in the morning. It might give us a better idea of where to start looking."

"I think you already know where to look," Sara asserted.

Kerney gave her a wry smile and shook his head. "I don't know where to *start.*"

Sara stood up. "I'll let the service club NCO know you're coming."

"Thanks." He walked to the bookcase and picked up a framed photograph of four riders on horseback, a man, woman, young boy, and girl. The girl, with pigtails dangling down under the brim of a cowboy hat, had a broad, happy smile. From the looks of it, Sara must have been no more than thirteen years old when the picture was taken. "Your family?"

"Yes."

"Where was the photograph taken?"

"Montana. North of Livingston on the Shields River. My parents are sheep ranchers. My brother and I are the fourth generation. Paul runs the ranch now. Mom and Dad work part-time, and head south in the winter. They call themselves snowbirds."

Kerney looked at the photograph again before replacing it on the bookcase. If Sara's mother was an indication of how her daughter would age, it was clear Sara would be very lovely for many years to come. "They look like good people," he said.

"They are."

"Do you think you can locate Bull McVay?" he asked.

Sara smiled. "Already done. Meet me at my office at noon and we'll drive up to see him."

"I'll be there. Is the BOQ available, or am I still out of time?"

"I think we can forget the clock, Lieutenant. I'll let them know you're staying over another night."

"Can you lose the tail on me?" he asked.

"Good night, Lieutenant," Sara said sweetly, brushing off the request.

She watched Kerney limp to his truck with his half-rolling, busted-up gait and smiled in spite of herself. It probably hurt him like hell, but the walk reminded her of home and the men she had grown up with. She watched him drive away, called the BOQ, sat at the dining-room table, opened her briefcase, and took out the memorandum prepared by the post historian.

Patrick Kerney (born Live Oak County, Texas, 1872; died Albuquerque, New Mexico, 1964, age 92) came to the Tularosa Valley at the age of thirteen, as a horse wrangler for one of the original Texas cattlemen. He was a contemporary of Eugene Manlove Rhodes (see W. H. Hutchinson, *A Bar Cross Man*, University of Oklahoma Press, 1956), a cowboy who became one of the best-known western novelists of the early twentieth century.

Both Rhodes and Kerney worked at the Bar Cross Ranch as wranglers and hands. Kerney took a patent on six thousand acres in the foothills of the San Andres Mountains about the same time that Rhodes laid claim to his land in what is now known as Rhodes Canyon. Both ran longhorn cattle, hired out to other spreads and broke mustangs to make ends meet. Patrick Kerney hauled freight from the railroad in Engle to the Mescalero Apache Indian Reservation on a contract with the Army for several winters.

Kerney and his son, Matthew, played a significant role in the resistance by the local ranchers to the military takeover of the valley. The Kerney family was one of the last to move off the range and one of the few to continue operations on a co-use arrangement with the Army into the early 1960s. Court action mounted by Kerney and his neighbor Albert Jennings, who ranched on the west slope of the San Andres, was dismissed after several years of litigation.

The last confrontation between ranchers and the government occurred at the Prather ranch in 1959. In spite of a court order, John Prather had refused to accept a writ of eviction served by military police and United States marshals. Word of the standoff spread to friends, relatives, and neighbors, who flocked to assist old John Prather. For hours the group kept a large Army contingent at bay. The writ was reversed and Prather was allowed to remain at his ranch until he died. It was the last property seized on the original installation under the eminent domain condemnation proceedings.

Patrick Kerney, age 87, his son, Matthew, and his grandson, Kevin, took part in the Prather showdown, armed with repeating rifles. (Attached are archive photographs.) The incident made national news and was covered by the wire services, newspapers, and broadcast media.

The Kerney family moved to the Jennings ranch, where Matthew was employed as foreman. Patrick Kerney resided with the family until 1963, when deteriorating health forced his son to place him in an Albuquerque nursing home, where he died the following spring.

She skimmed through the eight-by-ten black-and-white photographs once more, stopping at the picture of a young Kevin Kerney sitting against the rock exterior of the Prather ranch house, with his arms wrapped around his knees and his hands clutching the barrel of a rifle. He was dressed in faded jeans stuffed into scruffy boots and a wide-brim cowboy hat pulled low. His eyes were wide open and filled with innocent determination. It was both charming and touching.

Despite the lateness of the hour, more work needed to be done. Kerney's breakthrough was progress, and it started Sara's wheels turning. It was time to do something equally innovative about the missing Navy enlisted man. She opened the case file on Petty Officer Third Class Alan Yardman and started to read it, looking for anything that might give her a new strategy.

* * *

Strong upper-level winds cleared the last of the haze from the sky and chilled the night air. A crust of fresh sand crunched under Kerney's feet as he walked to the steps of the barracks. According to his watch, PFC Tony should be about to get off work. As tired as he was, Kerney didn't dare sit down. The knee felt as if it would lock up. It would take a lot of painful stretching to get it to work in the morning without killing him. He was grateful when Tony rounded the corner of the building.

"More questions, Lieutenant?"

"Just a few. Did you go with Sammy on any of his excursions into the desert?"

"I don't know nothing about that." He nervously took out a cigarette and lit it.

"I'll be checking the records at the service club in the morning," Kerney countered. "Why not make my job easier?"

Tony exhaled and stayed silent.

"Look, Alonzo, protecting Sammy because he may have broken a few stupid rules doesn't help him. We both know Sammy's a good guy. I'm not here to get anybody in trouble."

"Why should I believe you?"

"I'm Sammy's godfather." Kerney took out his wallet, found the high school graduation picture Sammy had sent him, and handed it to Tony.

Tony cocked his head and looked at it. "You expect me to believe a Navajo has a white guy for a godfather?" Tony questioned.

"Sammy isn't a Navajo; his father is. Sammy's Tewa and belongs to his mother's clan."

"That's right," Tony replied.

"I've known Sammy since the day he was born. Turn the picture over."

Tony flipped over the photograph, read the inscription, gave it back to Kerney, and smiled. "A Tewa with an Irish-American godfather. Damn. Sammy didn't tell me about that.

"Okay. I went with him a few times. We would check out a jeep from the service club and take off. You're supposed to stay on certain roads, but Sammy drove wherever the hell he wanted to. I kept warning him the MP patrols would catch us, but he said he would just tell them we got lost."

"What did Sammy do when you were with him?"

"He had this real nice thirty-five-millimeter camera he bought at the PX. It had a telephoto lens. He took a lot of pictures. Scenery. Birds. Whatever he liked."

"Do you remember where you went?"

Tony lifted his head in the direction of the San Andres Mountains. "Up on some mesas. A good thirty miles out."

"Do you remember any place-names?"

"Just one. Sheep Mesa, Big Sheep Mesa, or Big Mesa. Something like that. It's north of an old ranch."

"Where did Sammy keep his camera?"

"I don't know, but he almost always had it with him when he was off duty." Tony stubbed out the cigarette on the heel of his boot and field-stripped it.

"Did he develop his own pictures?"

"Yeah, but he didn't use the darkroom on the post. Once in a while he'd come back from Las Cruces with developed prints." He looked over

89

Kerney's shoulder, came to attention, and snapped off a salute.

Kerney turned to find Captain Meehan returning the acknowledgment. He was in uniform and wearing an Army-issue sweater to ward off the chill.

"I wonder if you would give me a few minutes with Lieutenant Kerney," Meehan said to the young soldier.

"Yes sir."

"Very good," Meehan answered cordially. He waited for Tony to salute again, returned the courtesy, eyed Kerney speculatively, and waited to speak until Tony went inside the barracks. "I thought you'd finished your investigation."

"Almost," Kerney replied. "Just some wrap-up questions."

"Any interesting developments?"

"Nothing at all."

"Will you be coming back?" Meehan inquired.

"Probably not."

Meehan smiled. "If you do, check in with my first sergeant or company clerk before you talk to the personnel."

"I apologize for the omission."

Meehan laughed. "No harm done, but I want to keep things settled down around here. Troop morale is important to me. From Captain Brannon I'm aware that you saw service as an Army officer. I think you know what I'm saying."

Kerney decided to push Meehan's button. He was growing tired of the man's supercilious attitude. "Is troop morale a problem for you, Captain?"

Meehan stiffened and became more formal. "This is an isolated, secure military base. Most of the men who live in the barracks are young, horny, and usually flat broke two weeks after they get paid. Any AWOL situation can become infectious. I do not plan to be called on the carpet to explain an unacceptable AWOL rate."

"I see your point," Kerney responded affably.

"Good. I'll walk with you to your truck," Meehan announced, guiding Kerney along with a touch on his arm. "I'm sure the Army will find Specialist Yazzi. Captain Brannon has some very experienced personnel."

"I'm sure she does," Kerney agreed.

At Kerney's truck Meehan said goodbye, patting the driver's door to speed him on his way. Kerney gave him a wave and drove out of the parking lot. He circled the compound, killed his headlights, and coasted to a stop in time to see Meehan going through the back door of Alonzo Tony's barracks. He restarted the engine and headed toward the BOQ.

The soldier on duty at the BOQ gave Kerney the irritated, barely compliant look enlisted personnel reserve for VIPs who take advantage, and told him Captain Brannon had ordered him to stand by until Kerney arrived. Kerney apologized for holding the soldier up, took his key, and found his way to his room. At the end of the hall the lobby lights went off before he had the door open.

He stretched out fully dressed on the bed, with a pillow under his knee. Where was Sammy's camera? That, and the film and photographs, along with any additional sketchbooks, needed to be found. And why was Captain Meehan interrogating Alonzo Tony? Kerney doubted it had a damn thing to do with troop morale. What was Meehan doing in the compound so late at night in the first place? The company headquarters had been dark and quiet during the time Kerney waited for Tony. Meehan's arrival and his little chat seemed more than coincidental.

He shifted the position of his leg on the pillow and groaned. The last question for the evening was personal: how in the hell did he expect to raise beef cattle and ranch when he got so damned exhausted doing absolutely nothing?

CHAPTER

5

— · — · — · —

Corporal Eddie Tapia stood in front of Captain Brannon's office door worried about orders he had received to report to her on the double. The duty sergeant at the desk shrugged when he asked why the captain wanted to see him. He didn't think he'd screwed up. On the promotion list for buck sergeant, Eddie couldn't afford any mistakes. He needed that third stripe and the pay raise that went with it. It wasn't easy to support a wife and a new baby on an E-4 salary.

After spending the night in a car outside the BOQ, trying to stay awake while the civilian cop from Las Cruces slept in a warm bed, he felt rumpled, groggy, and in need of a shave. He knocked on the door and entered quickly when the captain responded.

Captain Brannon stood with her back to Tapia, rummaging through a metal file cabinet. She was wearing cowboy boots, blue jeans, and a white, silky kind of blouse. Eddie had never seen the captain in civvies before. She had a very nice ass.

He stood in front of the desk and waited for her to turn around. She glanced over her shoulder and looked him up and down before speaking.

"Sit down, Eddie," she said, as she came back to her desk and lowered herself into her chair. "Thanks for coming so quickly."

"No problem, ma'am." Inwardly, Eddie sighed with relief. He wasn't in trouble after all. Bone-tired, he sat, folded his hands in his lap, and tried to look as alert as possible.

Sara took time to arrange the paperwork on the desk, using the moment to consider Tapia. He would do, she decided. Dedicated to his work, Tapia was solid and dependable. Of Mexican and Indian heritage, he was bilingual, had a guileless face and streetwise smarts.

"I'm closing the Benton case."

Surprised, Eddie became more attentive. He had been working the Benton case, checking every gym in El Paso and Las Cruces, trying to catch a break, until the Kerney assignment came up. Benton was a physical fitness nut and ladies' man who liked to hit on women at health spas. The case was going nowhere. Two months ago, for no apparent reason, Benton had resigned unexpectedly and left work that same day, never to be seen again. By the time the defense contractor reported him missing, Benton had moved out of his apartment and left no clues as to his whereabouts.

"Has he been picked up?" Eddie asked.

"Intelligence has him in custody," Sara replied. "That's all I know."

"I'd sure like to know where they found him," Eddie mused. "And how."

"So would I," Sara agreed. "I have another job for you. Are you familiar with the Alan Yardman case?"

"A little," Tapia responded. "Yardman worked at the Naval Space Satellite Surveillance Station as a repair technician. He went AWOL after his commanding officer ordered him to submit to mandatory drug screening. If I remember correctly, he went home to South Dakota, cleaned out his mother's jewelry box, and vanished."

"That's right," Sara confirmed. "I've been studying Yardman's personnel jacket. He had good efficiency ratings and a clean record until his transfer to the missile range. Within six months after his arrival, it's downhill all the way: poor job performance, uncooperative attitude, conduct bordering on insubordination.

"The assumption," Sara continued, "is that Yardman was an addict who went AWOL, paid a visit to his mother, and ripped her off to buy drugs. Yet, all his drug-screening results from every duty station, including White Sands, were negative. We know he wasn't a womanizer, yet he spent a lot of time in Juárez. If he wasn't getting high or whoring around, what was he doing?"

The third most popular vice, Eddie thought. "Gambling?" he suggested.

"Exactly."

"Is there any evidence that he liked to gamble?"

"Circumstantial only." She handed a sheet of

paper to Tapia. "I asked for Yardman's credit union account late last night. Take a look."

Tapia studied the statement. Yardman had made frequent deposits, in different amounts, many of them near the end of the month when most people were short of cash. The withdrawals, some identical to the deposits, seemed to occur without any pattern. It didn't mean squat, Eddie thought, unless Yardman was a loan shark. But sharks don't collect until after paydays, and they don't put their working capital in credit unions.

"Seems odd," Eddie said, trying to sound positive.

Captain Brannon agreed with Tapia's skepticism. "It tells us nothing until you compare Yardman's duty schedule to the transaction dates. Money out when he's leaving the post; money in when he returns. Not always, but consistently enough to suggest that he was banking his winnings for the next go-round. And when he won big, the next withdrawal matched the deposit exactly."

She passed him more papers. Yardman's days off were circled in red. He compared the two documents. The month before he split, Yardman had been taking cash out of his account and not replacing it, until all the money was gone. "You think he hit a losing streak?"

Sara nodded. "That's the way I read it. Two days before he left, he applied for a personal loan at the credit union, but didn't stick around to find out if it got approved. I think he robbed his mother because he was either in debt to a loan shark or had simply lost control completely. What do you think?"

"It's a possibility, Captain," Eddie replied. "If it's

true, we've been looking for him in the wrong places."

"That's right. Gamblers are superstitious. What if Yardman returned to Juárez to try his luck again? Does that seem likely to you?"

"He could be anywhere," Eddie answered cautiously.

"True enough, except for one point. He was rock-solid with his money at his previous duty stations. Didn't spend much and saved a regular amount each month. If Yardman is a compulsive gambler, it's a fairly recent development. I think he might go back to familiar surroundings."

"That makes sense."

Sara stood up and gave the Yardman file to Tapia. "I'm glad you think so. I want you in Juárez as soon as possible. There's two thousand dollars in that folder, along with a copy of my orders. Improvise, Eddie. This is an undercover assignment. You are to report only to me and tell no one about this."

Eddie opened his mouth, swallowed hard, and clamped his jaw shut.

"What is it, Corporal?"

"I have to tell my wife something," Eddie responded.

"Has Isabel been home to show off your new baby to her parents yet?"

"No, she hasn't."

"Use some of the money in the envelope and send her for a visit."

"Can I do that?"

"This time you can. You have my written permission to spend the cash as you see fit, including dependent travel. It's spelled out in the orders."

Eddie grinned. Isabel would love it. She'd been bugging him to go home since the day his son was born. "Anything else, Captain?"

"Be careful."

"I grew up on the border, ma'am. It's my old stomping grounds."

"That's why you're going," Sara said. "You know the drill on how to contact me. I'll expect reports at twenty-four-hour intervals. As of now, you're officially on leave. You're up for a promotion review next month. Clear this case and I'll make sure you get those new chevrons."

Eddie's grin widened. "Yes, ma'am."

"Enjoy your time off, Corporal."

Corporal Eddie Tapia did an about-face and left Sara's office, feeling a hell of a lot better about himself, his job, and his prospects. He had a plum assignment, an unexpected surprise for Isabel, and a chance to climb another step up the ranks. He hurried out, anxious to get home and pack Isabel and the baby off to her parents.

Major Thomas Curry, the post provost marshal, walked to his staff car in the parking lot humming the melody to "Blue Rondo à la Turk." Every morning before work, he spent thirty minutes at his piano. Today's session, an attempt at the driving chords and difficult time signature of the Dave Brubeck composition, was a technically demanding exercise, and it had gone very well.

Curry's fine spirits weren't dampened by the prospect of his regularly scheduled monthly briefing with the deputy post commander, at which Curry presented updated crime statistics. Curry's report was tolerated solely because the commanding general had decided to fight crime on the base and had made his second-in-command, who disliked the assignment, responsible for the initiative. It made for an uncomfortable half hour. No matter—only a few months away from retirement, Curry would muster out as a lieutenant colonel. Not bad for a man who came up through the enlisted ranks. As a survivor of the reduction-in-force purge, he was gratified to have made it to full retirement.

He heard Sara Brannon call out to him. He put his briefcase on the hood of his staff car and waited as she jogged toward him. Curry felt somewhat fatherly toward Sara. A reliable officer, she kept him fully informed, a characteristic he valued highly, and her criminal investigation unit produced the best rate of cleared cases among comparable commands, which was part of the reason he would wear the silver oak leaves of a lieutenant colonel at his retirement ceremony. Aside from all that, Sara bubbled with high spirits, boundless energy, and a well-founded confidence in her abilities that added to her attractiveness.

He was delighted to see her in civvies. "Day off?" he asked, in mock disbelief, when she reached him. Curry wondered if Sara had finally hooked up with one of the many eligible bachelors who were constantly trying to corral her.

"Not really," Sara replied. "I'm taking over the Yazzi investigation. I'll be away from the base most of the day."

Curry checked his wristwatch. "Fill me in later."

"My report is on your desk."

"Good enough. Can you handle the extra load?" he asked.

"I think so," Sara responded. "Has Jim Meehan talked to you about the case?"

Curry laughed. "Captain Charisma? No, he hasn't. Is he giving you trouble?"

Sara hesitated. "No, just acting like himself. I wanted you to know I'm sending an investigator undercover into Mexico to see what he can dig up on the Yardman case."

"I thought that case was stalled. Have you caught a lead?"

"More like a slim possibility."

Curry raised his eyebrows. "Is it worth the effort?"

"I'll shut it down if nothing materializes."

He nodded in agreement and picked up his briefcase. "I'm off to see our crime prevention czar."

"Have a good time, Major," Sara replied, her green eyes sparkling with humor, knowing how much Curry loathed the tedious meeting.

Curry grimaced. "Next month I'll send you in my place."

"You wouldn't," Sara protested.

"Watch me," Curry promised.

Kevin Kerney's internal clock brought him out of a sound sleep at five. A touch of pink was in the clear eastern sky, but the mountains would hold dawn back long enough for him to run without making a spectacle of himself with his awkward gait. An unmarked surveillance car was parked across the street. The man behind the wheel smirked as he ran past. The hell with him, Kerney thought. He jogged one mile down the gravel road to the water tower and a mile back. He returned to the BOQ as the morning orderly was coming on duty.

By the time he showered and dressed, the post canteen was open for business. He ate a light meal and watched the customers drinking their morning coffee before heading off to work. He trailed behind a group of office workers, entered the headquarters building, and found his way to the public information office.

The public information officer, a plain-looking female first lieutenant with a pinched face and mousy brown hair, was cooperative. Kerney learned that the only visitors allowed uprange during the time of Sammy's disappearance were a group of treasure hunters digging for lost gold at Victorio Peak and members of the Audubon Society conducting a semiannual bird survey west of Three Rivers. Neither place was anywhere close to Sammy's duty station.

He asked about outsiders with uprange access and learned that state and federal game and conservation officers were allowed in. All carried law enforcement commissions and had security clearances. The lieutenant didn't know who among them had been around when Sammy went AWOL, but she pulled out a file folder with names and phone numbers, explaining with great seriousness that conservation and the environment were of vital concern to the Army.

Kerney copied the list into his notebook—two

dozen names, including a wildlife specialist who came down from Santa Fe to manage the bighorn sheep herd, a National Park Service ranger who supervised the wilderness area, and a Bureau of Land Management officer who looked after the wild mustang herd. He thanked the lieutenant for her time and left wondering how the Army kept track of two dozen men and women roaming around the five thousand square miles of the missile range.

Probably with satellite locators, he decided, as he parked outside the service club. The club was closed, but the office at the back of the building was open. The young woman inside gave him an annoyed look when he entered. She covered the open paperback book on her desk with a piece of typing paper. Kerney introduced himself and showed his credentials.

"Captain Brannon said you'd be coming by." She had a flat midwestern voice, thin lips, and a pageboy hairdo.

"What can you tell me about the jeep excursion program?" he asked.

"It's very popular," the woman replied, her hand resting on the covered book. Her long fingers flowed down from a skinny arm and bony elbow. "Base personnel and their dependents may sign out to use service club vehicles for wilderness excursions and recreational trips. I'm usually booked solid a month in advance."

"The paperwork must really pile up," Kerney suggested.

She smiled briefly in agreement. "It does. I have to complete a monthly report that records vehicle mileage, trip destination, all drivers and passengers, times in and out, and gasoline consumption."

Kerney asked to see the records.

"How far back did you want to go?" she asked.

"Ten months."

"That's a lot of paperwork," she cautioned.

"I don't mind."

She scooted her chair to a bank of file cabinets behind the desk, searched through a drawer, extracted two thick accordion folders, held them out for Kerney to take, and tilted her head at an unoccupied desk. "You can use the sergeant's desk. He doesn't come in until noon."

Kerney took the files and sat at the desk. He read the material carefully, jotting down each of Sammy's excursions. His trip tickets showed that he went in all directions, but none listed Sheep Mesa or Big Mesa as a destination, where Alonzo Tony said he'd gone with Sammy. Finished, Kerney raised his eyes. The secretary was reading a romance novel. He coughed to get her attention, and the paperback book quickly disappeared from sight.

"What is it?"

"If I signed out for a jeep, how would I know where I could and couldn't drive?"

"You get a map with everything clearly marked."

"Can I see one?"

Wordlessly she held up a map for him to fetch. He took it from her and returned to the desk. Sheep Mesa was definitely off-limits, as was all "casual and recreational" travel from Big Mesa, once part of the old 7-Bar-K Ranch. Sammy definitely liked to go where the spirit moved him.

In one accordion file was a folder marked "Special Events." Sammy had gone on only one such outing. The trip ticket and an attendance roster were stapled to a flyer. It read:

KNOWN SURVIVORS

A ONE-DAY TOUR OF NATIVE AMERICAN

SPANISH AND ANGLO HABITATION

IN THE TULAROSA BASIN

CONDUCTED BY

DR. FRED UTLEY

FEBRUARY 5

PARTICIPATION LIMITED

SIGN UP BY JANUARY 15

BROUGHT TO YOU BY YOUR SERVICE CLUB!

He decided to pay Dr. Utley a visit and found him loading provisions in a four-wheel-drive utility vehicle in front of a prefabricated metal building. Utley stopped and gave Kerney a friendly handshake.

"Lieutenant Kerney, isn't it?" Utley asked.

"That's right."

Utley looked relieved. "I'm bad with names. What brings you out to my shop?"

Behind Utley an overhead door opened to a storeroom filled with rows of shelves filled with tools, climbing gear, water cans, camping equipment, and boxes.

"I'd like to know about the tour you put on through the service club," Kerney said.

"You mean 'Known Survivors'? I do that twice a year. It's very well attended." Utley adjusted his glasses. "Can I ask what this is about?"

"A missing soldier. Maybe Captain Brannon mentioned him."

Utley smiled. "Sara doesn't talk to me about her work." He leaned against the door of the vehicle, resting his arm on the bracket of the side mirror. "How can I help?" he asked.

"I'd like to know where you went on the field trip."

Utley pushed some hair away from his forehead. "Easy enough. Come inside and I'll show you on the map."

Utley and his team shared a chaotic work space, dominated by a large trough table with dividers in the middle of the room. It held pot shards, hand-forged nails, rusty shell casings, pieces of old machinery, fragments of rope and leather, and human bones, all sorted according to type and size. A woman at a work table labeled bits and pieces of rusty tools from a cart next to her. She looked up and smiled as Kerney and Utley walked by.

Utley guided Kerney through a clump of desks to a large map of the Tularosa Basin mounted on the far wall and started pointing. "It's a one-day excursion. I don't go too far out—otherwise the time would be eaten up by travel."

He traced his finger up a primary-road course. "I take them to an old Spanish site called Black Bear Mine, back down to the 7-Bar-K Ranch site on the east slope of the San Andres—the wildlife and conservation people use it as a base camp—and the last place we visit is Indian Hills, where I'm doing an excavation." Utley poked the map at Indian Hills. "I think I mentioned that when we first met."

"Indian Wells?" Kerney asked. The background in Sammy's painting of the Bobcat had to be Indian Wells.

"There is an Indian Wells, but it's completely off-limits, and you can only get to it by foot or horseback. It's an interesting site if you like geology or petroglyphs. Have you heard of it?" Utley asked.

Kerney shook his head. "I just thought you said Indian Wells. My mistake."

Utley nodded. "The place-names can get confusing." He made a circular motion with his finger over the map. "The Indian Hills excavation is east of Cottonwood Canyon. A stand of trees gave me the first clue that I might find something. Cottonwoods need a lot of water, so I went looking for the source. I found gray quartz and white gypsum sand accumulations early in the dig. The winds move the sand toward the Sacramento Mountains, away from the San Andres, so it was a real anomaly. We hit a rock foundation and an underground spring that once fed into a pond. It's definitely a semipermanent Apache campsite." Utley's voice rose in satisfaction. "A very important find. I'm heading back out there today." Utley's expression changed and became apologetic. "I'm boring the hell out of you."

"Not at all," Kerney assured him, rushing his question before Utley had a chance to continue talking. The man was a self-absorbed motormouth. "Do you remember Sammy Yazzi? Specialist Fourth Class. He went on your last field trip."

Fred nodded and repositioned his eyeglasses on his nose. "I do. I was delighted to have him on the tour. He gave us a real interesting perspective of the Apache from a Pueblo Indian point of view."

"Did you know him before the tour?"

"Never saw him before or after," Utley responded. "Sorry I can't be more helpful."

"That's okay." Kerney replied.

"I don't envy you your job." Utley walked with Kerney to the open door. "If you're still on the base when I get back, I'll buy you a drink at the officers' club."

"Sounds good to me," Kerney said, squinting at the whiteness of the day that greeted him outside.

He left Utley to finish his loading chore and drove away. It was time to meet Sara at her office.

"Did you notice that the watercolors were numbered in sequence?" Sara inquired, one foot curled under her knee, her back resting against the passenger door of Kerney's truck. A slight road breeze from the partially open window rippled through her hair. They were halfway to Elephant Butte Lake.

"No, I didn't."

"On the back of each sheet: two numbers separated by a slash. There should be thirty pictures. Only twenty-five were in the portfolio."

Kerney drummed his fingers on the steering wheel in response as Sara watched him. He had long fingers, perfectly proportioned. Kerney had taken care to dress for the occasion, Sara thought, with a private smile. He wore a light gray cowboy shirt with pearl buttons, black jeans, and freshly polished boots.

"No comment?" Sara nudged.

"I feel like we're chasing our tails," Kerney answered. "Lots of leads going nowhere."

"Frustrated?"

"So far." He smiled in her direction. "It's a big chunk of land out there. Lots of places where a person can get lost and disoriented."

"Or have an accident," Sara added.

"That too," Kerney agreed glumly, "but I still cling to the hope that Sammy's alive and kicking up his heels somewhere off the base."

"You do think that's realistic?"

"Not really. Sammy isn't the type. But without hope there can be no endeavor," Kerney quoted. "Some dead English writer said that. I can't remember which one; Samuel Johnson, Walter Scott."

Sara laughed. "Tell me something. Why did you drop out of graduate school to become a cop?"

Kerney shot her a sideways look. "You have done your homework."

"Of course."

"After Nam, I thought I needed peace and quiet. Graduate school seemed like a safe place to be."

"Was it?"

"Sure, if you believe that intellectual sharpshooting and belligerent superior attitudes are part of a quiet life. To me, it was just a mind game, so I decided to do something more real."

"I take it your wife didn't approve."

"Hell, no. When I told her what my intentions were, she decided I wasn't committed to maintaining a parallel career path with an equitable income that would match her anticipated earnings. She granted me an uncontested divorce."

"Was it that simple?"

"Nothing is that simple. She didn't want a husband with a second-class profession, and I didn't want a marriage that felt like a business arrangement. Otherwise, we were completely incompatible."

"Are you a romantic, Kerney?"

"I was. Now I'm a hermit. What about you?"

"There's very little time for romance in the military."

They drove in silence through Truth or Consequences, a town with no definition that spread out along a bypass looping the interstate. Main street, lined with dreary cafés, dress shops posing as boutiques, shoddy secondhand stores, and run-down tourist cabins bunched around empty parking lots, took on the stunted, meager personality of the sand hills above the town. Only the touch of green from the thick bosque that concealed the Rio Grande gave relief to the eye, pulling attention to the mountains east of the river.

According to Sara, Bull McVay worked as a maintenance man at a vineyard in Engle. At the only stoplight in town, Kerney turned toward the mountains, and soon they were on a curving road cutting through the foothills. Elephant Butte, a startling blue-green manmade lake, spread out in front of them just before the highway dipped into a narrow, sheared-off granite pass, climbed again to meet the *Jornada*—the ancient route of the Spanish into North America—and ran straight toward the San Andres Mountains. Cactus savanna flowed across the desert interrupted by large thickets of creosote brush and mesquite. The long plumes of the sotol cactus rose on thick bases, protected by hundreds of spiny leaves, bearing the first signs of flowering growth. Clumps of green grama grass, pale rabbitbrush, and yellow wildflowers erupted wildly on the flat plain.

Sara remained quiet, gazing out the window and thinking how pleasant it was to rubberneck. The need for more of a personal life outside of her job had to be given greater attention, she decided.

A large billboard sign came into view, heralding the turnoff to the vineyard. "I'll question McVay," she said, regretting the curt tone.

"Yes, ma'am," Kerney replied obsequiously. "Shall I wait for you in the truck, ma'am?" His blue eyes crinkled at the corners in a smile.

Sara punched him on the arm. "Don't be a smartass. Let's go."

In the processing shed, Bull McVay worked alone, cleaning up the debris left over from a newly installed vat storage system. He dumped some scrap metal in the cart behind a small tractor and noticed a man and woman standing in the wide bay doorway. Tourists, McVay thought, returning to his work. The winery attracted visitors intrigued by the idea of a champagne vineyard in the middle of the desert owned by real Frenchmen who pumped water thirty miles from the lake in order to grow grapes. He was sweeping up when the woman approached.

"Hello, Bull," Sara said.

"Captain Brannon." Bull resisted the impulse to snap to attention. The man wasn't somebody Bull knew. He hung back a little from the captain, just within earshot range. "What brings you here?"

"One of your old ballplayers went AWOL."

"Which one?" With huge shoulders, no neck, and

a bulky frame, Bull had a nickname that was a perfect match for his body.

"Sammy Yazzi."

"I heard about that. I thought everything had worked out for him."

"What do you mean?"

"Sammy was hot to take some art classes at the university. All his sergeant had to do was change the duty roster. Steiner wouldn't cooperate, and Sammy was really bummed out about it. I came up with an alternative—almost by accident."

"What alternative?"

"A lady at church taught art at the university in Las Cruces before she retired. I mentioned Sammy's problem to her in passing. She told me to have Sammy call her, so I did. Sammy started studying with her."

"You know that for a fact?"

"Absolutely," Bull answered.

"When did this happen?"

"Just before I moved up here."

"Did Sergeant Steiner know about it?"

"I don't think so. Sammy told me as a way to say thanks for the favor, but I doubt he made a big deal out of it with anyone else. That's not his style."

"What's the woman's name?"

"Erma Fergurson. Sweet lady. In her seventies but still a ball of fire."

"Thanks, Bull," Sara said.

"Sure thing, Captain." The man with Sara, a rugged-looking guy, turned and walked away without saying a word. His right leg had been busted-up big-time. Probably the knee, Bull decided. He shook Sara's hand with his beefy palm and watched her walk away. She stopped at the door, looked around, and stepped into the sunlight with almost a girlish skip.

Kerney stood at the end of the parking lot, oblivious to Sara's presence, looking at the small cluster of houses and shade trees that marked the remains of Engle, now a town in name only. The pavement ended at the Southern Pacific railroad tracks, and a dirt road took over, thrusting east toward the San Andres Mountains. Gone were most of the private homes, the general store, the post office, and the abandoned hotel, which had still stood when he was a boy. The one-room schoolhouse endured, moored on a wide rock foundation. The long, narrow window casements started a good eight feet off the ground and ran nearly to the top of the building.

"What do you see out there?" Sara asked.

Kerney's blue eyes smiled again. "An eighty-pound boy full of piss and vinegar who thought he would be a runt forever."

"What happened to him?"

"He grew up and found out nothing is forever. I think you're going to enjoy meeting Erma Fergurson," he said with a delighted laugh.

"You know her?"

"Damn straight I do. Let's go find out if she remembers me."

Erma Fergurson opened her front door holding a writing tablet in one hand and a pair of reading glasses in the other. Dressed in a paint-splattered man's shirt and a pair of black slacks, she carried her age beautifully, slender and erect. Her delicately lined face took them in with clear eyes. She wore her gray hair pinned in a bun at the nape of her neck.

She glanced nonchalantly at the badge in Kerney's hand. "You're here about the burglary," Erma said.

"What burglary, Aunt Erma?" Kerney asked.

"Oh, my goodness," she said, her hand flying to her mouth. "Kevin Kerney, is that you?"

"It's me," Kerney answered with a boyish smile.

"I don't believe it." A smile bubbled on her lips. "Let me look at you." She stepped back. "You're still a handsome rascal." She turned to Sara, the excitement of the moment ringing in her voice. "Kevin's mother and I were college roommates. When he came to the university I was asked to keep an eye on him. When he'd act like a young buck, he would beg me with those beautiful blue eyes not to tattle on him to his parents."

"I'm sure he was quite persuasive," Sara replied.

"He was indeed," Erma agreed happily. "Who is this pretty woman, Kevin?"

Sara blushed.

"Erma Fergurson, meet Sara Brannon," Kerney said.

"A pleasure," Erma replied. "Are you also a police officer?"

"Yes."

"So you are here about the burglary," Erma said.

"We know nothing about it, but it may be important," Sara responded. "We came to ask you about Sammy Yazzi."

"Oh, yes, I would like that. I've been very worried about him. Come in and make yourselves at home."

She ushered them through a curved archway into a

studio space washed in north light from a high
clerestory. Large landscapes, six feet high and wide,
filled the walls with vibrant colors of foothills ablaze
in a blanket of wildflowers, silvery tufts of Apache
plume dappling the desert, and shimmering golden
aspen rolling up mountainsides. Erma gestured at
the two love seats separated by a print cabinet that
served as a coffee table, and got them settled in.

"You haven't found Sammy, have you?" Erma
guessed.

"No," Kerney replied, "but we did find some
watercolors."

Erma nodded. "Excellent work. A wonderful series."

"We're missing five paintings," Sara said.

"I have them." She slid open a drawer to the print
cabinet and spread out each watercolor on top of the
chest. All five were of bighorn mountain sheep.
"Sammy left them with me to be framed. We were
planning a showing at a local gallery."

Kerney studied each picture, trying to get a sense
of the location. A cliff face with a ram on the summit
looked familiar. He was sure it was somewhere near
the ranch, but couldn't place it.

"Did he work from photographs?" he asked.

"Yes. His camera was stolen in the burglary."

"Tell us about the burglary," Sara prompted.

Erma shook her head in exasperation. "My fault
entirely. I ran out to the grocery store this morning
and didn't lock up. They came in through an open
window."

"What was taken besides Sammy's camera?" Sara
queried.

Erma picked up the notebook and put on her

reading glasses. "I just made a list. Two more cameras, a bedroom television, a VCR, and several pieces of jewelry I left out on a dresser. That's all I've found missing so far, and I've been through the house twice.

"The officer who came said it was probably a drug addict who robbed me. I guess they just take what they can carry out quickly and sell for money."

"Do you know where Sammy developed his photographs?" Kerney asked.

"Here," Erma replied. "I have a darkroom in the corner of my garage."

"Are his prints and negatives there?"

"I'm sure they are," Erma said, rising to her feet. "Shall we go and see?"

The darkroom had a sink and a long counter with shelves above containing all the necessary chemicals and bins below for equipment and supplies. A cardboard photo storage box sat on the counter. While Sara and Kerney watched, Erma searched the contents once, and then a second time.

"My mistake," she said. "Sammy must have taken them."

"Probably," Kerney agreed. "Were the cameras stolen from the darkroom?"

"Yes."

"Are your prints intact?" Sara asked.

"As far as I can tell, yes. Should I search to see if anything else was taken?"

"I don't think you need to do that," Sara answered.

"Did Sammy leave anything else with you for safekeeping?" Kerney asked.

Erma withdrew her attention from Sara and

looked at Kerney. "The theft is connected with Sammy somehow, isn't it?"

"We don't know that," Sara said.

Erma's back stiffened, and she raised her chin. "Kevin?" she demanded.

"It might be, Aunt Erma."

"Now I am upset."

Kerney took her hand and gave it a gentle squeeze. "I want you to call someone to come and stay with you for a while," he said.

"That isn't necessary."

"Then how about a cup of tea?" he suggested.

Erma brightened. "That *is* necessary."

Over tea, Erma learned what she could about Sammy's disappearance from Kerney while Sara carefully wrapped the watercolors in clear plastic sleeves. When Erma expressed the hope that Sammy would be found alive and well, Kerney's attempt at reassurance felt forced. It only made her more worried about the boy.

"He has such a rare talent," she said wistfully.

At the front door, Kerney promised Erma he would come back for a long visit.

"See that you do," Erma replied, reaching up to give him a motherly hug. "In fact," she said to Sara, "I want both of you to come back for a nice dinner so you can tell me exactly what this is all about."

"Sounds like bribery to me," Sara said. "I accept."

"It's a date," Kerney said.

Walking to the truck, Sara looked back at Erma. "What an exquisite lady she is. I hope I have that much class when I'm her age."

"I don't think you have a thing to worry about," Kerney said.

Sara didn't break her stride. "Do you think Andy has a deputy he can spare? I'd like your Aunt Erma to have some protection for a few days."

"That's a good idea," Kerney allowed, "but you'll have to ask very nicely. He's still smarting from that tongue-lashing you gave him."

Sara frowned. "I forgot about that."

CHAPTER

6

Andy Baca studied the five watercolors that were spread out on his desk. "I don't know anything about art, but I know what I like. These are good," Andy said. "The question is, will they help you find Sammy?"

"Maybe," Kerney answered. The picture of the ram on the cliff held his attention. Sammy had put three petroglyphs at the base of the cliff that didn't belong there: an Apache devil dancer, a rider on horseback, and a stylized sheep with a heart line. The arrangement of the petroglyphs matched perfectly with the rock art at Indian Wells, a place Kerney knew well.

Kerney tapped the picture of the ram on the cliff.

"I've seen this cliff. I just can't pin it down. See the petroglyphs? They don't belong there."

"You're sure?" Sara asked.

Kerney nodded. "The grouping is perfect. That's Indian Wells. Sammy's been there. So have I."

"Where is it?" Andy asked.

"North of Rhodes Pass, in the San Andres."

"That's a start," Andy suggested.

"Not much of one," Kerney countered. "It's a hell of a long way from the test facility." He returned his gaze to the watercolor. "Was Big Mesa covered by the search teams?" he asked, looking at Sara.

"No, they stopped at the 7-Bar-K Ranch," Sara replied. "Is Big Mesa where you think the cliff is?"

"It's possible. The landform in the picture fits the area."

"You could spend a month in those mountains and find nothing," Andy speculated.

"I know it," Kerney replied. He waved his hand over the watercolors. "Alonzo Tony said Sammy took him to Big Mesa or Sheep Mesa—he wasn't sure which—and from the looks of it, I'd guess Big Mesa."

"Where do we start?" Sara asked.

"We go where Sammy has been," Kerney proposed. "I've got a fairly good idea of three or four locations."

"Can you get us into that area undetected?" Sara asked.

"You're kidding," Kerney said. "You want to sneak onto the base?"

"That's the idea," she replied.

"Why?" Andy asked.

"I have my reasons."

"Is the Fergurson burglary one of them?" Andy prodded.

"You bet it is," Sara shot back. "Let's leave it at that, okay?"

"I'd rather not," Andy retorted.

"Bulldozing me isn't going to get you an answer."

Andy waved off the argument and grinned. "Bulldozing? I'm just testing the waters."

"For?" Sara shot back.

"Your reaction. Is somebody nipping at your heels?"

"I don't know," Sara answered flatly, and turned her gaze to Kerney. "Well? Will you do it?"

"It may amount to nothing more than a wild-goose chase," Kerney replied.

"Yes or no?" Sara demanded.

"Yes."

"Good." She gathered up the paintings from Andy's desk. "When can you be ready?"

"At first light."

"Where do we meet?"

"Engle," Kerney replied. "Be there at four in the morning. Bring the portfolio with you, wear your riding gear, and pack a change of clothes."

She gave him a curt nod and turned back to Andy. "Can I get a ride home from one of your deputies?"

"Absolutely." He walked to his desk, made a short telephone call, and hung up. "It will be just a few minutes."

"Thanks. I'd like Erma Fergurson to have some protection for the next few days. Can that be arranged?"

"I'll put somebody on it."

"That about covers it for now," Sara said, extending her hand to Andy. "Thanks again, Andy."

Andy covered her hand in his and gave it a gentle squeeze. "Anytime, Captain."

After Sara left, Andy and Kerney sat silently. Kerney seemed lost in thought.

"It looks like you get to go back to your old stomping grounds," Andy finally said.

"I never thought I would." Kerney shook his head.

Andy skipped over it. "Do you think Sara is holding something back?"

"She's got a fire lit under her," Kerney commented. "That's for sure."

"Do you trust her?"

"I do."

"So do I," Andy agreed with a grin. "She's a piece of work, isn't she?"

Kerney nodded and grinned back.

"We need to get you outfitted," Andy remarked, walking to the office door. "How long do you plan to be gone?"

"Twenty-four hours. We'll leave from the Rocking J Ranch on the *Jornada*. Dale Jennings's place. Do you know it?"

"Tell me how to get there and I'll be waiting when you get back." He let Kerney pass in front of him and closed the door. "You could both get your asses in a sling. You know that, don't you?"

"That's a reassuring thought," Kerney replied.

Sara rang the bell to the communications center security door. It was after normal working hours, and the headquarters staff was gone for the day. She pushed hard on the buzzer until the door opened.

"PFC Tony?" she asked, her open badge case at eye level for the soldier to see.

"Yes, ma'am."

"Do you know who I am?"

"Yes, ma'am."

"Did you speak to Captain Meehan last night?" Sara had the facts at hand: the surveillance team shadowing Kerney had duly noted the event.

"I've been ordered not to answer any questions," Tony said haltingly.

Sara snapped at the young soldier. "If you don't tell me what I want to know, I'll make sure every damn day you spend in the Army is very unpleasant. Do you understand that, soldier?"

"Yes, ma'am." Tony looked very unhappy.

"Well?" Sara demanded.

Tony licked his lips. "I spoke to the captain."

"Did you tell him that Sammy Yazzi owned a camera?" Sara demanded.

Tony nodded. "Yes, ma'am."

"Did you mention the jeep trip you took with Sammy to Big Mesa?"

"No, ma'am. He didn't ask me about that. Am I in trouble, Captain?"

Sara's smile was tight-lipped. "Not if you cooperate. What else did you tell him?"

"He asked me if I knew where Sammy stayed when he was in Las Cruces."

"And?"

"I told him I didn't know, but that his sergeant had a phone number for how to reach him."

"Why would Sergeant Steiner have a number for Sammy in Las Cruces?"

"Sammy told me that Steiner chewed him out once when he got back from town. Steiner needed him at the test site and couldn't find him. He made Sammy give him a phone number where he could be reached in case it happened again."

"What else did you tell Captain Meehan?"

"That's it, ma'am."

"Tell no one about this conversation. No one. Understood?"

"Yes, Captain."

Sara turned on her heel and walked down the hall, unwilling to let Tony see how angry she felt. In her office, with the phone book open to the listing for Erma Fergurson, she called Sergeant Steiner. He told her Captain Meehan had called and asked for the number. He read it off to her. It matched the number in the book. She waited until Steiner hung up and slammed the phone into the cradle. Damn Meehan! she thought. If she could ever get him on a level playing field, she would clean his clock.

A thin ribbon of light flowed over the crest of the mountains, as the night sky began fading into lighter grays. Thick clouds moved rapidly into the mountains, blotting out the color on the ridgeline. Ahead, through the windshield of Kerney's truck, Sara could see the flicker of house lights in the foothills, like a beacon with no reference point. It was the first indication of human habitation in twenty miles. For a very long stretch along the dirt road, the truck headlights revealed nothing but desert; not even fences or utility poles.

Kerney had Bach's Brandenburg Concertos playing softly on the cassette deck, a perfect choice against the tapestry of the last gloom of night. They climbed out of the desert, the house lights above them appearing and vanishing as the road twisted gently, following the contours up the slope of a small valley pinched between outcroppings of the San Andres Mountains. The valley narrowed to a canyon that gave way to mountain meadows of grass and thickets of cedar trees.

A band of clouds passed over the mountains as they reached the ranch gate. A weathered board nailed to a fence post by the gate displayed the brand for the Rocking J Ranch. Beyond the gate, in a grove of pine trees, warm light poured from the windows of the ranch house. It was the centerpiece of the surrounding buildings, still hard for Sara to discern in the early light.

Kerney got out and opened the gate. Without giving it a thought, Sara slid behind the wheel, drove through the gate, and stopped. Kerney swung the gate closed, pointed to the corral, and started walking. She drove to the corral and waited for him to catch up. He walked past the truck and leaned on the top rail of the corral, eyeing the four horses inside.

Dale had saddled a bay and cinched a pack frame to a slightly sway-back roan. The bay was perfect for Kerney; it had high shoulders, big hips, and a nicely proportioned frame. The horse would move smoothly, with good speed if needed. That left the gelding and the mare for Sara to choose from, Kerney thought. He wondered which one she would select.

From the truck, Sara studied the horses carefully.

A mare like that would do nicely when she was ninety years old and needed to ride in a surrey. It had a potbelly and weak hindquarters. The gelding's deep chest, flat back, and thick haunch showed the promise of endurance and quickness.

The first moment of true daylight touched the crowns of the pine trees as the sun crested the mountains. The foreman's quarters, within easy hailing distance of the main house, was a small cabin with a narrow porch running the length of the building. A hay shed sat conveniently next to the horse barn and corral. The windmill by the water-tank grabbed Sara's attention. Old, squatty, and made of wood, with a small platform beneath the blades, it creaked and hummed in the slight breeze. She loved the sound of it.

A screen door at the ranch house slammed shut, and they both turned toward the sound. Dale Jennings strode toward Kerney, one hand grasping a large coffee thermos and the other hand juggling three mugs. Dale put his load down on the hood of the truck and bear-hugged Kerney.

"I didn't think anything would ever get you back here," he announced, grinning affectionately as he released Kerney from his grasp.

Kerney grinned back. "Strange things can happen. Thanks for doing all this." He gestured at the waiting horses.

"Nothing to it. Coffee?" he asked Sara, as she stepped out of the truck.

Kerney broke in. "I'm forgetting my manners. Dale Jennings, this is Sara Brannon."

"Ma'am," Jennings acknowledged, picking up a

mug and holding it out to her. Dale Jennings was in his forties, maybe an inch under six feet tall, dressed in work boots, a western shirt, a goose-down vest, and faded blue jeans, topped off by a cap with a feed store logo. His eyes were widely spaced under a long forehead. His mouth seemed set in a permanent smile.

"I'd love some coffee, Mr. Jennings," Sara answered, taking the mug. She watched Dale pour it carefully, so as not to spill a drop, thinking she had been too long away from home and the company of people like Dale Jennings.

"The name's Dale," he said as he finished.

"Call me Sara," she replied, unable to contain a smile. The coffee smelled wonderful.

Dale repeated the ritual with Kerney, then poured a mug for himself, and together all three watched the sunlight spread into the canyon, the warm mugs cupped in their hands, the coffee quietly sipped and savored.

Kerney broke the pleasant silence. "Where are Barbara and the girls?"

"In town," Dale responded. "I'm a bachelor during the week. Both girls are in high school now. You know how that goes. They can't stand to miss any of the socializing and such. Barbara's renting an apartment and working part-time at the flower shop." He put his mug on the top of a fence post and leaned against the railing. He caught Sara's eye, then tilted his head at Kerney. "The only time we see this fellow is when I take my family up to visit. We use him as a tour guide to show us *nouveau riche* Santa Fe and all those fancy places we can't afford."

Kerney, looking up the mountain behind the

ranch house, wasn't paying attention. "Can you get Sara saddled up, Dale?" he asked.

"Sure thing."

"I won't be long," Kerney said, walking in the direction of a glen behind the house.

Dale watched Sara's questioning eyes follow Kerney until he disappeared behind the house. He waited for her to speak. Instead, she gave him an uncertain smile.

"His parents are buried up in the grove," Dale explained. "He's never been back since the funeral. I watched him dig the graves myself. Wouldn't let anybody help him. Took him all day and into the night. He really loved his folks. His grandfather is buried with them, along with my parents."

"I know what happened," Sara said, trying to think of something to add.

Dale saved her from the struggle. "Then you know it was a damn shame. He didn't say a word; didn't cry—nothing. He put his Army medals in the graves before we covered the caskets."

"Why did he do that?"

Dale shook his head. "Can't say for sure. He wrote me a couple of letters from Vietnam. Said the only thing keeping him going was the thought of getting back home. With his parents dead and all, I guess he figured he didn't have a home anymore."

"He couldn't stay?"

"Hell yes, he could stay. I wanted to take him on as a full partner, but he wouldn't hear of it. He left the morning after the funeral. This is the first time he's been back."

"How sad," Sara said.

Dale shook his head in agreement and changed

the subject. "Tell me about this trail ride you're taking."

"It's best that I don't," Sara responded.

Dale laughed. "That can only mean one thing. Kerney's taking you onto the missile range."

"Is that so?" she asked, unwilling to admit the truth.

"Hell, it was our favorite sport when we were growing up. I've bragged on it so much over the years, now my girls do it and give me grief when I crab at them to stop. It's gotten to be like a tradition." He pointed up the dirt road running past the ranch to the outline of a white sign by a cedar-post gate. "There it is. White Sands Missile Range. Half a mile away. The start of Rhodes Pass. It's our backyard."

"Did you and Kerney ever get caught?" Sara asked.

"Not once. Fifty-three hundred square miles is a lot of territory to protect. You'd have to put the whole damn Army inside the Tularosa to seal it off completely.

"Hell, we even used to try and get ourselves caught. Once in a while we'd let them Army boys catch a glimpse of us just to make the game more exciting, hoping they'd chase after us. I think they knew who we were and decided it wasn't worth the effort. There are ways into the range from here I bet the military have never figured out."

He opened the gate, stepped inside the corral, and reached for a saddle blanket. "I think the mare will do you."

The mare stood passively, head lowered, while the

gelding skittered away, spooked by Dale's sudden presence.

"What's the terrain like?" Sara inquired, unconvinced.

Dale had the blanket in one hand and a saddle in the other, ready to cinch up the mare. "Rough country. The mare's surefooted. You'll need that, especially in the mountains."

"She's slow, I bet," Sara countered, "and won't keep up with the bay." She climbed the railing and joined Dale in the corral. She took the bridle off the fence post. "I'll try the gelding," she announced.

"That's no horse for a lady," Dale said.

"Maybe I'm no lady," Sara said, picking up the bridle. She cornered the gelding and put the bit in his mouth, talking to him softly. When he took the bit, she worked her hand down his neck until he stopped snorting and put his ears forward. Still talking, she reached up for his mane and vaulted easily onto the gelding's back. The gelding trembled, bent his hindquarters almost to the ground, and started a counterclockwise spin. Sara leaned into the movement, her head low against the gelding's neck. After six rotations, the horse stopped twisting and settled into a mild canter around the fence perimeter. It had a comfortable, smooth gait.

"He likes to turn to the left," Dale allowed, pleased at the sight of a good rider.

Sara patted the neck of the gelding and slid to the ground. "He'll match the bay," she predicted.

"That he will," Dale agreed, walking to her with the saddle and blanket.

They saddled the gelding and loaded the gear on

the swayback roan. From the looks of it, Kerney had brought all of the essentials for the journey and then some. He rejoined them as they were finishing up.

"The lady can ride," Dale remarked as he opened the gate to let the small caravan out of the corral.

"I'm not surprised," Kerney replied. He lifted his head toward Rhodes Canyon. "Does the pass get much use?"

"Three vehicles a week is a traffic jam," Dale joked.

"Any regulars?"

"Military police. State Game and Fish. Some Bureau of Land Management types."

"Any one in there now?" Kerney asked, walking his horse to the dirt road. He stopped and mounted the bay. Sara was already astride the gelding.

Dale nodded. "Eppi Gutierrez went in yesterday. Manages the bighorn herd for Game and Fish. Should be back out in a day or two. How are you going in?"

Kerney looked down at his boyhood friend and winked. "Washout Gap, if it's still open."

"The worst trail in," Dale declared. "Why that one?"

"We're going to Indian Wells first," Kerney explained.

"Well, that's the shortest way." His hand ran down the withers of the bay.

"We'll be back no later than tomorrow morning, early," Kerney told his friend.

"I'll be looking for you." Dale moved his hand to the bridle to hold Kerney back. His voice dropped to a whisper. "I don't know what made you come back, but I'm glad you did."

Kerney felt the horse under him and looked at the expanse of desert and mountains that ran out from the canyon below. The turquoise sky rolled with cumulus clouds, heavy and moist.

He smiled at his friend. "So am I. Thanks for the loan of the horses."

Dale smiled back. "Watch out for rain," he said, looking skyward.

"Yeah."

Mountains tinged with red earth, richly forested in the protected canyons, rose to serrated peaks. Only the clatter of hooves on the rock-strewn trail, the breathing of the horses, and the occasional call of the waking birds in the evergreen forest broke the silence.

Kerney led them away from Rhodes Pass, down a gradual limestone staircase into a long, deep ravine that seemed to cut into the heart of the mountains with little chance of an outlet. There was no trail to speak of at the bottom, rather a confusion of loose rock, gravel, sand, and deadwood washed into the draw by countless flash floods. The gelding moved easily through the maze, relaxed under Sara's confident touch. The walls of the canyon were as finely etched as a delicate cameo, with veins of strata running through the rock at sharp angles.

They continued down, descending into the shadows of narrow-walled bedrock, sidestepping large boulders polished smooth by torrents of floodwater. She saw absolutely no way out and wondered if Kerney's memory of the trail was flawed. A cluster of boulders, each taller than a man, blocked their passage.

Kerney dismounted and motioned for Sara to do the same. "The horses won't like this," he said to her. There was a faint echo that bounced off the walls. "I'll walk them through."

Sara joined him by the rocks. He pointed to a jagged cutout in the ledge, barely distinguishable in the indigo shadows, exactly the height of the large boulder embedded in the gravel. The vent showed the crushing impact of the boulder, which had hollowed out a passage before recoiling off the wall. She peered into the opening; a slash of blackness with a gleam of light at the end. It rose precipitously on rough-hewn, chiseled steps, with scarcely enough room for a horse to pass. The packhorse won't make it, she thought, and turned back to see Kerney already busy uncinching the straps to the pack frame. She helped him unload and carry the gear through the opening.

She walked in deep gloom for a good twenty paces before she could see her feet. The crevice widened to meet a small ledge on an abrupt precipice that dropped at least a hundred feet straight down. Looking over the edge, she could see the faint outline of a trail.

"Where are we?" she asked, setting her cargo on the ground.

"Bear Den Canyon is below us. The ledge gives way to a good trail around the corner. Wait for me there. I'll get the horses."

"I'll bring the gelding through," she announced firmly.

Kerney began to argue, thought better of it, and said, "If it suits you."

The gelding made the journey nervous and snorting. Kerney left Sara holding the bridles and went back for the roan. Remounted and repacked at the trailhead, they rode down to the east, the blockading mountains occasionally dipping to give them a view of the immense Tularosa Valley and White Sands National Monument, sparkling brilliantly in the distance. North of the monument, huge manmade swaths cut into the desert floor defined the space harbor where shuttle pilots practiced landings.

At the bottom, Kerney turned them out of the canyon floor and up a dry streambed that snaked back into the high country. Once again on a crest, they stopped to rest the horses. The morning sun's heat shimmered up from the desert floor in waves. The blackness of the lava flow at the northern end of the basin spread across the valley. The Malpais, the Spanish called it, bad country, where a horse could break a leg and a rider could break a neck. Behind the sharp coils of lava, snow still capped the twin peaks of Sierra Blanca, the centerpiece of the Mescalero Apache Reservation, and in the depressions where the basin dipped, shallow salt lakes held the residual water of winter, not yet evaporated by the furnace of a summer sun.

They moved beneath the timberline in old-growth evergreens, breaking into the open only once to cross another knuckled canyon before the final push to Indian Wells. Sara could see game trails converging at the base of a mountain. There were spoor and sign of coyote, deer, and rabbits along the trail, but no prints of man or domestic animals.

The horses smelled water and picked up the pace,

breaking into a gentle trot as the hill leveled out to form a saucer at the foot of the mountain. Kerney dismounted and Sara followed suit. He led her through a small grove of cedar trees and into a clearing against the mountainside. Indian Wells, a pool of water in a rock catchment basin at the base of the mountain, seemed to have no source. The water overflowed into a natural causeway and quickly disappeared into a rock crevice.

They let the horses drink before tethering them. A search of the pool and surrounding area turned up nothing of interest. They ate a light lunch under the weak shade of a tree.

"How long would it have taken Sammy to hike in?" Sara asked. She had the open portfolio in her lap and was perusing the watercolors.

"Not long, if he drove partway up the last canyon we crossed," Kerney speculated. "Two hours, maximum, on foot, I guess. The game trails make the hike reasonable."

"I didn't see any tire tracks in the canyon," Sara noted, as she rose and walked to the edge of the pool.

"Washed away," Kerney called after her, chewing on a cracker. "All the canyons carry water east into the basin. There's no other outlet. It's a closed system." He got to his feet gingerly and joined her at the pool.

Squatting, Sara inspected the petroglyphs just above the water line. "Here they are," she said, pointing at the rock face. She looked again, this time more closely, at some scratches in the stone next to the devil dancer. "Are those your initials?"

Kerney grimaced. "I'm afraid so. I got my fanny

warmed for that mischief. I thought this was a magical place when I was a kid."

"It still is," Sara replied. "The pictographs are wonderful. I'd love to know what they mean."

"I'm not real sure anyone knows, except the Apaches. I used to study them and try to figure out the symbolism. I think you have to know the story."

"I would love to," Sara reflected, getting to her feet. "So where's the cliff from here?"

"I have no idea," Kerney said. "Somewhere near Big Mesa, I think." The clouds had turned the sky a solid gray. "Time to go. There are two old mines close by at Sweetwater Canyon I want to check out. Sammy may have used those locations in several of his paintings. We'll cut up there and then come down to Big Mesa."

"And after that?" Sara inquired.

"It depends on the weather. We'll stop off at the 7-Bar-K."

"What did the family brand stand for?"

"The seven was for luck and the K stood for Kerney. The lucky Kerneys. What a joke that turned out to be." He looked skyward again. "We need to get moving. I don't want us caught in a gully washer."

Kerney pushed along at a faster pace; he could smell the faint tinge of salt in the air. Gray clouds were foaming into black tiers, building up to an angry squall, and canyon winds were whipping tree branches, whistling through the gullies. The storm could hit at any time or jump right over them.

They moved along the back side of stair-stepped

mesas, through troughs that plunged into stands of virgin forest. Climbing again, they reached the first mine site only to be greeted by horizontal lightning in a thick sky, the cracking sound muffled in thunderheads. Kerney knew he was searching for Sammy's body, but it was hard to say so. He appreciated Sara's silence.

A light rain was falling as they finished searching the caved-in mine and moved downslope to the next shaft. The wind pushed the rain against their backs with enough force to soak through to the skin. They stopped briefly below a ridgeline to don rain slicks.

The tunnel to the second mine, partially open and buttressed by large beams, had enough space beneath a rockfall for a person to crawl through. Sara dismounted, gave Kerney the reins to the gelding, got the flashlight from the packhorse, and wriggled cautiously into the cave before he could take the lead. She stopped, half in, half out, to sweep the blackness with light, looking for rattlesnakes and rats. A scurrying movement and the flash of red eyes at the edge of a vertical shaft made her freeze. It took all her self-control to keep from flinching while she waited for more movement. She fanned the light slowly over the floor of the cave. There were no snakes that she could see and no evidence of any two-legged visitors. She wormed completely inside the tunnel, stopping at the sound of scampering beyond her line of sight. The noise ended and the beam of her flashlight caught a pack rat frozen in the light. She sighed with relief and switched her attention to the shaft. It was filled in with rubble.

Kerney scouted the outside area on foot as the rain came down harder and harder. He smiled when

Sara emerged. There was dirt on her chin and the tip of her nose. She shook her head back and forth.

"Nothing?" he asked.

"Just a pack rat."

"Let's move on."

The wind roared up to gale force, pelting them with cold rain as they mounted their horses.

Sara shouted over the gale, "We've got to get out of here." Lightning cracked above her. The gelding reared, ears back, rotated in a quick counterclockwise spin, and slammed into the packhorse. The roan backstepped and went down. Sara was out of her saddle, fighting to stay seated. The gelding spun in a tighter circle, whirling into a juniper tree at the fringe of the trail. The branches whipped Sara's face, and she tumbled off the gelding, trying to take the fall on her shoulders and get away from the horse. She landed hard, the breath jarred out of her. The gelding, snorting with fright, reared above her. She could barely see through the sheet of rain as she rolled to avoid the hoofs. The impact never came. Kerney had the bay between her and the gelding, switching it with his reins. He got it settled down and hitched securely to a tree, tied off the bay and the roan, and ran to her.

Sara struggled to sit up.

"Are you all right?" he demanded.

"I caught my foot in the stirrup and twisted my ankle." She held out her hand so he could help her to her feet. "That's all."

"Let me look at it," Kerney ordered, holding her firmly in place. There was a red welt on her forehead.

"It isn't broken."

"Which ankle?"

"The right one." She shook off Kerney's grip, tried to stand on her own, grimaced in pain, and sank back to the ground.

"Stay put. I'll tape it."

He got the first-aid kit, took off her boot, and inspected the ankle. It was sprained but unbroken. He wrapped it tightly and got the boot back on before it would no longer fit over the swelling. He supported her as she stood up and took a few tentative, painful steps. Then he laughed.

"What's so damn funny?" Sara demanded.

"You and me," he said, still chuckling, as he walked her to the gelding. "Now we're a matched pair."

They hurried across Sweetwater Canyon. There was no time to stop. The storm covered the range from north to south. Any runoff would catch them before they could reach the desert. Kerney led the small caravan to the side of a high mesa, into the stinging rain of a low cloud. There was nothing above them but the blackness of the storm.

Big Mesa curved between two canyons, encased in the cloud that spilled over into the basin and blocked the basin floor from view. Fog came at them from every direction and wrapped them up. It was gray and wind-lashed, with fleeting breaks in the cover that brought a glimmer of creamy light into the haze.

The horses, jaded from the ridge-running, needed rest. Kerney had pushed hard to leave the low ground. It was none too soon. They could hear the growing roar of the torrent below them, crashing through the rocks, sweeping toward the wide mouth of the canyon. He dismounted and dropped the reins over the head of the bay. The horse stood still, legs quivering. Hunched over, eyes cast downward, he went looking for the footpath that would get them off the mesa. The trail started at a rock face along a narrow ledge, then made a series of sharp switchbacks. The old ranch road intercepted the trail on the first step up the mesa. They would have to walk the next two miles, leading the horses. Kerney found the trailhead and returned to give Sara the news.

She groaned silently at the prospect and dismounted without comment. As she hobbled behind the packhorse she wondered if she would ever get dry and warm again. She assumed Kerney was taking them to shelter, but she had no idea where they were going or how long it would take to get there. She damn sure wasn't going to ask. There was no way Kerney would hear a whine or a whimper from her.

The two of them trudged along on gimpy legs, waterlogged, leading miserable, tired animals. There was enough humor in it to make Sara smile every now and then, in spite of the pain shooting up her leg.

The switchback trail was barely passable and in places only faintly discernible. Scattered rocks and saturated earth along the way made for tough going. The mud turned to thick slop as the intensity of the rain increased. The cloud sank lower and the rain turned to hail. Sara's only reference points were the trail at her feet and the backside of the packhorse in front of her. She sighed with relief when Kerney signaled her to stop. He stood between two superficial ruts filled with water, intersecting the path. It had to be the jeep trail.

When he failed to move on she joined him and asked what was wrong. The hood of his rain slick dripped water down the brim of his hat as he bent to study the tire tracks in the mud.

"These are recent," he said. "It looks like somebody's cut a new route."

"Going where?"

"As far as I know, nowhere. It dead-ends up at the rock face." He pointed up the trail. She might have missed it in the rain. "Drops straight off or goes straight up. There's no way out."

They were quiet for a moment, neither one of them enthusiastic about the obvious need to follow the tracks.

"The storm should break soon," Kerney suggested, wiping his nose with a damp hand.

"Let's go have a look," Sara said, with as much energy as she could muster.

The tire tracks gave out in a circle of flattened grass where the vehicle had turned and backed up near two twisted, intertwined cedar trees close to a seamless cliff that cut off forward movement. At the base was a steep plummet to a smaller mesa below. On the canyon floor a bighorn browsed serenely within yards of a cascading flood of water rushing toward the mouth of Sweetwater.

Kerney looked at the cliff. It matched perfectly with the bighorn watercolor. They tied the horses to the trees and took a closer look. The lower branches had been cut away to allow passage to the rock face. A tent-shaped crevice in the granite had been carefully filled in with stones and small boulders. It took only a few minutes to remove the rocks. The air that wafted out of the darkness brought the smell of decaying flesh with it.

Standing at the entrance, Sara used her flashlight to illuminate the cave. It was high enough for Kerney to stand upright and deep enough to hold two dozen or more people. The ground was smooth stone, except for a pile of loose shale at the back of the cave. They walked to the mound, and Sara held the flashlight while Kerney removed the shale. Under layers of rock the outline of a body emerged, wrapped in a tarp. Gagging on the stench, Kerney peeled back the sheath. Escaped gases from the decomposed body had blistered Sammy's face so that it looked burned. He was barely recognizable.

"Shit, shit, shit, shit," Kerney said, spitting the words out. He turned away, gasped for fresh air, and looked at Sammy's face again.

"Let me help," Sara said.

Kerney brushed her hand away. "I'll do it," he said hoarsely.

He felt around Sammy's neck until his fingers touched the dog tags, undid the clasp, and carefully pulled loose the chain. The canvas beneath Sammy's head, crusted with dried blood, claimed tufts of hair as Kerney turned the rigid body on its side. The back of Sammy's head was crushed. Kerney's breath whistled out of him through his clenched teeth. Underneath Sammy's torso was a sketch pad. He handed Sara the pad and the dog tags, fished Sammy's wallet out of his back pocket, and gave it to her.

With her mouth covered to fight off the stench, only Sara's angry eyes showed. "This sucks," she said.

Kerney said nothing. Slowly, he wrapped Sammy in the tarp, his hands tucking the material as though he were putting the boy to bed.

Standing, he swallowed hard against the bile in his mouth and the piercing anger in his chest. "Let's get out of here," he growled, pushing past her and into the moist, fresh air that smelled like earth, pine needles, and cedar.

Sara's flashlight beam caught a dull glitter in the fine dust near the feet of the corpse. She picked it up and held the light close to inspect it. It was an old military insignia, two crossed cavalry sabers with a company letter beneath the sheathed blades. She put it in her pocket and joined Kerney outside.

Savagely, Kerney restacked the rocks to seal the entrance. The violence in his movements as he worked warned Sara that no help was wanted. Finished, he walked to the edge of the mesa. The high winds and rain were gone. Dreamlike on the skyline, the Sierra Blancas gathered the last of the clouds to their crowns. The basin, damp in wet tones of brown, green, and gray, glistened in the sunlight. Below him on a sprawling foothill, the shape of the 7-Bar-K ranch house jumped out at him. The living windbreak his grandfather had planted on the north side of the house was now a dead row of cottonwood trees. A pile of lumber was all that was left of the horse barn, and a few random fence posts marked the remains of the corral. The stock tank, almost covered by drifting sand, showed a rusted lip to the sky. A truck was parked in front of the log porch.

East of the ranch, on the flats in the distance, sunlight bounced off a cluster of metal roofs. It had to be the test site. The sound of Sara's voice startled him.

"Are you all right?"

"Not by a long shot," he answered.

"Kerney . . . I'm sorry."

"I know." He refused to look at her. "You'd think this old place had seen enough suffering over the years." He pulled himself together and forced a smile.

"I know it must hurt, but . . ."

His interruption came before she could continue. "It's okay." Tears made lines in the dirt on his face. He blinked more away. "Let's dry out, clean up, and get some rest. I don't know about you, but I'm a complete wreck."

They rode down toward the ranch in the unusually cool air the storm had left behind, Kerney in the lead. Sara prodded the gelding along until she was even with Kerney's shoulder. He would not look at her.

CHAPTER

7

The small desk, positioned with a view out the window, gave Eppi Gutierrez a clear line of sight to Big Mesa. He made his last entry in the daily log on the status of the bighorn herd, closed the book, and looked up. Coming down the old trail, two riders on jaded horses trailing a pack animal picked their way through the sandy bottom. His apprehension grew as he watched them come closer. In all his overnights at the 7-Bar-K he'd never seen anybody come down that trail—it went nowhere. He put his logbook in a metal box, found his holstered sidearm, and watched their approach through the front window, nervously snapping open the hammer flap. The riders dismounted at the tailgate of his truck and walked the horses to the porch. Both were limping, the man rather badly, the woman less so. They looked exhausted. He unholstered the pistol, hid the weapon behind his right leg, and stepped outside. The man spoke before he could challenge them.

"Are you Eppi Gutierrez?"

"Yes, I am. Who are you?"

"Lieutenant Kerney, Doña Ana County Sheriff's Department." He held out his badge and gestured at Sara. "This is Captain Brannon, Provost Marshal's Office. Do us a favor and put the gun away."

Eppi blushed and stuck the pistol in the waistband of his trousers. "Sorry about that," he said. "I didn't expect to see anybody riding out of the mountains, especially after the storm that just blew over. How did you know my name?"

The two began unsaddling the horses. The woman, her face dirty and with a welt on her forehead, was still a looker, Eppi decided.

"The truck gave you away," Kerney replied.

"Did you come through Rhodes Pass?"

"More or less."

"Through the storm?"

Kerney nodded. "Had no choice. Do you think we can bunk here tonight?" He pitched his saddle onto the porch railing and Sara followed suit.

"Sure. No problem. Let me help you unload."

Kerney nodded wearily. "I'd appreciate it."

They relieved the roan of its burden and bedded the horses under the dead windbreak trees after Kerney ran a string line. Eppi helped them carry water to the animals.

Sara's butt was sore, her legs were cramped, and the twisted ankle throbbed. She finished watering the gelding, grabbed her sleeping bag and day pack, and walked toward the ranch house. It was a long, wide rectangle, easily sixty years old, with a shallow veranda, partially screened at one end.

Sara couldn't resist the temptation to snoop around. The inside contained practical living spaces; an oversized living room and country kitchen on the front side, with a door opening to the partially screened porch, bedrooms and a single bath arranged in a row down a hallway at the rear of the house. She heard Kerney clomp across the oak floor of the front room and dump his gear in one of the empty bedrooms. She caught sight of him leaving. She decided it had to be his childhood room: a rusty horseshoe nailed above the door confirmed it. She spread her sleeping bag on the floor, unpacked a change of clothes, brushed her hair, and washed her face in the cold tap water from the bathroom sink.

Kerney waited for Sara in the living room. A crudely fashioned desk made of a single piece of thick plywood, supported by two small filing cabinets, was jammed against a sill under a window. A camp stool, too small to make working at the desk comfortable, was pushed under the plywood top. Below the ceiling light in the middle of the room, two army surplus office chairs facing each other served as the lounging area. An army cot against the back wall completed the furnishings. While old memories clattered through his mind, he was struck by the realization that his cabin at Quinn's ranch had the same feel to it, and in some ways mirrored his childhood home. He wondered why the similarity had escaped him. Maybe he had needed to see the old house before he could fully admit to the dream that constantly chased him to get a place of his own. He couldn't help but smile, a little painfully, at his silliness.

Sara came into the living room, her eyes searching Kerney for signs of residual shock. The numbness was gone from his face. "There's indoor plumbing," she said quietly.

"You can thank my father for that."

"He didn't install any hot water," she replied.

"To my mother's irritation."

"You're feeling better," Sara announced.

Her diagnosis earned a wan smile. "Barely."

Together they went to the kitchen, where Gutierrez had turned his attention to making sandwiches: cold cuts and cheese on sliced white bread.

"It's nothing fancy," he announced, smiling at them over his shoulder. "But you two look hungry."

"Ravenous," Sara replied. The grimy wood cookstove stood proudly on ornate cast-iron legs. The handmade cupboards and cabinets, some without doors, were painted a faded, chipped yellow. Sara wondered what the room had looked like when Kerney's mother ruled the nest. Probably warm and inviting, she decided.

They sat at the kitchen table on mismatched cast-off chairs, Sara sinking gingerly onto the unpadded seat. The table, a pine creation fashioned out of planks and rough-cut lumber, wobbled radically.

Kerney watched Gutierrez as he worked at the counter. In his early thirties, Gutierrez had thick lashes, dark eyes, and large ears. His short neck and wide nose gave his face a fleshy look.

"Can I ask what you're doing out here?" Gutierrez inquired as he brought them their plates.

"Purely pleasure," Sara replied. "We just needed a few days by ourselves, away from the grind." She brushed her fingers across Kerney's cheek and looked at him lovingly. "Isn't that right, dear?"

Kerney, almost blushing, nodded and bit into his sandwich.

"It's turned into quite an adventure," Sara added.

"I believe it," Gutierrez replied. "I didn't know there was a trail that came through Big Mesa."

"There isn't," Kerney replied, swallowing. He could still feel Sara's touch on his cheek. "We got lost in the storm."

"That can happen," Gutierrez said, pouring fresh coffee, serving the cups, and joining them at the table, his smile sympathetic.

To Sara, Gutierrez seemed affable and rather ordinary. "You run the bighorn program on the range," she said, making small talk.

Gutierrez nodded. "Going on five years now. I work out of Santa Fe but spend a lot of time down here. Especially this time of year." He took out his wallet and gave Sara a business card. "If you'd like to see the herds, give me a call. We do periodic flyovers to track the herd and check on the new lambs. I took the commanding general up last year. He enjoyed it."

"That would be fun," Sara admitted. "Can I heat some water? I'd like to wash up."

"I'll put the pot on for you."

"Thanks."

After eating, Sara took the pot of hot water into the bathroom, stripped out of her clothes, and sponged off the sweat and dirt, feeling better by the minute. She wondered what Kerney must feel like to see the ranch for the first time in so many years.

She dressed in fresh clothes, barely managing to get the boot on her injured foot, and limped out of the bathroom. The living room and kitchen were empty. The packhorse gear was on the living-room floor. She searched through it for the handheld radio. Andy needed to know they would be late getting back to the Jennings ranch. The case, seriously cracked, came apart in her hands. The radio was dead as a doornail. Probably damaged when the gelding slammed into the roan during the storm, she thought, returning it to the pack. She went looking for Kerney and found him stretched out on his bedroom floor, his jacket stuffed under his head, fast asleep, and breathing generously through his mouth. She brought her gear into his bedroom, spread it next to him, and shook him gently with her hand. He woke up quickly.

"So we're a couple now, are we?" he said, sitting up.

"In your dreams, Kerney."

"How did you guess?"

Sara suppressed a blush and gave him an unreadable look. "Did you question Gutierrez?"

"No. I fell asleep." He rubbed his face with his hands and looked at the sleeping bag and pack on the floor next to him. "Are you bunking with me?"

She poked his arm with a warning finger. "Only for appearance' sake. Go back to sleep. I'll talk to Gutierrez."

Kerney nodded and rolled onto his side. "Thank you, dear."

Sara stuck out her tongue and left.

Gutierrez, stretched out over the seat of his truck, was cleaning out an accumulation of trash. As Sara approached, he climbed out and moved the bench seat back as far as it would go. "Hi."

"Hi," Sara replied. "I wonder if you have time to answer a few questions."

"Sure. What's up?"

"Did you know Sammy Yazzi?"

"I never met him, but I know who he is," Eppi answered. "I was uprange when the search team started looking for him. I heard all the radio traffic. I stay tuned to the military police channel whenever I'm on the range."

"Where were you?"

"Camped out up on Sheep Mesa, identifying animals for a relocation project. I was stopped and questioned by a patrol when I got back down here, the day after the search started." Gutierrez chuckled. "They even searched my truck."

"Did you ever have any unexpected visitors at Sheep Mesa?"

Gutierrez shook his head. "I would have remembered something like that. The areas I work in are mostly off-limits. The only people I see are military police and other wildlife officers."

"Thanks. Would it be all right if I used your radio?"

"Go ahead." Gutierrez started to move away, then stopped. "I guess you haven't found that soldier yet."

"No, we haven't."

"Well, good luck with it. There's fresh coffee on the stove. Help yourself."

"I'll do that." She waited until Gutierrez left, keyed the hand mike to the radio, called the base dispatcher, and left a message to be passed on to Andy Baca that they would be late returning.

Inside the house, Eppi looked up from the desk, closed his notebook, and put down his pen. "That was fast," he said conversationally.

"How long will you be on the range?" Sara asked.

Gutierrez gave a harried sigh. "You'll have the place to yourselves in the morning. I'm heading back to Santa Fe. We've got a drawing for bighorn hunting licenses this week." His expression brightened. "I could get you a VIP permit, if you like."

"I'll pass, but thanks just the same."

He shrugged. "If you change your mind, let me know."

Kerney emerged from the back of the house into the kitchen, scrubbed and clean, wet hair plastered to his forehead, carrying his boots in one hand and his still-damp cowboy hat in the other. Sara was drinking coffee at the table.

"I couldn't go back to sleep," he admitted, sitting down. He shaped the hat to get the right crease back in the brim and placed it on the table. "Andy's going to start looking for us in the morning unless I give him a call."

"I took care of it," Sara said.

"Good." He started pulling on his boots. "Did Gutierrez have anything interesting to say?"

"Let's talk outside," Sara suggested, nodding at Gutierrez through the open kitchen door.

Kerney grabbed a small kit from the pack, and they left the house, walking toward the horses. The bay lifted his head as they approached. Kerney brushed him down with a curry comb and checked his legs for soreness.

"Well?" he asked. "What did Gutierrez have to say?" He handed Sara the comb.

"Not much," she answered, brushing the gelding while Kerney rubbed some antibacterial ointment into a small scrape on the animal's neck. "I asked if he knew Sammy, and he said he didn't. But he was on the base when Sammy turned up missing."

Kerney worked on the gelding's hoofs, brushing a dressing under the hair and into the band. "Was he questioned?"

"Stopped, questioned, and searched," Sara answered. "Nothing suspicious was uncovered."

The packhorse rolled in a patch of wet grass. Sara got the animal to its feet, and while Kerney treated a sore rubbed raw by the pack frame, she gave the roan a fast brushing.

"We know Sammy was in the area, and Gutierrez sleeps at the ranch when he's on the base," Kerney commented as he repacked the kit. "Should we question him some more?"

"He seems straight enough."

"It's your call," Kerney noted.

152

"I'd rather wait and do it later, when we're back at the main post."

They left the horses and walked to a sheared-off dead cottonwood that had been struck by lightning. One thick branch remained on the tall stump; it bowed and touched the ground. It had the shape of a wizened woman bending over, extending a long hand to the earth. It was the witch tree of Kerney's childhood, a favorite hangout where he would perch with a book and read until sunset.

Sara reached in her pocket for the cavalry insignia and held it in her open palm. "Any ideas about this? I found it in the cave."

Kerney took it, turned it over several times, and shook his head in wonderment. "Right in my backyard."

"What?"

"Apache plunder. Mexican silver. The Lost Bowie Mine. The treasure at Victorio Peak. I used to sit on the witch tree, read Frank Dobie books, and dream of finding riches." He tossed the pin in the air and caught it. "Dale and I would spend days on end searching. We never found a damn thing." He handed the insignia to Sara. "Amazing."

"This type of insignia hasn't been used since the nineteenth century," Sara said.

"Did you find anything else?"

"No. We'll see what the crime scene unit uncovers."

"Let me guess," Kerney speculated. "We'll wait to send them out until after we get back."

Sara laughed. "That's an excellent idea."

* * *

After Kerney and Sara Brannon were asleep, Gutierrez crept quietly out of the house. He took an alternate route to the cave, picking his way carefully to avoid leaving footprints. The nearly full moon gave him enough light to confirm his fears. The two cops had been nosing around. He stepped cautiously from rock to rock until he reached the cave entrance. The stones were not in the same order he had put them in. It made him sick with worry.

He knew the law. He could be charged with murder. He was as guilty as the man who had killed Yazzi. No one was supposed to get hurt. It wasn't his goddamn fault the soldier had showed up at exactly the wrong time. Hiking in the boondocks with a sketchbook, for chrissake. Nosing around where he had no business being. Walking into the cave with a wide-eyed, shit-eating grin. Asking questions.

Gutierrez retraced his steps until he dropped below the rim of the mesa and sat on a rock, looking at the ranch below. What the fuck was he going to do? The story about a pleasure trip was pure bullshit. He might have bought it if Brannon hadn't asked all those questions about Yazzi. He'd almost shit a brick when she brought the subject up.

Damn it! If they had only listened to him and let him move the rest of the stuff right away. That was the smart thing to do. No, no, too risky, too soon, let it quiet down, they said. Shit!

In too deep to back out, he almost wished he'd never found the cave. Can't cry over spilt milk. The last load was behind the seat of his truck. Two thousand gold and silver coins and a leather dispatch case filled with historical military letters.

Worth plenty. Fuck the others! He didn't need them. He'd sell it himself in Mexico and just disappear.

As far as he could tell, he wasn't under suspicion, but that could change. He looked down at his shaking hands and clasped them together to stop the trembling. He needed a plan. Something he could pull off. There was no way in hell he was going to prison.

"I've got to improvise," he whispered to himself.

It was still dark. The bare ceiling light cast a harsh glow throughout the kitchen, and the aroma from a wood fire in the cookstove filled the room. Sara, drying two plates at the sink, turned and looked at Kerney as he came in.

"Is Gutierrez gone?" Kerney asked. There was a pot of coffee and pan of scrambled eggs on the top of the cast-iron stove. He was stiff from head to toe, but rested.

"Before I got up," Sara reported, putting the plates on the table. "Coffee?"

"Please."

"How long will it take to get back to the Rocking J?" She asked, putting a mug of coffee in front of him.

"We can make good time if we run the ridges over Rhodes Canyon."

"That may not be wise," Sara said.

Kerney sipped his coffee and laughed. "Trust me, your people won't even see us coming. I watched the Army build that concealed outpost in the canyon when I was a kid."

"You're not supposed to know about that," Sara chided, half-jokingly.

"I won't tell a soul."

They ate breakfast, enjoying each other's company, cleaned up the dishes together, and headed out to saddle the horses.

Gutierrez watched the three horses and two riders leave the ranch veering south and west. At first light he had picked a vantage point that would keep them in view for some time. His plans depended on the route they took.

He would use his knowledge of the terrain and his speed to his advantage. He knew the mountains and could outrun them easily in the truck. Yesterday's storm had brought a blessing. The usual telltale funnel of dust thrown up by the tires would be missing.

He followed them with his binoculars. Going southwest was good, he thought. It would take them to Rhodes Canyon, probably above the pass. Anything farther on was more than a day's journey by horseback. They weren't provisioned for another night. He had searched the pack and knew what supplies they carried. He just had to be patient. He held their shapes in the lenses until they turned into dots, then fired up the truck.

He got in position just in time to watch Kerney bypass the canyon that ran out of Tipton Spring. They were running the ridge tops to Rhodes Canyon. Had to be. From where they were now, they had no alternative. Water still filled the washes from the storm. It would be too dangerous to ride through the draws.

Two canyons over they'd hit Amole Ridge. There would be two steep steps up and down. They would have to break trail and lead the horses through it on foot. Above the eastern scarp of the ridge they would reach high country of broken benches, cedar breaks, and gentle slopes. After that, they could easily pick up the road through Rhodes Pass.

He moved the truck again and watched until they entered a stand of cedars. He held his breath as he scanned the prehistoric reef Kerney had to use to scale Amole Ridge. They came back into view just where he had his glasses trained. He watched them weave slowly back to the west. Gutierrez was starting to feel good. He would be way ahead of them when they reached the road.

Sara held the horses while Kerney fed them the last of the oats from the bag Dale Jennings had provided. The view was stunning; so completely different from the slashing gorges and mean canyons on the ride in. On both sides of the tight pass the land rolled in soft hills that hid the vast desert from sight.

The road below her, carved and blasted out of the mountainside, clung to the edge of a drop-off dotted by the crowns of tall pine trees, rising seventy-five feet from the canyon floor, that formed a natural border along the shoulder. Here the turns in the road were gradual. Farther along it slashed in a series of cutbacks that pierced deeper into the canyon.

Sara had traveled the road many times before, but the vantage point from the top of the canyon threw her off. She asked Kerney to locate the MP outpost for her. He smiled and pointed at her feet. They were standing on top of the outpost, which was carved out of the mountainside.

Kerney finished with the horses and swung into the saddle. She mounted the gelding and took one last look at the breathtaking beauty around her before moving her horse down the slope to the road.

Gutierrez surveyed the roadside patiently before selecting his spot. Where the granite changed to limestone, the ground was still soggy from yesterday's storm. At a blind corner, a large slab of limestone had separated from the top of the cliff. Chunks of stone and earth partially blocked the roadway. He drove around it carefully, the truck tires inches away from the fall-off into the canyon, found a place to turn around, and parked close to the rock wall below the slide. He climbed to the top of the cliff and scanned in all directions. Above him, there was no possibility of passage down to the pass. Kerney and Brannon would have to join the road long before they reached his position.

He stayed back from the ledge, stretched his arm over the crevice, and poked at the crumbling limestone. A small clump broke away and dribbled down the bluff. He kept working on the slab until rock blocked the entire road.

After climbing down he moved rocks into a pile, then stopped to think things over. His back ached and his shirt stuck to him like a wet rag. He walked around the blind corner and then back to his truck, studying the road. He got a shovel from the truck and moved dirt and rocks from the lip of the road, leaving just enough space to allow foot traffic around the rockpile. He sprinkled earth and pebbles over it to make it look natural.

He put the shovel in the bed of the truck and walked back up the road, pacing off five-yard increments, marking each with a small rock until he was fifty yards from the corner. He turned and examined his labors. The slide would look passable to anyone approaching on horseback. He went back to the slide and eyed the height of the pile. He needed it to be at least to the top of the truck's bumper and loosely packed. He threw some of the bigger stones over the side and hollowed out a peephole where he could watch the road without being seen.

Judging the timing and the amount of force he would need was the only remaining problem. He estimated distances and moved the truck farther down the road. He walked from the farthest marker, timing himself as he went. He did it once more, walking backward to erase the footprints. It might be a Rube Goldberg scheme, but it would work. Shit happens, Gutierrez thought, smiling to himself. He spread some damp dirt over the rocks to make the pile look more natural. Kerney and Brannon would have to ride single-file to get around it.

He stretched out at the peephole, still sweating from the exertion, and waited. When everything was over, he would erase any traces of his presence and be on his way. He checked his watch. He would be long gone before anyone came looking. Maybe to Yucatán or Veracruz on the Gulf of Mexico. He had visited both areas before, and Spanish was his first language. He'd blend right in.

An hour passed. He was starting to get restless when Kerney came around the last bend. Kerney reined in and stopped, the roan packhorse siding up to the bay. Gutierrez held his breath. Finally Kerney moved and Sara Brannon came into view, closing the gap between her and the roan. Gutierrez counted off the seconds as Kerney passed the first marker. The pace of the animals was perfect. He forced himself to wait, timing Kerney's progress over the next thirty yards. Still perfect. He crawled backward and scrambled to the truck. It was going to work! He started the engine, jammed it into gear, and plowed it into the rockpile, only a second or two faster than planned.

Kerney was past the nose of the truck and on Gutierrez's right side, but the rocks still splattered his horse. Kerney spurred the bay desperately and dropped the reins to the roan. The bay was flying, landing with forefeet on tumbling rocks, fighting for solid ground, hind feet flailing in the air. The packhorse dropped over the edge, making sounds Gutierrez had never heard from a horse before.

Amazingly, the truck continued to roll. He braked hard, fishtailed into the wall, bounced over the remains of the rockpile, and landed hard on the undercarriage, the front wheels dangling over empty space. On his left, Sara Brannon and the gelding were spinning counterclockwise in a tight circle away from the scatter, out of danger. Gutierrez wondered how she was able to do that.

He cursed and looked for Kerney. A few feet from the truck the riderless bay, eyes wild, ears back in fear, pawed the ground. Hatless, facedown on the roadbed, Kerney pushed himself upright and started running toward Gutierrez with murder in his eyes. How could the lame bastard move so fast? Gutierrez panicked, reached for the door handle, and heard a sharp, splintering sound from above. He twisted around to look out the rear window. The cliff gave way, burying the truck with rock, crushing his skull, and pulverizing his chest against the steering wheel.

Kerney watched the last of the rubble trickle over the truck, the thick limestone dust rising in the air like a plume of smoke. The roar of the slide gave way to the sound of stones careening into the canyon below. He scrambled over the truck looking for Sara. She stood with her back pressed against the rock face, holding the skittish gelding by the bridle.

"Are you okay?" he asked.

She took a breath, held it, and exhaled slowly. "Let's not do this anymore."

"Not enough excitement?" Kerney inquired, holding her arm to keep her steady.

"Too much of a good thing can be dangerous," she said.

"That's almost funny."

Sara coughed and rubbed the tip of her nose. "It's the best I can do under the circumstances. Gutierrez?"

"Dead," Kerney answered.

"We lost the roan." She was covered in limestone dust from head to foot.

"I know."

The landslide completely blocked the road. "I can't get the gelding across," she said.

"Cut him loose. He'll find his way home."

She removed the bridle and wrapped it around the pommel. Unrestrained, the gelding wheeled and trotted up the pass. Tentatively, she walked to the edge of the road and looked down. Seventy-five feet below, the dead roan was wedged between the base of two pine trees, surrounded by supplies from the shattered pack.

She stepped away from the edge and looked at Kerney. He had lost his cowboy hat, and his hair, flattened by the hatband, curled up into wings above his ears. He was covered from head to foot with fine limestone dust. "You look like shit," Sara commented, the fluttery feeling in her stomach subsiding.

"I suspect you're right," he answered, brushing off the front of his shirt. Puffs of limestone dust floated into the air. "Seems like we upset Gutierrez. Let's see if we can find out why."

They cleared away enough rubble from the truck to uncover and pry open the passenger door. The seat, thrown off its tracks by the impact, pinned Gutierrez to the steering column. His shattered skull dripped blood and brains, soaking his clothes and the floorboard.

Behind the seat were ten packages, wrapped and taped shut. Kerney reached in and handed them to Sara one at a time. He was searching the glove compartment when, with an incredulous whistle, Sara made him stop.

"Look at this," she said, holding out an open package filled with gold coins. "The mint dates are all from the eighteen hundreds. Do you know what these are worth?"

"I don't want to think about it," Kerney said sourly. He opened a flat, rectangular box that had slid under the seat. It contained a military dispatch case, the leather desiccated and veined with cracks, filled with faded documents.

Sara moved next to him. "What is that?"

Kerney shrugged and closed the flap. "Just some old letters."

"Don't tease," she chided, pulling the case out of his hands. She sat on the ground and skimmed through the documents. Gingerly, she detached a letter and read it with growing amazement. She studied two more papers before speaking. "Incredible. These are letters written by General William Tecumseh Sherman and President Ulysses S. Grant." She patted the case. "This has to be General Howard's official document file."

"Who?" Kerney inquired.

Sara replaced the letters, closed the pouch, stood up, and brushed off the seat of her pants with a hand. "The letters are addressed to O. O. Howard. He was a Civil War general. Grant sent him west during the Indian Wars. He negotiated a treaty with Cochise. These letters are historical treasures."

"It looks like Gutierrez found the mother lode. Isn't that the luck of the Irish?"

"Stop feeling sorry for yourself. Do you think Gutierrez killed Sammy?"

"It's possible," Kerney allowed, "but not likely. I don't think murder was Gutierrez's strong suit."

"Sammy found the coins and documents and recruited Gutierrez to help him," Sara proposed. "Instead, Gutierrez decided he wanted it all for himself."

The theory didn't sit well with Kerney. "Why would Gutierrez wait almost two months after he killed Sammy to move the merchandise?"

"Caution?" Sara suggested. "He wanted things to cool down."

"This case cooled down a month ago. If you had a

clear shot at making tens of thousands—maybe hundreds of thousands—of dollars, would you wait any longer than absolutely necessary? Especially if you had a dead body concealed with the goodies? Wouldn't that make you anxious?"

Sara nibbled her lower lip. "Maybe Gutierrez was forced to wait until he found someone to handle the transaction. It can't be easy to convert this stuff into cash without raising a lot of eyebrows."

"Which means somebody may be expecting a delivery and might get worried if it's late."

"Exactly." Sara grinned. "Do you want to play it out?"

"Why not?"

She flicked a glance at the truck. "What we have here is a tragic accident. Not quite what Gutierrez had in mind. Let's put it back the way we found it and see what happens."

"Including the coins and letters?" Kerney inquired.

Sara paused to think about it. "We'll give those to Andy for safekeeping."

"Let's do it and get the hell out of here."

Together they restacked rocks around the truck. Kerney wrapped the treasure in his rain jacket and tied it to the saddle on the bay. They walked down the road, the bay favoring a bruised hind leg, until the grade dipped enough to let them cut back in the direction of the dead roan. They dug a shallow trench in the soft earth under a stand of trees that blocked any view to the road above, gathered up the debris, and dumped it in. Sammy's portfolio was intact and the watercolors undamaged.

Kerney hitched a rope to the bay, tied it off on the dead animal, and had to quirt the bay to drag the carcass to the trench. They covered the roan with dirt and rocks to keep the coyotes away and retraced their route to the road.

"I'm taking the portfolio to Sammy's parents," he announced, looking at Sara for a reaction.

She sensed his decision was not negotiable. "When?"

"Today."

"What do you plan to tell them?"

"I'll think of something."

"When will you be back?"

"Tomorrow."

"Good."

"I'll ask Andy to get a search warrant for Gutierrez's house."

Sara nodded her approval.

They lapsed into silence. The bay snorted in discomfort, and Kerney stopped to give him a rest, stroking him gently on the forehead. "Dale isn't going to like the way we've treated his horses."

"The Army will pay full damages," Sara promised.

"That'll be a first," he said, as he got the animal moving again.

"I expect you're right."

They walked down one last sharp series of turns before entering the rolling hills of the western slope. The *Jornada* fanned out in front of them. Kerney hobbled and Sara limped along. The bay favored his bruised leg, snorting in annoyance. Still crusted and streaked with rock dust, they looked like pale apparitions. Dale's ranch came into view. He was at the fence line with Andy, both scanning the pass with binoculars. Dale saw them first and waved.

"What a sight we must be." Sara began to laugh, and before he knew it, Kerney was laughing with her.

CHAPTER

8

The only sound on the deserted plaza was the idling engine of Kerney's truck. The tourists were gone for the day and the pueblo was quiet. Kerney stopped at the end of the dirt lane that bisected the plaza. Across the empty square was the tribal administration building where Terry had his office. A long, squat structure with a series of narrow doors and small windows, it looked like an unfriendly sanctuary built to keep out intruders. At one end of the building, three squad cars were parked in front of the police station door.

Kerney turned his head and looked over the line of adobe houses that bordered a section of the plaza. Against the western mountains, the setting sun seemed cold in the pink light. He tried not to think about the pain that faced Terry and Maria. His own sadness felt like a sharp wound cutting through him. How much worse it would be for Terry and Maria he could only imagine. He touched the portfolio on the seat next to him. The five thousand dollars was safely tucked inside. He put the truck in gear and coasted to a stop in front of the building.

From the moment Kerney stepped through the door of the one-room office carrying the portfolio, Terry knew his son was dead. A phone call would tell him Sammy was alive, but only his death would bring Kerney to his door with that grim look. His heart sank and he stood up slowly, testing the steadiness of his legs. The two young officers in the room were suddenly quiet, shoptalk frozen in the air like hot breath on a cold winter's day.

Terry tilted his chin in a wordless greeting, afraid to speak, his unblinking dark eyes locked on Kerney's face.

"I came here first," Kerney explained.

Terry nodded his appreciation and cleared his throat. No words came. He unbuckled the Sam Browne belt that held his holstered pistol and stowed it in a desk drawer. "Will you walk with me to Maria's?"

"Of course."

"I will be with my son's mother," he told the officers, not seeing them at all. "Ask her family to join us there."

The two officers nodded wordlessly as Terry walked out the door with Kerney.

Crossing the plaza, Terry felt detached from his surroundings. The familiar buildings looked strange, and his heart pounded in his chest like a powerful drumbeat. Oddly, he thought of cornmeal and pollen. He needed to gather both for the burial ritual. He didn't realize he was holding his breath until he reached Maria's front door. She looked at him, glanced at Kerney, and her hand flew to her mouth. Terry opened his arms and she exploded against him, small and vulnerable. She buried her head in his chest and sobbed.

He looked for Kerney, and found him at his side, fretfully shifting his weight, staring at the ground. When Maria stopped crying and relaxed her grip, he spoke to Kerney. "Come inside and tell us what happened." His voice sounded gruff as the words tumbled out. Supporting Maria, he led the way.

In the small living room, Kerney listened to the sounds of the house while Terry and Maria waited, dull-eyed and stunned, for him to speak. A breeze sighed through an open window, the old wood ceiling creaked, and the hum of the refrigerator drifted in from the kitchen. Kerney wanted to melt away with the sounds.

Maria and Terry sat close together on the small love seat. Terry's hand clutched Maria's.

Maria spoke first. "What happened to my son?"

The truth would only send Terry on a rampage. "It was a hiking accident," Kerney lied. "In the mountains. On the missile range."

"When did you find him?" Terry asked.

"Yesterday."

"Did he suffer?" Maria asked.

"No, I don't think so."

"And his body?" Terry asked. "Is it . . ."

"Intact," Kerney replied quickly.

169

Terry looked relieved.

Maria smiled bravely, her gaze riveted on empty space. She touched her hair, pinned casually into a loose bun, and quickly forced her hand back into her lap.

"He was saving his money for a new car," she said in a faraway voice. "He wanted to pay for it himself. He was so proud about doing things on his own. I kept asking him to come home for a visit, but he wouldn't. Not until he could take me for a ride in the car."

Kerney picked up the portfolio from beside the chair and handed it to her. "For you."

Maria took the case, put it on her lap, stroked it gently, and with a shaking hand unzipped it. Terry leaned close as Maria unfolded the portfolio. For a very long time, they examined Sammy's work without speaking. It seemed so personal, Kerney wanted to vanish. When they finished, Maria closed the case and smiled in Kerney's direction, her mouth a razor-thin line of grief.

Terry held the envelope with the five thousand dollars in his hand. "This is your money," he said hoarsely.

"No," Kerney replied.

"Take it, please," Terry countered. His face looked ready to shatter into pieces. He was barely in control.

Kerney shook his head. "I can't do that."

Sounds from outside the house intruded; cars arriving, subdued voices, footsteps on the gravel path. The family was gathering.

Kerney stood up. "I have to go."

Maria held him from leaving with a gesture. "Do

you know when they will send Sammy home to us?" she asked.

"Soon," he promised.

Maria stood and hugged him, patting his back as though it would ease her pain.

"I'm sorry," Kerney said.

Maria looked up and released him. "I know." She walked away to greet her guests.

Old and young began to fill the front room, children hushed, adults somber. Condolences expressed in several languages floated on the air.

Terry was at Kerney's side. "Thank you," he said.

"I did nothing."

Terry grunted in disagreement, searching for more to say. "I'll call you about the services."

"I'll be there."

He smiled dismally. "Sammy would like that."

"Will you be all right?"

He rubbed the back of his hand across his mouth before answering. "I need a drink. A dozen drinks."

"Will you take them?" Kerney asked.

"I won't."

"Good. Call me if you need to talk."

"You mean that?"

"Yes, I do."

Terry held out his hand. Whatever rancor Kerney felt about Terry was gone, part of a dim, unimportant past. He pulled Terry to him in a hug, and held him tight while his old friend finally cried.

Kerney slipped through a group of people waiting outside and walked up the dirt lane. On the plaza, filled with people moving in small groups toward Maria's home, he felt even more like an intruder. Some of the older women were veiled, and several elders were wrapped in ceremonial blankets. All looked at him with sidelong, passive glances. At the front of the police station, the two young tribal officers were in their squad cars, emergency lights flashing. As he drove away, he looked in the rearview mirror. The officers had blocked the plaza with their cars. The pueblo was now closed to outsiders.

Andy came through with a search warrant, signed by a local judge and delivered to Kerney by a bored city patrol officer who was parked in front of the apartment complex where Eppi Gutierrez lived. Kerney thanked the patrolman, turned down his offer for backup, and went to find the apartment manager. He showed the warrant to the man and learned that Eppi lived alone in a one-bedroom apartment on the second floor. He got the key and directions to the unit.

The complex, on a main throughway of Santa Fe, had been built by an out-of-state developer. Gutierrez's apartment was a string of three boxy rooms on the second floor, the layout dictated by the developer's computer program and slapped up with a few touches to create a cut-rate Santa Fe style. Gutierrez liked his toys: the living room had a big-screen television and a costly rack sound system, the kitchen counter held a variety of expensive gourmet appliances, and the bedroom contained a king-size water bed and a top-of-the-line mountain bike. The bike was against the wall, used as a dirty clothes rack.

Kerney tore the place apart systematically. There was nothing taped under the dresser drawers, no incriminating notes in the pockets of clothing, and no coins and letters like those found in Gutierrez's truck. He dug through clothing, shoes, boxes, and papers. The living room, bathroom, and kitchen yielded the same dismal results. Packages in the refrigerator and kitchen cabinets held nothing but food. A high-powered hunting rifle and a set of golf clubs were in the hall closet, just where a burglar would expect them to be. The bathroom, including the toilet tank, held no surprises. What jewelry Gutierrez owned was scattered on the top of the sink counter, in plain view. Either Gutierrez had nothing to hide or he was an expert at concealment.

He started over again, reversing the search. He upended the living-room furniture and pulled apart all of the cushions. He dug through the dead ashes of the fireplace, turned over the pictures on the walls, and looked through every book on the bookshelf. Gutierrez's taste ran from horror novels to popular mysteries.

He took one last look around the room, put the couch upright, and sat down in disgust, thinking maybe there was absolutely nothing to find. On the carpet by the overturned lamp table was a stack of unopened mail, mostly bills and advertising flyers. He flipped through the accumulation. One thick envelope had a return address from Gutierrez's office and carried first-class stamps instead of the usual metered imprint government agencies use. He opened it. Inside was a handwritten list on sheets of lined yellow paper. Kerney read it with growing awe. Rifles, pistols, saddles, uniforms, sabers, holsters— all in quantity and all dated as over a hundred years old. Many were brand-new, according to Gutierrez's estimate.

If the list was real, and there was no reason to doubt it, Gutierrez had been moving truckloads of material off the base. He read on.

Military clothing: boots, coats and hats, dress uniforms, greatcoats were listed by the dozens, all packed in the original crates. There was enough to outfit several squads of pony soldiers and their horses. The tack list was just as impressive: saddles, halters, bridles, saddle girths and blankets, saddler and blacksmith tools.

The inventory went on for pages, written in Gutierrez's compulsively neat script: leather cartridge boxes, forage sacks, waist and saber belts, fatigues and stable frocks, halter chains, gloves, cartridge belts, and spurs.

Kerney stopped reading and visualized the cave at Big Mesa. It must have been packed to the ceiling. He returned to the list. Gutierrez had recorded every coin and letter recovered from the truck. Each coin was described by type, denomination, date, and condition. Each letter was summarized by author and subject. The last entry was for another mail pouch. Again, Gutierrez provided a summary of each letter; most of them were from members of the 9th Cavalry to family and friends back home. Gutierrez had added a note in the margin, written with a different pen. It read: "Delivered to buyer to prove authenticity."

Kerney folded the list and put it back in the envelope. Gutierrez had hit a treasure trove; definitely the spoils from at least one Apache raid—maybe more. He couldn't begin to estimate the value, but people paid enormous sums of money for rare historic objects. He needed to get a general idea of the value, just to be sure. The next question was equally simple: where would Gutierrez find the most likely buyer? Probably through a broker, eager to do business with him. It was stuff that museums, universities, and individual collectors would drool over.

There was no sign of activity at the ranch when Kerney got home. His arrival was greeted by the whinnying of the mustang in the horse barn. It was the lonely sound of a neglected animal. He chastised himself for keeping the horse penned up for no good reason other than his own convenience. He apologized with fresh oats, a clean stall, and some soothing words, which didn't seem to be quite enough. The mustang snorted and turned away. He got a halter from the tack room and slipped it over the animal's head.

"You deserve better," he said, leading him out of the corral.

There wasn't going to be any breeding stock on Quinn's ranch for a very long time, if ever. No big deal. It was just another setback.

He opened the gate to the north section, where the grass was best and the restored windmill fed clear water into a stock tank. The horse picked up his ears in anticipation. Kerney scratched the mustang's nose and apologized again. Halter off, he wheeled through the gate and galloped into the darkness. Silently he watched until the thought struck him it was time to give the mustang a name. He'd call him Soldier, in honor of Sammy.

It wasn't very imaginative, but he hoped Sammy, wherever he was, approved.

* * *

Greg Benton picked the lock to Gutierrez's apartment, flipped on the light, and surveyed the mess. Not good, he thought to himself as he closed the door and eased the semiautomatic out of the pocket of his windbreaker. He did a quick room-to-room search, encountered nothing except more disarray, and left the apartment complex, hurrying quickly to his car. Two blocks away he stopped at a convenience store, dialed a long-distance number, let it ring three times, and disconnected. He repeated the process, got back in his car, an inconspicuous compact rental that was too cramped for his large frame, and headed for the interstate.

His mind was racing. It was bad enough that Gutierrez had blown the rendezvous to deliver the merchandise, but now it looked as though Eppi had flapped his mouth and queered the whole gig.

Time for damage control, Benton decided, with a tight smile. He held the car at 65 and settled back to think things through. Traffic on the interstate was light. In the distant Jemez Mountains, Los Alamos winked down at Santa Fe. The piñon-studded hills along the right-of-way were filling up with subdivisions, and across the valley, streetlights lined new roads to new neighborhoods outside the city limits.

Too much was riding on the deal to let it go sour now. Benton wondered if Eppi had decided to keep the last shipment for himself and do a little freelancing. A dumb move. But the apartment had been tossed by a pro, probably looking for the goodies.

Benton had to find Gutierrez.

Leonard Garcia smiled warmly at his visitor and had him sit by the window with the nice view of the interior courtyard of the Palace of Governors Museum. The morning sun barely touched the tops of the trees and the robins were undisturbed, yet to be chased off by museum visitors.

As a high school senior, Leonard had persuaded a small band of his friends to help him protest the closing of the last drugstore on the Santa Fe Plaza. Armed with a truckload of cow manure, they waited for the day the new art gallery was to open in what had once been their favorite hangout. In the middle of the night they dumped fresh dung against the entrance and drenched it with gallons of water. It was so much fun they did it again the next night.

The daily newspaper carried the escapade as front-page news. It was the talk of the town. It was heady stuff for the anonymous heroes or villains— depending on the point of view. Leonard had plotted a third foray against Santa Fe gentrification and been caught in the act by the man sitting in his office.

Leonard owed Kerney one very big favor. Officially, he and his pals were never apprehended. Kerney took them one by one to their parents and had each boy confess. Punishment was left up to the family. Leonard lost his driving privileges for the summer, which, in turn, resulted in the loss of his girlfriend. For that he was grateful. He might never have started college if Loretta hadn't broken up with him in order to date Roger Gonzales, who, at the time, owned a very fine raked and lowered Chevy. Roger was now paying considerable child support to Loretta for their three children.

He asked Kerney what he could do for him.

"You're the only delinquent I know who has a

doctorate in archaeology, runs a history museum, and owes me a favor," Kerney replied.

"I'm rehabilitated," Leonard countered. "Anyway, there isn't enough cow shit left in Santa Fe County to cover all the boutiques, galleries, and tourist shops. What can I do for you?"

He handed Leonard the inventory. "Take a look at this."

Kerney watched Leonard's eyes widen as he read through the list. "Is this real?"

"Yes."

He read the list again while Kerney waited. Garcia had red hair and classic Castilian features. He could trace his family roots in Santa Fe to the Spanish reconquest of New Mexico.

He tapped his finger against the papers. "This is a major find. One any curator would give his eyeteeth to acquire. If it was purchased intact, I could get the museum foundation to build a new wing to house it."

"How much would you be willing to pay?"

Leonard studied the list again. "On the open market, who knows? It would be a bidding war. If I had an exclusive option, I'd offer three million dollars and probably go as high as four. Maybe more."

"And if the collection was sold piecemeal?" Kerney ventured.

"It would take longer to dispose of it, but you could make even more profit. Add another million," Leonard answered. "Everything on the list has value. Especially now that anything to do with the frontier west is such a hot commodity among collectors. For example, the letters from Grant and Sherman to General Howard: it's correspondence about Grant's peace policy regarding the Indians. Howard was a crusty, one-armed, pious son of a bitch who served with Grant in the Civil War. His men called him the praying general. Grant made him a presidential emissary. Any presidential correspondence of historical significance commands top dollar. Those letters are even more valuable because they fill in some gaps. Historians would kill to have them. I wouldn't sneeze at the Sherman letters, either. He ranks right up there as an important American personality of the time. The letters alone could bring hundreds of thousands of dollars."

"Thanks, Leonard." Kerney reached across the desk and retrieved the list.

"I'd love to have an opportunity to make an offer. Do you know who the buyer is?"

"Not yet," Kerney replied. "Any ideas where I should look?"

"It depends on the type of buyer. I'm assuming this isn't kosher."

"It isn't."

Garcia gazed at the ceiling. "Unfortunately, it isn't that hard to find unscrupulous dealers. If I was in the market to sell something illegally, I'd lower the risk and ship the merchandise out of the country. Western Americana is a hot item among collectors in the Far East and Europe. Especially the Japanese and Germans. They couldn't beat us in the war, but they sure can outbid us in the marketplace."

"Would that be likely?"

Leonard nodded. "With the quantity and quality of the list, I would say it's very likely. The megabucks are overseas, and once the items are on foreign soil, the chances of getting caught are almost nil."

"Could an average citizen pull it off?"

"I don't think so. Not without a broker. There are too many complexities to deal with. If your crook isn't an expert in the field, he's going to have to split the profits with somebody who has the right contacts."

Eddie Tapia felt right at home on the Juárez strip. The gaudy, hot colors of the buildings, the rawness of the streets, the carnival atmosphere of the hustlers, whores, and street urchins, and the smells from the street vendors hawking food to pedestrians combined into one loud pulse of Mexican life. The streets were crowded with drivers playing a mad game of bumper cars. Shills made bilingual pitches along sidewalks, selling fake designer watches and gold jewelry that would turn green within a week. Bars cranked out loud Tex-Mex music to attract attention. The hookers wore dresses that stopped at the ass and pranced around in their spiked heels and cowboy boots working the streets. Open stalls in alleys displayed velvet paintings of Elvis, cheap sombreros, and piñatas.

Tapia soaked it all up. The first twelve years of his life he'd grown up in Mexican border towns along the Rio Grande. From Matamoros on the Gulf to Piedras Negras, he moved with his family from job to job. His father, who rebuilt generators, particularly those for prized American-made cars, could always find work. Still, it was necessary for Eddie and his brothers to make money. At the age of five, he became a beggar's apprentice, working for his Uncle Adolfo.

Every day Uncle Adolfo put on a harness with a padded hump and transformed himself into a *jorobado*—a hunchback. To Mexicans the *jorobado* brought luck. Gamblers, whores, housewives—even the priests—would touch Adolfo's hump for luck and give him money for the privilege. Eddie shilled and sold talisman jewelry.

After putting Isabel and the baby on a bus to Brownsville, Eddie had purchased all the material needed for his transformation: soft cowhide, which must feel like skin under his shirt; padding, which had to be firm yet pliable; a harness to round his shoulders; and finally the clothes of a beggar. He crossed the bridge into Juárez as a hunchback. Neither his wife nor Captain Brannon would have recognized him.

Finding Petty Officer Yardman's trail hadn't been all that difficult. Concentrating on the GI hangouts and clip joints, Tapia quickly learned that Yardman had won a considerable amount of money and had stayed in Juárez for over a month. His winning streak was remembered by the dealers in the clubs he favored. There was talk that when he started losing, Yardman borrowed heavily to keep gambling, before dropping out of sight. Some people thought he was still in Juárez, hiding from a loan shark, while others reported he'd left town. If he was still around, nobody knew where.

After a long night, Eddie left the strip and walked through a working-class neighborhood. The *casitas* were small and packed tightly together along the street, but the sidewalks were clean and the houses well cared for. There were no whores, hustlers, or junkies in sight. He came to a small plaza with a gingerbread bandstand in the center, a wrought-iron fence around the square, and tall shade trees. He sat by the gate of an old hacienda with high, white-washed adobe walls and watched the morning parishioners on their way to early mass. The church, with two tall spires and a bell tower, also painted white, gave the neighborhood a small-town feeling. Opposite the church, the largest building fronting the plaza was a converted general store that had been turned into a nightclub, restaurant, and gambling parlor. Lettered in Spanish on the door was the name of the establishment: the Little Turtle. It was open for business, and morning customers—mostly locals on their way to work—ducked in for a quick roll of the dice, a cup of coffee, or breakfast.

It was a relief to get off his feet. Eddie's muscles ached, and the straps around his shoulders had rubbed the skin raw. He wanted a shower, with lots of hot water and clean, dry towels. It would have to wait. He rubbed the stubble on his chin and checked the grime under his fingernails.

Next to the gambling house was a boarded-up cantina. The two front windows were covered with plywood. On the sidewalk, padlocked to a street-light, was a homemade food cart. It had automobile tires for wheels, a tin awning supported by metal brackets, and a screaming-pink paint job.

A stern voice interrupted Eddie's preoccupation. "Move on, *jorobado*. You cannot beg here."

The policeman standing over Eddie had small eyes above full cheeks, thick jowls, and a head much too big for his body. A pencil-thin mustache under a fat nose drew attention to his crooked teeth.

Eddie smiled, reached into his pocket for some bills, and held out his hand. "Perhaps you would allow me to stay."

The cop took the *mordida*. With the bribe transacted, he smiled at Eddie. "What is your name?"

"Eddie."

"I am Dominguez." The cop was burly, broadchested, and had a huge gut. "You will not make much money this time of day."

"No matter," Eddie replied. "I will rest for a while and be on my way."

Dominguez nodded and rubbed Eddie's hump for luck. "Don't stay too long," he warned, before lumbering away in the direction of the gambling house.

Eddie watched Dominguez enter the nightclub. The door to the adjacent cantina opened and a man in a white apron hurried out carrying trays of food. He was a fair-skinned, blond gringo with a full beard that hid his face. Yardman was blond and the same size as the man in the apron. The man placed the trays in the cart and went back into the cantina. Soon a street vendor emerged, opened a compartment at the rear of the cart, and put a box inside. Then he removed the padlock and pushed the cart down the street.

During the next half hour, carts arrived at the cantina on a regular basis and the same routine occurred. The gringo brought the food, and the vendors stowed boxes in a compartment of each cart. To Eddie, it looked like the cantina was used to distribute more than just tacos to sell on the streets.

He decided to get a closer look. He crossed the plaza, sat on the curb, and watched the next group of vendors. They stocked the carts with bags of marijuana and cocaine.

"Get out of here, *pendejo.*" The gringo was behind him. As Eddie hurried to his feet, the gringo kicked him in the butt and shoved him off the curb into the street, glaring at him with bloodshot eyes. Keeping his temper, Eddie shuffled away, convinced the gringo wasn't Yardman. He decided to move on, find a telephone, and report in to Captain Brannon.

Dominguez stopped him as he crossed the square. "Did you have a problem with the gringo junkie?"

"Who?"

"Duffy. I saw him kick and push you." Dominguez shook his head. "That was wrong of him to do. I will tell Señor DeLeon."

"Señor DeLeon?"

"A very important man. Well connected. He owns the Little Turtle."

"Does he also own the cantina?"

"Of course. It is one of his businesses."

"There is no need for you to tell the señor," Eddie replied.

"You are wrong, my friend. If I do not tell him, someone else will, and I could lose a *mordida* I have come to depend on." Dominguez stopped at the corner. "Will you come back?"

"Perhaps."

"I will look for you."

"I welcome your protection," Eddie said.

Tom Curry sat at the conference table with Sara and an FBI agent named Johnson, a dour man with thin lips and a long, serious face, matched by a lanky frame. He wore a brown suit, white shirt, and regimental striped tie.

"Who found the body?" Johnson asked, tapping the tip of his pen on the desktop, prepared to take notes.

"An MP on patrol," Sara answered. "He found tire tracks in a restricted area and followed them. Specialist Yazzi's body was in a cave, wrapped in a tarp. The back of his head was crushed. Possibly by a rock or some other blunt object. From the appearance of the body, Yazzi has been dead for some time. We have the area cordoned off."

Johnson wrote a note and looked at his wristwatch. "My people should be landing there right about now," he said. "Was anything found with the body?"

"A sketchbook, his dog tags, and his wallet," Sara replied. "Nothing else."

"I'll need those," Johnson said.

Sara slid a manila envelope across the table.

Agent Johnson picked it up and set it next to his elbow. "Was there any indication that Yazzi was killed elsewhere and his body moved to the cave?" Johnson inquired.

"None that we could find," Sara answered.

"Weapon?" Johnson asked.

"We didn't find one."

"Suspects?" he inquired dryly.

"One possible," Sara noted. "There was a vehicle accident in Rhodes Canyon yesterday. A state Game and Fish officer, Eppi Gutierrez, was killed by a rockslide. He had been staying at an old ranch that's used by wildlife and conservation officers when they're on the range. It's approximately ten miles from where Yazzi's body was found."

Johnson smirked. "A dead suspect isn't much good. What do you know about Gutierrez?"

"The usual background information," Sara answered. "He was a wildlife manager. Single. Never married. No military experience. No police record. No traffic tickets in the last five years. He held a degree in biology from New Mexico Highlands University. Started working for Game and Fish right after college. Had slightly over ten years on the job with steady promotions. I've ordered a deeper background check on him."

"Was anything found in the vehicle?" Johnson asked, writing in his notebook.

"We don't know that yet," Sara replied. "His pickup is buried in rock from the slide. The site is under guard with instructions to leave everything as is until further orders. I'd like you and your people to look at it, if that's possible."

Johnson nodded and closed his notebook. "Be glad to."

"Excellent," Major Curry responded, rubbing a hand over his bald head. "Do you have any more questions, Agent Johnson?" Curry's eyebrows were almost an invisible white against his pale complexion, which made his eyes seem huge behind the reading glasses. There was no humor in his gaze.

Johnson shook his head. "Not right now."

Curry stood up. "Keep Captain Brannon informed."

"I'll be in touch," Johnson said, rising and reaching across the table to shake hands with the officers.

As the door closed behind him, the smile dropped off Tom Curry's face.

"What in the hell are you doing, Captain?" Curry demanded, yanking off his glasses and leaning across the table.

"Sir?"

"Don't 'sir' me, Sara." He waved his glasses at her. "I read the dispatcher reports every day, just like you do. Gutierrez's radio had the same locator chip that every MP unit on the base carries. I know exactly where you were when you called and left that message for Sheriff Baca."

She felt his rebuke like a slap across her face. "Sir," she said weakly.

"You found that goddamn body. Do you know how serious it is for an officer to falsify official reports and order subordinates to lie for them?"

"Yes, sir, I do." She was numbed by Curry's criticism. He had every right to slam her.

"Will your people stick to the line of bullshit you fed to Johnson?"

"Yes, sir, they will."

Tom got up from the conference table, walked to his desk, lowered himself into his chair, and stared at Sara across the room. "I want to know why you did this."

She told him about the burglary, her conversation with PFC Tony, the phone call to Sergeant Steiner, and her suspicions about Meehan's involvement.

Curry's look didn't soften. "You would jeopardize your career because of some stupid rivalry with Jim Meehan, who doesn't have to operate by the rules? There'd better be more to this fuckup than that. Tell me exactly what happened at Big Mesa and Rhodes Canyon."

Sara collected her thoughts. "I can tell you how we found the body. Or I could start with Gutierrez's attempt to kill us." She paused. "But perhaps the major would like to hear about the two thousand gold and silver coins and the letters from President Grant we found."

Incredulity spread across Tom Curry's face. "Jesus Christ," he muttered, stuffing the glasses into his shirt pocket. "Start at the beginning. And just who in the hell is *we?*"

"He had every right to jump down my throat," Sara concluded. She wrinkled her nose at the thought of it and twisted her class ring.

Kerney sat at the far end of Sara's couch, legs extended, feet crossed. His cowboy hat rested on the cushion, still dusty and slightly mangled-looking. He wore a collarless maroon pullover shirt with the sleeves pushed up to his elbows and a pair of blue jeans. Sara wondered if he owned anything but jeans. The shirt accentuated Kerney's well-formed upper body.

"I'm glad to see you're not feeling sorry for yourself." Gutierrez's inventory was in his shirt pocket, yet to be revealed.

"Don't be snide."

Kerney blinked in surprise at Sara's reaction. "I meant it as a compliment. What did Curry say?"

"I think my report dampened his enthusiasm to have me cashiered. I got off with an unofficial reprimand."

"Are you off the case?"

In the act of taking a sip of her wine, Sara pulled the glass away from her lips. "Um, no. Officially, the FBI has the ball. A special agent by the name of Johnson is heading up the investigation. Did you find anything in Santa Fe?"

Kerney grinned, took out the inventory, and waved it at her. "Gutierrez mailed an interesting letter to himself. Care to guess what was in it?"

"Don't give me a hard time." She wiggled her fingers at him. "Come on, fork it over."

Minutes passed after Kerney gave her the inventory before she peered at him over the edge of the paper. "This is incredible."

"Three to four million dollars' worth of incredible," he replied. "I had an expert give me a rough estimate. There's more. I stopped at the historical museum in Truth or Consequences. They have archival material on the history of Fort McRae, a post that operated on the north end of the *Jornada* during the Indian Wars. According to the records, in the spring of 1873 a detachment left the fort with military supplies bound for Fort Stanton. The convoy was attacked as it entered the Tularosa Valley. Eight soldiers were killed, along with three scouts, and all the mules and horses were stolen."

Sara waited for Kerney to continue. He didn't. She prodded him. "Is that all?"

"The entire supply train was sacked by a band of Warm Springs Apaches led by a chief named Victorio. Nothing was ever recovered."

"Does it match the inventory?"

"I don't know. That information wasn't available.

The person I talked to said it was probably in old War Department records. But I think Gutierrez found the spoils of that raid."

"That's extraordinary," Sara said. "If you're right, Gutierrez was moving the cache in stages."

"And we showed up during the last run," Kerney agreed.

She flicked the papers with a finger. "But moving it where?"

"Gutierrez would need an agent to manage the sale. The best way to sell it without getting caught is to a foreign buyer."

"Where does that take us?"

"Juárez," Kerney said. "We're only forty miles from the border. Mexico is too close not to be his first choice. Customs should be able to tell me who the big smugglers are. Chances are Gutierrez at least put out feelers in Juárez, trying to connect with somebody."

Sara shifted position and started pulling at her ring. "You're assuming the transaction hasn't been concluded."

"I am. The postmark on Gutierrez's letter is dated last week. His notes indicate that he sent some samples to a buyer to prove he was selling legitimate goods. Besides, why would Gutierrez have any inventory left if the deal had been consummated? It wouldn't make sense."

"I'm way overdue for a leave."

Kerney shook his head. "Don't even think about it. You've got a career to protect."

Her expression turned serious. "You shouldn't go in alone."

"There's no risk."

"I'll query Interpol and see what they can tell us." Sara chewed on her lip reflectively before continuing. "I've got an investigator in Juárez, Eddie Tapia, working an AWOL case. He knows the area like the back of his hand."

"That would help. Can you contact him?"

"I should hear from him by midmorning."

"I can't wait that long. When he calls, give him my description and ask him to keep an eye out for me."

"He knows who you are," Sara replied. "He was on your tail for two days."

Kerney laughed, stood up, and tested his knee. It almost buckled on him. He started for the door, a grimace of pain on his face.

"Where are you going?"

"It's late and I'm leaving."

Sara motioned for him to stay. "You can sleep in the spare bedroom."

The invitation was appealing for a lot of reasons, but he kept moving. "I don't want to impose."

"Don't be silly. You look like you won't make it ten feet without collapsing. The spare bedroom is made up and the hall bathroom is right next to it. You won't disturb me a bit."

"Okay, you talked me into it. I'll get my gear." He was almost dragging his right leg as he went out the front door.

Unable to sleep, Kerney flipped the covers back, sat up, and painfully lifted his leg over the side of the bed. His thigh and calf muscles were cramping badly, the result of too much time behind the wheel frozen in one position, no exercise, and the persistent strain on the leg from his unnatural gait. He turned on the lamp and stared at the leg with loathing; it hadn't hurt this much in over two years. Hobbling to the hall bathroom as quietly as he could, he sat on the toilet seat, ran hot water in the sink, soaked a towel in water that scalded his hands, and wrapped it on the leg, gently rubbing the warmth into the muscle. When the heat dissipated, he wrung out the towel, ran more hot water, and repeated the process. He was starting a third application when a tapping at the closed door came and he heard Sara's voice.

"Are you all right?"

"More or less," he answered.

"Can I come in?"

"I guess."

Sara slipped inside the small bathroom, misted with condensation. On the toilet seat, dressed only in a pair of boxer shorts, Kerney held his calf with both hands, a steaming towel against the skin, a look of pure suffering on his face. Kerney's rebuilt knee had an abnormal bulge. The scar on his belly seemed to cut his torso in half.

"Would a heat pad and some ointment help?" Sara asked.

"Very much."

"I'll get them. Go stretch out on the bed." She left quickly.

In the bedroom, Sara put a heating pad on his lower leg and rubbed ointment on his thigh. As she kneaded the muscles, her eyes drifted to the scar, but she said nothing. After switching the pad to the thigh, she worked on his calf before ordering him to roll over on his stomach. She rubbed more ointment on his leg and, using the heating pad and her strong hands, eased the tightness.

After a long time she stopped, and the room was silent except for their breathing. Kerney couldn't see her. He started to turn over and felt her hand pressing between his shoulder blades.

"How do you feel?" she asked.

"Much better," he said.

"How much better?"

"A lot."

"Good," she said softly.

The light went out, and he felt her weight on the bed. Her fingers traveled down his back and tugged at his shorts as she stretched out beside him.

CHAPTER

9

_ . _ . _ . _

Frustrated, Eddie worked the streets of Juárez near the bridge to El Paso, trying to locate Lieutenant Kerney. After a failed attempt to reach Captain Brannon by phone the previous day, Eddie had continued his search for Yardman. When he made contact with the captain at midmorning, she had told him to drop Yardman, find Lieutenant Kerney, and back him up.

Still in his humpback disguise, Eddie questioned street vendors, cops, cab drivers, and merchants along the boulevard, asking about a tall gringo cowboy with a limp. He kept his cover story simple—the gringo had ripped him off. It got him a lot of sympathy but no leads.

Captain Brannon hadn't given Eddie much to

work with. She had told him that Kerney was trying to get a line on the major smugglers in Juárez. That meant Kerney could be anywhere in the city, if he was in the city at all. Just about everything could be bought or sold on the Juárez black market, and you didn't have to cross the border to conduct business. With no clear direction from Captain Brannon, Eddie felt as if he were spitting into the wind.

Early in the afternoon, he gave up trying to find Kerney directly and started buying information about big-time smugglers, hoping he would get lucky and intercept the lieutenant. All it bought him was repeated opportunities to get thrown out of fancy clubs, trendy restaurants, and expensive casinos.

Eddie settled on the steps in front of the hacienda across from the Little Turtle, wondering how he could wangle his way inside without getting kicked out on his ass. He knew the Little Turtle was a front for drug distribution, and it had been mentioned frequently on the streets as an after-hours playground for the criminal elite in the city. It was worth a try to see if he could get in.

While he waited for the fat cop, Dominguez, to put in an appearance, Eddie made almost twenty dollars. The hacienda was a high-class whorehouse catering to a well-heeled clientele. Glumly, Eddie decided it was about the only interesting bit of information he had gathered during his search for Kerney. The day had been a complete bust.

At the end of the plaza, Eddie saw Dominguez strolling casually among the cars parked along the sidewalk, chewing on a toothpick. Halfway down the block, Dominguez spied him and hurried over.

Eddie waved, reached for some pesos, and had them ready for Dominguez when he arrived.

The money disappeared into a pocket and a smile crossed Dominguez's face. "Señor DeLeon wishes to speak with you, my little friend," he announced.

"Por qué?" Eddie inquired.

"A small matter. Come with me."

Dominguez waddled officiously toward the Little Turtle, and Eddie followed. At the entrance, Dominguez told him to wait and went inside. After a few minutes, he reappeared, looking quite pleased, rubbed Eddie's hump, and told him to go in.

Eddie stood in the open doorway. The Little Turtle was a long, deep, and softly lit hall with ornate chandeliers suspended over gaming tables. Dark mahogany dining tables circled the periphery of the gambling area, and an elaborate mezzanine with a polished staircase and railing jutted out over the room. A long antique bar with a full-length mirror behind it was under the mezzanine at the back of the hall.

The afternoon clientele was a prosperous group. Businessmen in suits sat at the bar, while artist types held court in the mezzanine, crowded together around small café tables. Several young couples were seated near the bar, enjoying drinks and appetizers. The gaming tables were busy. Most of the gamblers were middle-class, male, and fairly young.

For a fleeting minute, Eddie wanted Isabel at his side, wearing her prettiest dress. They would have dinner, dance to some music, play a game or two at the tables and meet new people.

"Jorobado," a voice said, pulling Eddie away from his thoughts. "I am glad Dominguez found you."

The man looking down at him was in his mid-thirties, with a fair complexion, brown curly hair nicely trimmed, and prominent blue eyes. His nose was narrow and his strong jaw ended at a square chin. A purely Hispanic face, Eddie thought, without a drop of Indian blood.

"Señor?" Eddie replied deferentially. It had to be DeLeon, Eddie thought. The unbuttoned sport coat was silk, the trousers hand-tailored, and the linen shirt was open at the collar to display an expensive gold chain around DeLeon's throat. He wore a Rolex Oyster watch on his left wrist and a large diamond ring on his right hand.

The man smiled casually. "Dominguez tells me that one of my employees was rude to you. More than rude. You are owed an apology. Come."

Eddie didn't move. "It was a small matter, señor, easily forgotten. It is of no consequence."

DeLeon turned back. "But it is, my friend. Tradition is very important to me. No one who works here may insult a *jorobado*. It could bring misfortune. Duffy must be taught a lesson."

"Who, señor?"

"The gringo," DeLeon explained. "Come."

Eddie followed him through a door by the bar into the old cantina. The former saloon had been gutted to create a large modern kitchen, an employee dressing room, and two small partitioned sleeping quarters at the front of the building on either side of the door to the street. Duffy was in one of the partitioned areas, asleep on a cot, his face buried in a pillow, his leg chained to the bed frame. The cot was bolted to the floor.

DeLeon shook Duffy roughly to wake him. The

man rolled over, opened his eyes, and sat up quickly. He had the look of an addict who had gone too long without a fix: sunken cheeks under the beard and bleary eyes that blinked rapidly.

"Mr. DeLeon," the gringo said in English, scurrying to his feet. "What is it?" The leg chain clanged against the metal frame of the cot as he got up.

DeLeon pointed to Eddie. "You were rude to the hunchback. Apologize to him immediately. Wait one minute." He switched back to Spanish and asked Eddie if he understood English.

"A little bit," Eddie answered haltingly in English.

"Go ahead," DeLeon ordered Duffy.

"What did I do?" Duffy asked.

"It is a tradition in my country to treat hunchbacks with courtesy. You spoke harshly, and attacked him for no reason. Apologize," DeLeon demanded.

"He was outside the cantina," Duffy explained, whining. "I just told him to get out of the way."

"Apologize," DeLeon repeated.

"Sorry," Duffy mumbled to Eddie.

DeLeon slapped Duffy hard across the face. "Be more respectful, Duffy," DeLeon said sarcastically. "He cannot possibly believe you if I do not. Humbly ask his forgiveness." There was ice in DeLeon's voice.

Duffy did as he was told, his eyes searing into Eddie's.

"I hope that gave you some small satisfaction," DeLeon commented, as he walked Eddie back into the Little Turtle.

"You were most kind to do it, señor."

DeLeon brushed aside the comment. "I have a

dilemma about you. I would invite you to stay as an entertainment for my customers, if you were not quite so threadbare. You can see the Little Turtle is neither a clip joint nor a bordello." He put his hand into his pocket. "Let me give you something for your trouble."

Eddie wavered for a moment before responding, searching for the right gambit. If he could stay, it might get him closer to finding Kerney. "I cannot take your money, señor, unless I earn it. If you will allow me to make myself more presentable, I would welcome the opportunity to entertain your customers."

DeLeon's smile returned. "What is your name, little man?"

"Eduardo. Most people call me Eddie."

"You may stay, Eddie. Use the dressing room to clean yourself. All profit that you make, you can keep."

"Thank you, but the sight of me undressed usually offends. Perhaps I could bathe elsewhere and return later."

"That is not necessary. I will have the door guarded to protect your privacy. If you are provided with the implements, can you sew?"

"Yes, señor."

"Good. We will dress you in a cook's uniform. I may call upon you to serve a special guest or two, as a diversion."

"I would be delighted to do so."

"Excellent!" DeLeon said, clapping his hands together. "Come to my table when you are ready."

"Gladly, señor," Eddie replied.

* * *

Eddie wanted desperately to stand under the shower until the ache in his back went away. He didn't dare do it for fear that the guard at the door would get impatient and come in to hurry him along. He washed quickly, grateful to at least feel clean, then put on the artificial hump, tightened the harness, and dressed in the cook's uniform. It hung loosely on his frame, so he undressed, tacked the sleeves and cuffs with a needle and thread, put it back on, tucked in the shirt, and inspected himself in the mirror. He looked comical but not disreputable.

The cook's helper guarding the dressing-room door took Eddie to the kitchen, where the staff teased him good-naturedly about his costume. He gladly accepted the offer of tamales, frijoles, and strong Mexican coffee, eating the meal with a gusto that pleased the cooks. He stayed with them until the bartender came to tell him DeLeon was waiting.

His entrance into the casino caused quite a stir. Wearing a chef's hat provided by the chief cook, he paraded behind the waiters, mimicking their movements. Two small children, sitting with their parents in the dining area, giggled at the charade. They came running up when he finished, clutching coins to give him. Eddie let them rub the hump and promised they would have good fortune. He got a round of applause from guests in the mezzanine and gamblers at the tables. He picked up the coins from the floor and went to DeLeon, bowing formally.

"Señor? I am respectable now, *qué no?*" he asked. DeLeon sat at his private table at the end of the bar next to a small dance floor and bandstand.

DeLeon's laugh was hearty. "Yes. Very much so.

You are a very amusing *jorobado*. I may have to give you a job. You make my place a carnival. I could use you in the evenings and perhaps even later, after hours."

"I could stay for a few days," Eddie countered, "until I must leave to be with my family again."

"You have a wife?" DeLeon inquired.

"No woman would have me," he answered. "I live with my brother and his family."

"And where do you live, Eduardo?"

"Piedras Negras."

"Your home is a far distance."

"It is a poor place with few opportunities. I must travel to earn a living." Eddie turned his palms up to signify resignation to his lot in life.

DeLeon toyed with the cellular phone on the table, his eyes reflective. "You must let me decide what is best for you, Eduardo. Consider seriously my offer of a job."

Eddie kept smiling, but he heard the warning in DeLeon's velvet words. There was only one response he could make. "I am at your disposal, *patrón.*"

"Good." The cellular telephone rang. DeLeon dismissed the *jorobado* with a wave of his hand. "We will talk later about the terms of your employment."

Eddie thanked DeLeon for his kindness and was sent back to provide more entertainment for the customers. He worked the gambling tables and the bar with all the peppiness he could muster, wondering what in the hell he'd gotten himself into.

Enrique Deleon stood on the freight dock behind the Little Turtle watching the off-loading of a panel truck of computer electronics. It was a special order of single inline memory modules, expansion boards, and microprocessors, hijacked from a semitrailer on a highway outside of Phoenix. The driver had been paid well to orchestrate a breakdown and leave the truck unattended.

The electronic components would go to a Mexican assembly plant and ultimately wind up in cut-price computers shipped back to the United States. Besides the money he would make, DeLeon enjoyed the knowledge that he was helping Americans cut their economic throats. The current trade agreement with the United States was nothing more than exploitation of Mexican businesses. Most of the profits flowed north.

He checked the paperwork brought to him by the warehouse foreman. Everything was in order. The *mordidas* he paid to make the shipment legal and untraceable were minor compared to the profits. Delivery to the assembly plant was scheduled for the morning. Enrique employed a Japanese style of management. He stocked no unnecessary inventory and shipped only at the point of need. It made his business even more profitable by cutting the overhead for labor and storage.

He walked through the warehouse, greeting the few employees on duty. Aside from the computer consignment, the only other scheduled delivery for the next day was VCR components to another large American company operating in Juárez. He used the old mercantile storeroom only for small, highly valuable commodities. It was made of hand-cut stone, three feet thick, and supported by huge timber beams. His other facilities, sprinkled throughout the city, were much larger but held no charm. He admired the old stone walls, the floor paving bricks, and the roughcut beams in the building. The restoration was expensive but the results were splendid. He must do more with old buildings. When the hacienda was rebuilt, he would look around for another project. It gave him a feeling of fulfillment to preserve the heritage and history of the city.

DeLeon had decided to add one of the swords and scabbards from the missile range shipment to his collection of antiques. He would hang it over the fireplace at the hacienda. He also decided to keep Eduardo, the *jorobado*. The hunchback seemed intelligent. He would house him in the old cantina with Duffy until he was sure Eddie was trustworthy. If it worked out, Eduardo could do small, useful errands for DeLeon when he wasn't entertaining customers. DeLeon liked his decision. Now that the Little Turtle was fully revived and profitable, the hunchback would add good fortune to the casino.

Major Tom Curry felt particularly good. His daily session at the piano had been a resounding success. Finally he could approximate the unique left-handed roll of Erroll Garner. He was so pleased with himself he ran through five renditions of "I'll Remember April" before his wife told him it was time to get dressed and go to work.

He entered Sara Brannon's office humming the bridge to the melody. She swiveled her chair away from the desk and stood up, her expression guarded.

"Relax, Sara," Curry said. "I'm not here to chew you out again."

"Major . . ."

Tom cut her off with a wave of his hand. One

apology was sufficient. "It's a new day, Sara. Let's leave it at that. I have news for you. Our sister service, the Navy, has just informed me that Petty Officer Yardman turned himself in to the San Diego shore patrol a week ago. Your analysis was right on. It seems he went on quite a crime spree in Mexico to support his gambling habit. The police chased him from Juárez to Tijuana before he crossed the border. Nice of the Navy to let us know so promptly, wouldn't you say?"

"That is good news," Sara said, her voice brightening. She sat down at her desk and changed the subject. "Agent Johnson called and gave me his preliminary findings."

"Did your story hold water?"

"So far. But there's more I need to tell you."

Curry sat down in the chair in front of Sara's desk, his good mood evaporating. "What is it?" he asked tersely.

Sara took a deep breath and started talking. She held nothing back about Kerney's discovery of Gutierrez's inventory, his theory of the source of the treasure, and his decision to try to find the pipeline into Mexico.

After the briefing, Curry left Sara's office feeling relieved and damn glad that this Kerney fellow was in Juárez, and not Sara. If what she said was true, and he had no reason to doubt her, the value of the treasure, historically and monetarily, was astounding. If artifacts of such importance vanished from the missile range, he would have to explain it to some very unhappy people with stars on their collars. And it wouldn't make a damn bit of difference that nobody knew about the treasure until it was stolen. The case was either a career-maker or career-breaker for Sara.

Failure to solve a case of such importance would dampen Curry's retirement party, which was not that far off. Curry didn't like that thought; it would be much better to go out on a high note. He went back to Sara's office and told her he wanted all available investigators assigned to the Yazzi homicide, and every piece of evidence, every interview, and every report gone over with a fine-tooth comb.

"Keep Tapia in Juárez," he ordered. "Tell him to back up that sheriff's officer, if he can find him. And not a word to anybody about the treasure, Sara," he cautioned. "Keep it under wraps."

"Yes, sir."

When Curry left, Sara almost whooped with delight as she reached for the phone.

After midnight, the clientele at the Little Turtle changed, this time dramatically. The bohemians, young couples, families, and run-of-the-mill gamblers were gone, replaced by fashionable men and sleek ladies, some with bodyguards. The women were as elegant as any Eddie had seen in the fashion magazines Isabel brought home from the grocery store. The men were dressed in suits that cost more than Eddie made in three months, and sported watches of thick gold and jewels. The women favored diamond necklaces, pins, and earrings.

DeLeon had assigned a watchdog to Eddie, a middle-aged thug named Carlos. His face was pock-marked, his breath smelled of garlic, and he had an upper plate of false teeth that he constantly adjusted with his thumb. A bushy mustache completely covered Carlos's upper lip, and a low forehead gave him the appearance of a permanent frown.

Eddie was told to greet arriving guests at the entrance. Carlos stayed with him, twitching his fingers at the hem of his suit coat to keep the shoulder holster under his armpit hidden.

By two in the morning the Little Turtle resembled a commodities market for smugglers, drug wholesalers, and politicians. Deals were being made by men throughout the room, in person and on cellular telephones, while the women gambled, drank, and socialized in small groups. Eddie made good money at the door, by Mexican standards, most of it in American dollars. Carlos, as a payment for his attentiveness, took half of it off the top.

Enrique DeLeon moved among his guests, occasionally glancing at the door to watch the *jorobado*, who seemed to be a popular attraction. DeLeon wore a white linen banded collar shirt under a black linen jacket, with dark gray trousers. At his side, the director for cultural affairs solicited a donation.

"You know how important the García Mansion is to the people of Juárez. And so close to the mayor's residence. We cannot allow it to be razed," Ramón Olivares said.

DeLeon looked down at him. Olivares, short, pudgy, and sweating, smiled up at him.

"It would be a tragedy," Enrique said. "Have you plans for the building?"

"A fine arts museum. The mayor supports it."

DeLeon nodded approvingly. "Have you a sum in mind?"

"We're asking one hundred thousand dollars from benefactors," Olivares replied.

"Of course, I'll participate," DeLeon said, knowing Olivares would pocket 10 percent of the donations, "but Ramón, I'll want something more than my name on a plaque."

Ramón's smile turned into a knowing grin. "As always. I have a Spanish Colonial wardrobe from the seventeenth century in storage. A modest piece, but significant. I had planned to consign it for auction. It would look perfectly at home in your hacienda, once the renovation is complete."

"What was to be the minimum bid?" DeLeon asked.

"Five thousand dollars," Ramón replied, "but if it catches your eye, I would gladly present it to you as a gift."

DeLeon laughed and patted Olivares on the shoulder. "You must show it to me. Do you like my *jorobado?*"

"He's wonderful."

By the time Eddie was relieved of duty it was four in the morning and the crowd was rapidly thinning out. Carlos took him into the cantina and shackled his leg to the steel frame of the empty cot. Duffy, also chained for the night, was sprawled on his rack and snoring in spurts through an open mouth.

Eddie, exhausted, tried to stay awake. He loosened the harness slightly to reduce the pain in his shoulders and stretched his muscles as much as he dared. He covered himself with a sheet to hide the hump and rolled on his side. One more day in the disguise was all he would chance. But with Carlos as his jailer, he would need to figure a way to escape. His eyes were heavy. Just a catnap, he said to himself as he drifted off to sleep.

Sounds of pots and pans in the kitchen at the back of the cantina woke Eddie. He lay motionless, eyes shut, angry at himself for falling asleep. He couldn't feel the hump between his shoulders. The device had slipped out of place, and the sheet no longer covered him. He heard breathing and felt a slight movement next to his face. He opened one eye and saw Duffy kneeling, looking him squarely in the face.

"You ain't no fucking hunchback, are you?" Duffy hissed. His long, stringy hair and beard hid his face, except for the revengeful smile. "Just another wetback hustler, ain't you, Eddie? Too bad you don't talk English. I don't know if I should fuck you up myself or let DeLeon do it. He doesn't like bogus beggars. I think he'd hurt you pretty bad. *Comprende?*"

"*Que?*" Eddie said, staying very still.

"This shitty disguise," Duffy responded, reaching across Eddie to shake the loose hump, "is what I'm talking about. Plus you fucked me with DeLeon. I had to kiss your little Mexican ass. I got enough trouble without you giving me grief."

"*Donde es Señor DeLeon?*" Eddie replied, looking as confused as possible. Early-morning sun seeped through the cracks of the plywood-covered windows. The light from the kitchen spilled across the floor between the partitions to the sleeping area. The sounds from the kitchen continued. Maybe two cooks at work preparing food for the vendors, Eddie figured. No more.

"He ain't here, asshole, that's for certain." Duffy's smile turned wicked. "And I ain't gonna wait to tell him about you."

Duffy's right hand, out of sight at the side of the cot, came up fast. He slashed with a knife at Eddie's throat. Eddie blocked the path of the knife with his right forearm and took a deep cut below the elbow. He gouged Duffy's eye with his left thumb. Duffy pulled back, yelped in pain, and stabbed again, missing completely. Eddie flung himself at Duffy. The leg iron kept him chained to the cot. He sank the edge of his left palm into Duffy's throat, driving the blow as deeply as possible. Duffy choked and recoiled, rocked back on his knees, and pulled Eddie with him. Fighting to keep his leverage, Eddie reached up, grabbed Duffy's chin with both hands, and snapped Duffy's head with all his strength. Their faces were inches apart. He heard a distinct crack and let go. Duffy, still on his knees, fell over, gurgling through his shattered larynx, his eyes fixed on Eddie.

Eddie fell on top of him. He could hear Duffy's death rattle. He pushed himself off the body and crawled backward until he was able to get on the cot. His heart pounded in his chest and his ears were ringing. Reaching back with his wounded arm, he tried to tighten the harness under his shirt. The movement brought tears to his eyes. The knife wound hurt like hell. He used his left hand to fix the hump and pulled his shirt down. There was blood soaking through his sleeve and onto the sheet.

He heard footsteps. An old man wearing a splattered apron came around the partition. His wrinkled face was weary and dull-looking.

"What have you done to Duffy?" the man asked, looking from the body to Eddie. His voice was agitated.

"He tried to kill me. Call the *patrón.*"

The old man's mustache twitched. "You are bleeding."

"Yes," Eddie answered through clenched teeth. "The gringo tried to kill me," he repeated.

The old man didn't move. His expression was heavy with confusion. "Are you also dying?"

"No. Get me a towel to stop the blood and call DeLeon," Eddie snarled through clenched teeth.

The man slowly took a filthy hand towel from his back pocket and handed it to Eddie. "I must call the *patrón,*" the old man announced.

"Do that, by all means."

"José," the old man called out to his partner. "The gringo Duffy is dead and the hunchback is much wounded. We will have no help in the kitchen this morning."

José rushed in to see for himself. The men muttered, shook their heads, and said the *patrón* would not be happy. Eddie listened to their jabbering as they debated what should be said and who would speak on the telephone to DeLeon. After an agreement was reached, the cooks left to make the call. Eddie bound the wound with the towel, tying it off with his good hand and his teeth. When he finished, he looked at Duffy. He had never killed a man before. It was not pleasant. He couldn't tell Isabel about this, he thought. She would have him lighting candles for Duffy's soul for the rest of his life.

He wondered what Captain Brannon would think. He decided she would not like it at all. One dead man at his feet, no leads on Lieutenant Kerney, and he was chained to a frigging bed with no way to get help.

He could not risk discovery as an imposter. He worked on a story he could use with DeLeon. It took a long time before the two cooks ushered DeLeon and Carlos to his cot.

DeLeon took in the scene without comment. His face was harsh. Carlos, arms folded across his chest, adjusted his false teeth with his thumb and said nothing. The two cooks stayed back, out of DeLeon's range.

"Explain," DeLeon finally said to Eddie.

"I cannot. I awoke to find Duffy kneeling at the side of my bed. He spoke in English. He was angry about something. He had a knife. He attacked me."

"You understood nothing?" Enrique queried. His eyes searched Eddie's face.

"He said your name several times," Eddie answered. "I think he blamed me for getting him in trouble with you."

"How did the attack take place?"

"He tried to cut my throat. I threw up my arm to ward off the blade. I could not move away because of the chain. He cut my arm."

DeLeon turned to the pudgy-faced cook. "Was the hunchback chained?"

"Yes, *patrón*. I only released Duffy from his bed, as I do every morning."

DeLeon nodded and returned his attention to Eddie. "You killed him very neatly, *jorobado*."

"I did not know what I was doing. I am sorry, *patrón*."

DeLeon gave him a skeptical look and pointed at

the body. "You are not listening. You gouge Duffy's eye, shatter his Adam's apple, break his neck. These are not the skills of a beggar."

"It was by accident, señor." Eddie whined. "Truly. I only fought to defend myself. I was much frightened. I could not escape him. My finger poked his eye as I tried to push him away. I think maybe my elbow hit him in the throat as we struggled. We fell. I was almost off the bed, lying against him as he tried to stab me again. His neck twisted under my weight. I heard the snap. He did not move, and then the old man came to see what had happened."

DeLeon returned his attention to the cook. "Did you find Duffy where he now rests?"

The old man looked at the body. "Yes, *patrón*. Exactly."

"Where did the butcher knife come from?"

The old man blushed. "He stole it from the kitchen. I was unobservant." He wrung the towel he clutched in shaky hands.

"Go back to work," DeLeon ordered the cooks. The men scurried out of sight. "Carlos, give me your opinion."

"It is possible. An awkward struggle, perhaps."

"You are not convinced?"

"The *jorobado* has strong arms and a thick chest. He fought for his life. Perhaps it gave him added power."

"Perhaps," DeLeon reflected. "Let me see the wound. Carlos, unbind it."

Eddie raised his arm so Carlos could untie the bloody towel. DeLeon waited for Carlos to roll up the sleeve and wipe away some of the blood.

"It is a deep cut to the bone," Carlos reported. "Duffy damaged him."

"Very well," DeLeon said in a less caustic tone. "Call for the doctor to come and then remove Duffy's body."

Carlos nodded, adjusted his upper plate, stepped over the corpse, and left to do his chore.

"Were you not wounded, I would have you replace Duffy in the kitchen," DeLeon said, "to learn a lesson. As it is, you will stay chained to the bed until the doctor tells me whether or not you will require more extensive care."

"What will you do with me, Don Enrique?"

DeLeon sighed and prodded the body with the toe of his shoe. "Duffy is no great loss. He was not going to be with us much longer anyway. I do not tolerate those who lie or steal from me. Duffy did both. Have you lied to me, Eduardo?"

"No, Don Enrique."

"Very well. I will accept your story for now and pay for your care."

"I will work for you tonight," Eddie proposed. He had to get unchained. "I will work with one arm, if necessary, *patrón*. I will repay your kindness with loyalty and labor."

DeLeon chuckled in amazement. "Were you a whole man, Eduardo, I would have much better work for you to do. Your tenacity is strong. If the doctor agrees, you may work tonight."

"Thank you."

DeLeon gave him one last searching look and left. The subservient expression on Eddie's face vanished. He was getting tired of kissing DeLeon's ass.

The man was nothing but a gangster. More than ever, Eddie wanted to get back to the United States.

Carlos dragged Duffy's body away, and the cooks brought clean bed linens. They moved Eddie to Duffy's cot, secured him with the leg iron, and changed the bloodstained sheets, muttering to each other about the loss of Duffy's help in the kitchen and the unfair burden it placed upon them.

The doctor arrived promptly. He was a harried-looking man about thirty who talked to himself during the examination. Round-shouldered, wearing a rumpled suit, he had a narrow face, and his nostrils flared above a wide upper lip. He asked no questions about the knifing and deferred to Eddie's request to stay fully clothed. He cut the shirt sleeve away, studied the wound, and pronounced it non-lethal. He told Eddie he might lose some mobility in the arm if it wasn't quickly repaired. Eddie asked how long he could wait for the surgery.

"I would be reluctant to see you delay for more than two days," the doctor answered. "It would be best to fix the damage now so that the scarring will be minimized."

"How long would it take?"

"One night in the hospital."

Eddie could not risk going to the hospital. "I have promised Don Enrique I will work tonight. It is a matter of honor that I do so."

"Carlos said you were a tough *jorobado*." He raised a finger and shook it under Eddie's nose. "Do not use the arm. I will disinfect and tape the gash, bind it, and give you a painkiller. I will fashion a sling for you and tell Carlos to bring you to the hospital tomorrow morning." He opened his bag and began removing his medical supplies.

"Thank you."

"Do you fear the hospital?" the doctor asked, swabbing away the coagulated blood. So often, especially with the poor, it was hard to overcome a patient's apprehension of modern medicine.

"No. I wish to show the *patrón* that I am trustworthy."

The doctor nodded his head. "That is an important quality if you wish to work for Señor DeLeon. Prove yourself and he will reward you well." He worked quickly to close the gash. "The wound is away from the arteries. You are lucky."

"So far," Eddie allowed, wincing.

CHAPTER

10

Armed with a list of low-grade snitches grudgingly provided by a customs agent who wasn't about to turn over his most valuable confidential informants to a cop he didn't know, Kerney got to work.

El Paso filled barren hills stubbed up against the Rio Grande, and spread like a bloated octopus into the Chihuahuan desert north of Mexico. The city was hot, the traffic miserable, and the jumble of housing developments, barrios, and miles of strip malls depressing.

Kerney found Cruz Abeyta in his pawnshop, a seedy establishment filled mostly with stolen televisions, stereos, power tools, and weapons. Abeyta wore a Grateful Dead T-shirt, and a bandanna around his head to hold back his long hair. About forty years old, Cruz sported a two-day beard and had prison tattoos on both arms.

Abeyta smiled at the fifty-dollar bill, and a gold front tooth with a star flashed at Kerney. He picked the money from Kerney's fingers. "What do you need, man?"

"Information. I need to find someone to move some merchandise south."

"Ain't my specialty, man," Cruz replied.

"You must have friends in the trade," Kerney prodded.

"For fifty dollars, I'll give you a name."

"Fair enough."

With the name and address of Eduardo Lopez in his shirt pocket, Kerney left and drove to a barrio on the outskirts of the city. A *fronterizo* enclave of illegal Mexican and Central American refugees, the barrio was a string of tar-paper shacks along a dirt road, with no electricity, no sewers, and one community well. The place teemed with barefoot children, mangy dogs, and women with malnourished faces. Few young men were in sight.

Kerney found his way to Lopez's shanty, conspicuous by the presence of a half-ton Chevy truck adorned with running lights. Lopez was buff-waxing the truck by hand under a tattered picnic canopy held up by scrap lumber. Fifty dollars made him stop for a chat.

"I can deliver anything you want," he told Kerney. Lopez was short, about five feet five, and had jet-black hair greased down and combed straight back. "In or out of Mexico," he added.

"That's good to know," Kerney said. "But I need a buyer first."

"What kind of merchandise?" Lopez asked, licking his lips.

"Artifacts."

"Indian pots? That sort of stuff?"

"Close enough."

Lopez gave him a cunning look. "That kind of information is worth more than fifty bucks."

"If I make a deal, you can make the delivery," Kerney proposed.

"That's cool. Talk to Miguel Arnal. He owns a curio shop downtown."

By eight o'clock at night, Kerney was dejected, hungry, and tired. His attempt to move up the smuggler's food chain had resulted in being passed from one small fish to another, at a total cost of four hundred dollars. And he was no closer to getting the name of a major player than he had been when he started out.

On a boulevard driving back into the core of the city, Kerney stopped at a Mexican diner for something to eat. There were enough working-class cars in the parking lot to predict the food would be at least decent. Outside the building, an old adobe home painted white, was a row of newspaper vending machines. He popped some coins in a slot, pulled out the El Paso paper, and glanced at the adjacent machine. The headline story, in Spanish, was about the Zapatista revolutionaries in the Mexican state of Chiapas. He bought a copy just for the hell of it.

Over dinner, he skimmed the El Paso paper and set it aside. The Spanish paper, a left-wing weekly, was published in Juárez. The article on rebels in the state of Chiapas was well written and sympathetic to the cause.

The featured columnist, a woman named Rose Moya, presented the third in a series of articles on government corruption and the *Mafiosios* in Juárez. With a lot of bite, facts, and allegations the lady tore into the Juárez drug lords, smugglers, and malfeasant city officials.

Maybe Rose Moya was somebody he should talk to, Kerney thought. He tucked the paper under his arm and paid the bill. It would have to wait until the morning.

It was midmorning when Kerney stood at the bridge that connected El Paso to Juárez. He had five thousand dollars of his own money, wired from the bank in Santa Fe, in his pocket. It was the sum total of his wealth.

The Rio Grande, a sluggish brown stream, smelled of effluent and industrial waste. On each side of the river, chain-link fences defined the border. Vehicles on the bridge were backed up at the checkpoints, and pedestrians moving in both directions pushed through the gates along the walkways.

Kerney entered the procession and joined the tangled stream of people and cars along Juárez's Lerdo Street. The boulevard, lined with dental clinics, cut-rate pharmacies, bars, liquor stores, and tourist shops, was a conduit for day-trippers from the north looking for bargains or entertainment. The sidewalks were congested with hookers, street vendors, and musicians mixed in with tourists. A large plastic tooth hung suspended over the door of a dental office and neon signs blinked furiously along the strip.

Cars in the street, jammed bumper to bumper in both directions, lurched in and out of traffic lanes, horns blaring and drivers cursing. Kerney got a taxi and gave the driver the address for the newspaper.

The offices for the newspaper were on the Plaza Cervantine, a tiny square with a gold bust of the Spanish poet as its centerpiece. The buildings surrounding the plaza housed artist studios, workshops, apartments above, and an experimental theater that put on plays in a renovated cafeteria. The building for the newspaper had a number of passageways that took Kerney to a patio café in a central courtyard and up a flight of wooden stairs to a suite of offices that opened on a balcony.

The door was open, and Kerney entered to find an unoccupied room filled with books stacked haphazardly in piles on every available space. The walls were plastered with art and film posters. An enlarged photograph of Pancho Villa on horseback was tacked to a side door. Against one wall a desktop computer was running, the screen-saver pattern flashing a colored starburst on the monitor. A messy desk with a phone and ashtray filled with cigarette butts completed the decor.

Kerney called out in Spanish, and a very pretty woman opened the side door and looked out. She held a teapot in her hand. Her hair, cut just to the bottom of her ears and close to her neck, draped down to the top of her left eye. Her eyes, brown, speculative, and direct, were provocative. At the corner of her right eye was a small mole. Her full lips did not smile. She wore a pink top with a scarf over a long skirt and black hose.

"Yes?" the woman said, in English.

Kerney switched languages. "I'm looking for Rose Moya."

"One moment." She stepped back and closed the door. After a minute, the woman reappeared carrying a coffee cup in her hand. She paused to examine the man before moving to the computer table. He was tall and rather good-looking in a cowboy sort of way.

"Why do you want to see Rose?" the woman asked as she put the cup on the computer table.

"I would like to speak to her about the series on corruption."

"You've read them?" Her tone was skeptical.

"Only the most recent one," Kerney admitted.

"What is your name?"

"Kevin Kerney." He held out his badge case.

Tentatively, the woman crossed to Kerney, took the case, opened it, and looked quickly up at him, her expression cautious. "Is this real?"

"Yes."

She sized Kerney up one more time before speaking, switching back to Spanish. "I'm Rose Moya. What do you want?"

Kerney followed suit. "Information."

"What kind of information?"

"Everything you can tell me about the *Mafiosios*. Especially smuggling."

"And why do you need that information?"

"To catch a murderer."

Rose Moya gestured to a side chair filled with

books. "Sit down, Lieutenant Kerney, and tell me your story."

After an hour of conversation, Rose Moya came through with a confidential source. Kerney had the cabby stop along the Avenida 16 de Septiembre, where the cityscape changed from tourist sleaze to an upscale, cosmopolitan area of theaters, restaurants, and department stores. Using plastic, Kerney went shopping. From what Rose had told him about Francisco Posada, he needed to dress for the occasion.

According to Rose, Posada was an elderly, rich retired pharmacist who sold information to cash customers with good references, and asked few questions. Most of Posada's clients sought introductions to people who circumvented any number of Mexican laws.

He got back in the cab, and the driver sped past a row of old mansions under shade trees with deep lawns, rattling over cobblestone streets until the residential area gave way to auto junkyards, repair shops, garages, and car upholstery shops, all with signs painted in hot, screaming colors.

After a long stretch where the only scenery was the Juárez dump, they entered an opulent neighborhood of modern houses on winding streets in a series of low hills. The driver stopped in front of a two-story house with a tile roof, arched windows, and a wide set of granite steps leading to double entrance doors. The archway to the doors, supported by columns, was built of wedgeshaped stones, each cut individually. A burgundy Mercedes was parked in the curved driveway.

Kerney asked the driver to wait. The door opened almost immediately after Kerney rang the bell.

The houseboy, a young Indian in his late teens, dressed in an immaculate white shirt, trousers, and sandals, looked Kerney up and down without expression. "Yes?"

"I would like to see Señor Posada."

The boy studied Kerney, taking in the tailoring of the new suit and the shirt and tie that went with it. He dropped his eyes to Kerney's feet, clad in four-hundred-dollar Larry Mahan boots.

"Do you have an appointment?" the boy inquired. He was as slender as a girl, with the lithe body of a swimmer. His eyes, darker than the rich color of his skin, were soft and innocent. He had the most beautiful natural eyelashes Kerney had ever seen on a man.

"No."

"Who referred you?"

"Rose Moya."

The boy stepped back and let Kerney enter. He pointed to a chair in the foyer. "Wait here."

Within minutes Kerney heard padded footsteps on the marble floor as the houseboy returned.

"Follow me. The señor will see you."

The foyer gave way to a courtyard with colonnades that supported arches under a low veranda. Ornamental trees ringed the space, and in the center a fountain gurgled water from a fish mouth. The boy opened a door under the veranda, stepped aside, motioned for Kerney to enter, and closed the door, leaving Kerney alone in the room. It was a great room, bigger than Quinn's library; a large sunny space, with a wall of windows that looked out on an expansive patio, swimming pool, and cabana. The interior consisted of several conversation areas of plush off-white couches and easy chairs arranged to give the best view of the artwork on the back wall of the room.

A large Diego Rivera painting held center stage over the fireplace, illuminated by recessed lights. It was a portrait of a strikingly beautiful woman wearing a Franciscan habit. Her arms were folded below her breasts and she faced a distant, unknown horizon with passionate eyes. It felt both pious and pagan.

"It is compelling," a voice said, speaking in Spanish.

Kerney turned. An elderly man with long white hair, a waxed gray mustache, and a courtly manner, Francisco Posada smiled at him peacefully, his hand resting on the houseboy's thin shoulder. His fingers, grotesquely deformed, were twisted into a claw.

"Diego Rivera," Kerney said.

"You know his work," Posada said approvingly, continuing in his native tongue. He shuffled closer. "There is a story to the canvas. Diego fell in love with this woman, but she was fulfilling a *manda*, a promise to God to do penance. That is why she wears a friar's robe. Rivera could not have her physically, so he possessed her through his art."

"I have never seen this image before," Kerney said, using his best Spanish.

"Few have. It has always been privately owned and never exhibited or reproduced." Posada eased himself down to a couch and gestured for Kerney to sit across from him. "How did Rose Moya come to refer you? She has never sent someone to me before."

"I lied and told her I was a policeman working on a murder case involving the *Mafiosios.*"

Posada chuckled, but his eyes hardened. "I'm sure that appealed to her sense of social justice. Are you a policeman, Mr. Kerney?

Kerney laughed. "I was. Now I'm in business for myself. Imports and exports. I would like to expand into the Mexican market."

"What do you wish to export, Mr. Kerney?"

"Artifacts. Historical documents of great value. Military memorabilia and rare coins."

"An unusual assortment of merchandise," Posada commented.

"But quite valuable," Kerney replied.

"You need a broker, I assume," Posada noted. "Someone who will act on your behalf with discretion."

"Exactly."

"It might be possible to arrange an introduction," Posada said, with a serene smile.

"I would be grateful."

"But I am reluctant," Posada added. "You have come to me in a most unusual way."

"I am new to my profession, señor," Kerney replied. "It is difficult to find one's way without assistance."

Posada rubbed his mustache with a twisted knuckle. "How much is your merchandise worth?"

"It has been appraised at four million dollars."

The figure didn't startle Posada at all. "If you

agree to a two percent commission, plus my standard fee, I would be inclined to accept you as a client."

"What is your standard fee?" Kerney asked.

"Five thousand dollars."

The whole wad, Kerney thought. "I'll go one percent payable after delivery with the five thousand up front," he said.

"Agreed," Posada replied. He gestured to the houseboy, who stepped quickly to his side. The boy helped Posada to his feet. "Seek out Enrique DeLeon at the Little Turtle gambling house. I am sure he would be interested in your desire to do business in Mexico."

"Will you speak to Señor DeLeon on my behalf?" Kerney asked, as he stood up.

"Of course. Do you wish me to pass along a message?"

"No. I would like you to keep the details of our discussion confidential, if that is possible."

Posada nodded in agreement. "All my client conversations are privileged. Señor DeLeon will be satisfied with the knowledge that I have accepted you as a client."

"Excellent."

"Please pay Juan before you leave." He smiled lovingly at the young man.

"Thank you, Señor Posada," Kerney replied with a slight bow of his head.

Posada bowed back. "It is a pleasure to meet a *norteamericano* who speaks our language, admires our art, and knows how to conduct business. I look forward to seeing you again."

* * *

Greg Benton hung up the phone in disgust. He dug out the portable printer, hooked it up, disconnected the phone jack, plugged in the laptop computer, and accessed the fax modem program. The motel room phone had been rewired at the junction box the night Benton checked in. It was secure, direct, and untraceable.

He paced the room waiting for the fax. The whole fucking scheme had started to go haywire from the day he whacked the Indian soldier up on the mesa. And unexpected events kept floating in, like shit from a plugged-up toilet: the burglary at the old lady's house, Gutierrez's failure to make the final delivery, the tossed apartment in Santa Fe—all signs that the plan wasn't neat and tidy anymore.

Benton walked to the window and looked out. The motel was a dump; the whores kept him awake at night, and the air conditioner barely worked. He looked at his watch. Meehan wanted him to meet with DeLeon and tell him the delivery might be delayed.

Damn right it would be delayed, with Gutierrez dead and the last shipment missing. DeLeon would be pissed but probably wouldn't cancel the deal. Not with the amount of money that was at stake. He would have to come up with a good story for DeLeon.

Benton looked at his watch again. It was too early to catch DeLeon at the Little Turtle. He was never available until evening. There was time for a workout at Kiko's Gym and a good steak before crossing the border. He hated Mexican food.

In the bathroom, Benton stripped down and examined himself in the mirror. He liked what he saw.

His body was fit and hard, and his gray eyes under curly black hair drew a fair share of attention from the ladies. The small scar on his chin made his face interesting. He smiled at himself and put on his sweats. Then he pulled the fax off the printer, put the computer away, grabbed his gym bag, and walked out into the hot west Texas sun.

The garbage blowing down the street didn't bother him anymore, and the graffiti-adorned car wash, the boarded-up gas station, and the junked cars in the vacant lot were now just part of the normal barrio landscape. The street ended at a concrete abutment where the freeway cut off through traffic. The fat hooker in front of the Caballito Bar saw him and waved as he got into his car. He waved back. Each time he went to buy lunch at the bar, she showed him a different tattoo and offered to fuck him for ten dollars—the going rate for locals.

With all the low-riders, addicts, pimps, and whores in the neighborhood there was no difference between the barrio and Juárez. Benton thought it would be a good idea to give El Paso back to the Mexicans.

He drove toward the freeway on-ramp, looking at the fax picture. So this was the cop Meehan wanted him to find and kill. No problem, Benton thought to himself. After all, damage control was his specialty. It gave him something to look forward to.

The painkillers the doctor had given Eddie made him woozy. He had spent the afternoon either chained to the cot or throwing up in the bathroom. Now Carlos stood over him, a clean white cook's uniform in his hand.

"So, you are going to live, Eddie," Carlos predicted. There was a hint of friendliness in his voice. "Have you finished puking?"

"It would seem so," Eddie agreed, "although my stomach now thinks I am starving."

"There will be food for you." Carlos picked his nose with his forefinger while he pushed his upper plate into place with his thumb. "Are you well enough to work tonight?"

"Of course. I must. I gave my word to the *patrón.*"

Carlos bent over and unshackled Eddie's leg. "Friday night is very busy. Many of Don Enrique's friends come early before leaving for their homes in the country. Clean yourself. Can you do it with one arm?"

"I can manage," Eddie answered, swinging his legs off the bed.

"And your wound?" Carlos asked.

Eddie stood and wiggled the fingers that protruded from the sling around his arm. "I must thank the doctor when I see him. The arm feels much better."

"Tomorrow he will stitch you," Carlos reminded him. "Thank him then."

"I will," Eddie replied, determined that in the morning, at the latest, he would be at the Fort Bliss military hospital being treated by an Army doctor who wasn't on DeLeon's pad.

Carlos walked him to the dressing room and told him not to be long, as others might have need for the toilet. He would be outside, waiting. Eddie bathed quickly, keeping the wound dry as he sponged himself, washed his hair, and used his left hand to shave with a razor Carlos gave him, nicking himself several times. He dressed in the clean clothes—a much better fit than yesterday's apparel—dried his hair, and adjusted the sling and the hump. He felt good enough to think about escaping. His plan was simple: given enough of a distraction he would run away.

Carlos knocked at the door. Eddie opened it, and one of the cooks brushed by him on the way to the urinal, unbuttoning his fly as he went.

"Time for your meal, *jorobado*," Carlos noted, "and then to work."

"I am ready." Eddie smiled at the ugly man as he handed back the razor.

Kerney stood inside the Little Turtle and looked around the room. The gambling house was filled with well-dressed men and women busy placing bets, socializing, and milling about the casino. It had a party atmosphere to it, and from the way people mixed, it was not a gathering of strangers. Kerney picked out a bodyguard hovering near a man with a slick-looking woman draped on his arm, and another close by an older gentleman betting at a monte table.

He counted six more bodyguards in the room before switching his attention to the bar. More muscle, Kerney thought to himself, as he sized up the man standing directly behind a table at the corner of the bar. A thug with acne scars and a bushy mustache, the bodyguard carefully scanned the room with watchful eyes. At the table the goon guarded, a man and a young woman were talking. On a bar stool to one side sat a hunchback dressed in a cook's uniform, smiling stupidly at everybody.

Kerney walked toward the table, and the body-guard cut him off.

"What do you want?" Carlos asked in heavy English, looking the gringo up and down. The man wore an expensive suit with an Italian cut that accentuated his square shoulders. He was tall and deeply tanned, with blue eyes that crinkled at the corners. He's a big son of a bitch, Carlos thought to himself.

Kerney smiled. "I have an appointment with Señor DeLeon," he said in Spanish.

"Your name?"

"Kevin Kerney."

"You must wait, señor," Carlos said, nodding at the table. DeLeon was still talking with the girl, who wore tight designer jeans and a scoop-neck silk top that revealed remarkable breasts. "I will tell the señor you are here."

Kerney nodded, slipped onto the empty stool next to the hunchback, watched Carlos walk quickly to DeLeon and whisper in his ear. DeLeon looked up in irritation, glanced at Kerney, nodded to the bodyguard, and returned to his conversation.

Kerney watched DeLeon for a brief time and spoke to Eddie. "Are you bringing the customers luck?" he asked in Spanish, patting the hump.

"I hope so, señor," Eddie answered, trying to mask the astonishment he felt. Dressed up, Kerney looked like a major player, not at all like a shit-kicking cop from New Mexico.

Kerney pointed to the sling and held out a twenty-dollar bill. "It looks like you didn't keep any luck for yourself."

"A minor accident." Eddie put the money in his

pocket. "Thank you." He glanced at Carlos and decided he couldn't risk saying more.

The girl with DeLeon pouted, stood up, flipped her long hair over a shoulder, kissed DeLeon on the cheek, and pranced off to a monte table. DeLeon gestured for Kerney to approach.

"Señor Kerney," he said, rising. "Please join me."

"Thank you." Kerney studied DeLeon as he settled in. A good-looking man with pale blue eyes and strong features, freshly shaved and dressed in a tan business suit, DeLeon smiled back at him. His hands were soft and his nails manicured.

"Francisco Posada said you wished to secure the services of a broker."

"That is correct."

"What type of products do you wish to ship?"

"Artifacts."

DeLeon raised an eyebrow. "That covers a wide range."

Kerney handed DeLeon a typed copy of Gutierrez's list and waited for a reaction.

DeLeon scanned the contents and smiled warmly at Kerney, his mind racing. His chartered plane, scheduled to leave Mexico City for Hong Kong in two days, would carry an identical cargo. It was an impossible duplication.

"Where did you get such treasures?" DeLeon inquired.

"That's not important," Kerney countered. "Do you know anyone who specializes in such antiques?"

"A select few deal in antiques," DeLeon replied, tapping his fingers together in thought. "But all I see are items written on paper. Authentication would be necessary."

"I can provide samples," Kerney replied, "but there is some urgency to the matter."

"I understand," DeLeon replied. "Time is money, is it not? I have an associate who might be interested. May I keep the list to show him?"

Kerney didn't like the idea, but he had no choice. "Certainly."

DeLeon folded the papers and put them in a pocket. "Excellent. Could you return later this evening?"

"Will your associate be joining us?"

"Yes. Come back after midnight." DeLeon stood and offered Kerney his hand. "I'm sure we can accommodate you."

"I look forward to it," Kerney said.

He shook DeLeon's hand and left, walking past a man at the door entering the club. The man eyed Kerney intensely. He had a weight lifter's build, gray eyes, and a small scar on his chin. Kerney nodded and kept moving.

Benton pushed his way through the crowd to DeLeon, who whispered something to Carlos as the bodyguard leaned across the table.

DeLeon's eyes snapped when he saw Benton. "Wait," he ordered Carlos. He shoved some papers across the table at Benton. "What is going on?" he demanded.

"He's a cop," Benton said, thumbing through the inventory.

"How did he get the list?"

"Our courier died in a traffic accident. The inventory was in his vehicle, and the cop found it. He's just snooping around."

"And the last shipment?"

"Still on the base. We'll get it out."

"Are you lying to me, Benton?

Benton shook his head. "The cop's name is Kevin Kerney. He's a sheriff's lieutenant from Las Cruces. All he has is the fucking list. I swear it."

"Then you will dispose of Lieutenant Kerney, instead of Carlos."

"That's why I'm here."

"Do it," DeLeon ordered, his eyes narrow, "and clean up after yourself when you're finished." He walked toward the young woman in the scoop-neck top and the stone-washed jeans, who was still at the monte table, betting heavily.

Outside the club, Kerney looked for a taxi. Expensive automobiles were double-parked around the small plaza, blocking most incoming traffic, and there were no waiting or cruising cabs. A fat cop with an enormous head wandered between the cars, his hand resting on his pistol grip. Kerney gave him some money and asked him where he could get a taxi.

"I can call one for you, señor," Dominguez replied. "It can be here in less than ten minutes."

Kerney could see the thoroughfare about a mile in the distance, down the narrow residential street leading from the plaza. He didn't like the idea of waiting. It only gave DeLeon time to have him followed, which was a sure bet.

"The night air feels good," Kerney said. "I'll walk. Thanks anyway."

He started out at a brisk pace, looking for something he could use as a weapon if DeLeon decided to send some muscle after him, which was another possibility. What he really wanted was the pistol safely locked in the glove compartment of his truck.

Carlos watched Benton hurry from the club and felt Eddie tugging on his sleeve.

"I must go to the *baño*," Eddie announced, in a loud voice. Several people at the bar looked up from their drinks.

"Not now," Carlos answered.

"I will soil myself," Eddie rejoined shrilly, trying to look miserable. "My bowels are loose."

Carlos gave him a peevish look. "If you must go, be quick about it."

"I won't be but a minute." Eddie scooted toward the cantina, almost knocking over a waiter coming through the swinging door. He moved through the kitchen to the rear door and ran into the alley. No one tried to stop him. The lane paralleled the plaza and ran straight to the main drag. Eddie took off in a sprint, tugging his arm out of the sling. He ripped off his shirt, yanked the harness free, and threw the contraption to the ground. He veered through the backyard of a small house and onto the street, stopping to catch his breath. Ahead, he could see Kerney walking toward the strip, making slow progress. He stepped into the darkness at the side of a house and checked for Benton behind him. Nothing yet. The street was quiet. A few *viejos* were on the front steps of a house, enjoying the mild evening.

Eddie froze as a car drove out of the plaza coming

in his direction. As it passed under a streetlamp, Eddie recognized the driver and relaxed; it was one of DeLeon's customers. He started running again. He had heard DeLeon order Kerney killed, and he needed to reach the lieutenant before Benton showed up.

Greg Benton saw an obese cop at the end of the square chasing some kids away from a Range Rover. He called him over, gave him a fistful of dollars, and asked about a gringo in a suit with a limp. The cop pointed in the direction of the main drag and told him Kerney was on foot. He ran his car up on the sidewalk to avoid the parked vehicles on the plaza, found an opening, bumped into the street, and floored the gas pedal, burning rubber as he accelerated toward the strip. He flicked on his high beams and saw two men on the sidewalk about a hundred yards apart. He passed the first one; some punk in white pants running at full tilt. Up ahead Kerney moved in an awkward gait. Benton laughed; it was a ludicrous sight.

First Kerney, Benton decided. If the kid posed a problem, he would deal with it later.

Kerney heard the car coming and left the street at a run, disappearing between two houses. Tires screeched on the street, and he ran faster. He pulled himself over a backyard fence, ducked under the low branches of a tree, and doubled back down the cobblestone alley. He needed to find cover and something to use as a weapon.

Benton left the car in the street and gave chase on foot. He stopped at a backyard fence next to an alley, where the low branch of a tree moved gently in the still air. He listened for sounds and heard a slight clacking of heels on the cobblestones. Kerney was moving back toward the Little Turtle. Benton smiled to himself and reached for the knife in his ankle sheath. It would be a good hunt after all. He stepped into the alley and started stalking.

As far as Kerney could tell, he was alone in the alley. He found the jagged top of an oil drum that had been cut with a welding torch and a stubby piece of metal pipe. They would have to do. He stood with his back against the wall of a shed listening to the rats inside squeak at his presence. He knew someone was out there, going, he hoped, in the wrong direction.

He took a fast look down the alley. The light from the concourse gave him enough illumination to pick up any movement. Nothing. A car door slammed and he pulled back his head. The sound was followed by rapid, loud Spanish. Somebody wanted to know who the asshole was who had left his car parked in the middle of the street.

He looked again and saw movement, a shadowy ripple against the light. The movement stopped under a solitary tree, a good fifty feet away. Slowly Kerney crouched down, hoping his attacker would be searching at eye level. Risking one last glimpse, Kerney saw a discernible shape moving cautiously in his direction.

Kerney held his breath and waited until the man was almost on top of him. When he saw the knife, he came out of his crouch and swung the stubby pipe at the man's head.

Benton skipped back and kicked, the blow landing full force on Kerney's bad knee. The leg caved in and put Kerney on his back. Rolling to avoid another kick, he threw the lid as a distraction and scrambled to his feet, his back against the shed wall, waiting for the man's next move. He was the gray-eyed body-builder with the scar on his chin.

Benton laughed. He had a knife in his hand, held low so it could rip into the belly. "Can't you do any better than that?" he jeered.

Benton stepped in for the kill, feinting an over-hand lunge at Kerney's chest. He stopped the thrust in midair, rotated his wrist, and arched the blade up to slash Kerney's gut. Kerney slammed the metal pipe on Benton's wrist.

Benton grunted and sprang back as Kerney tried to swipe him across the face. "Now you're trying," he said indulgently.

The son of a bitch isn't even breathing hard, Kerney marveled. His knee locked up as he circled to the center of the alley.

Benton turned with him, relaxed and watchful. He came at Kerney in a textbook move: wheeling, faking a kick, driving the point of the knife at Kerney's exposed torso. Stepping into the thrust, Kerney turned sideways, caught the knife hand, locked the pipe against the wrist, and wrenched it back with all his strength until the bones snapped.

Benton yelled in agony as the knife clattered to the ground, and hammered a solid left into Kerney's eye with his good hand. Kerney held on to the wrist, trying to bend the man to his knees.

Refusing to go down, Benton hit Kerney again,

flush in the mouth, followed by a solid smash to the stomach. The blow put Kerney on his hands and knees, with a searing pain that exploded in his stomach. His vision blurred, he clawed desperately on the cobblestones, searching for the pipe. He had to get to his feet. He tried to push himself upright. The knee failed, and as he tried again he felt the knife against his throat.

"You son of a bitch," Benton rasped. "You broke my fucking wrist."

The man bent over him, his gray eyes locked on Kerney's face, savoring his victory. Get it over with, Kerney's mind screamed.

The jagged oil-drum top came out of nowhere, like a discus. The rusty, sharp edge caught Benton in the neck and severed the artery. Blood gushed over Kerney as Benton turned toward his attacker, both hands clutching his neck. He crumpled to the ground, his dying heart pumping blood into a pool that seeped into the porous cobblestones around his head.

Kerney clutched his stomach, blinked away the pain, looked at the man walking toward him, and didn't believe what he saw. It was the hunchback from the Little Turtle, only he wasn't a *jorobado* anymore. "Who the hell are you?" he asked, speaking between the jolts that ripped through his stomach.

"Eddie Tapia. Provost Marshal's Office. Criminal investigations. White Sands." He bent over Kerney. "Are you all right, Lieutenant?"

"No, I'm not all right."

Eddie inspected Kerney again, more closely. He

was beat up, but the damage seemed superficial. "You seem to be in one piece," he said.

"Hardly."

"Are you cut?"

Kerney shook his head. "Forget it. Just a private joke." He held out a hand. "Help me up."

"Can you walk?"

"Of course I can."

On his feet, Kerney felt light-headed. If he could puke, maybe he would feel better. He swayed, and Eddie grabbed him around the waist to keep him steady.

"Can you make it to Benton's car?" Eddie asked.

"Benton's car?" Kerney repeated vaguely, wondering if Benton was the dead man.

"Yeah. He left the keys in the ignition."

"Let's go."

At the car, Eddie checked for any sign of Carlos, hurried Kerney inside the vehicle, and drove to the main drag as quickly as possible. Surrounded by Friday-night traffic and heading toward the bridge, he risked a glance at Kerney. The lieutenant, doubled over with his head between his legs, seemed to be gagging.

Kerney sat up and rested his head against the back of the seat. "I just threw up," he said. "Sorry about that."

"I know how it feels," Eddie said. He sniffed, wrinkled his nose, rolled down the window, and turned on the air conditioner. "Mind telling me what the fuck is going on?" Eddie asked.

Enrique DeLeon paced on the loading dock waiting for Carlos to return with Eddie. Carlos would have to be punished. His inattentiveness had allowed the *jorobado* to flee. A beating would improve his attitude. He heard footsteps running down the alley. The warehouse foreman moved to his side protectively, pistol in hand. Carlos arrived winded, and stood looking up at DeLeon with a distressed expression. He placed a bundle on the dock at DeLeon's feet.

"The hunchback was a fake, *patrón,*" he said.

DeLeon knelt and inspected the bundle. Inside the arm sling was an elaborate harness and cowhide skin formed into a hump with padding. The cowhide, expertly tanned and supple to the touch, felt remarkably lifelike. "What else?" DeLeon said, rising.

Carlos held up a knife. "Benton is dead, Don Enrique."

DeLeon raised an eyebrow. "Really?" It was unexpected news. "How?"

"His neck was cut," Carlos replied.

"Tell Dominguez to remove the body from the alley and send men to look for the gringo and the *jorobado.*"

"Yes, *patrón.*" Carlos started to leave.

"Wait," Enrique ordered. "Bring Francisco Posada to me."

"Yes, *patrón.*"

DeLeon waved him away. "Go."

Carlos scurried off. DeLeon decided he would not have Carlos badly beaten. Eddie had fooled them both, along with dozens of customers and employees. A gifted young man, DeLeon thought dryly. He felt a need to know more about Eddie. Francisco might have information, and if not, he could get it. It was also vital to learn more about Kerney, now that Benton was dead.

Frustrated, DeLeon went back inside the Little Turtle.

CHAPTER

11

Seated at the table on the patio of Fred Utley's house, James Meehan watched the setting sun on the western horizon while Fred stirred the charcoal in the barbeque pit, his back stiff with irritation. Meehan smiled to himself and dropped his gaze to the foothills of the subdivision where Utley lived. The new single-family homes were gradually creeping up the hills toward Utley's lot. Fred had thrown up a six-foot wall to protect his privacy from the encroachment.

Meehan switched his attention back to Fred and watched as Utley plunged the poker into the hot coals one last time before walking to the table. He took his glasses off to clean them and peered near-sightedly at Meehan.

"How could Gutierrez lose the last shipment?" Utley demanded, his tone verging on a whine.

"Eppi got careless," Meehan replied. "He moved the merchandise to the ranch house before he went to play with his sheep. When he came back for it, it was gone."

"Where is Gutierrez now?"

"Sulking in El Paso with Benton."

"The stupid son of a bitch. What do we do now?"

"DeLeon expects a full shipment."

Utley held his eyeglasses close to his nose, decided they were still dirty, and cleaned them again. "How do we do that?" he grumbled.

"We get the merchandise back," Meehan said, rising to mix another drink at the wet bar near the patio door. "I know who has our property."

"Who?" Utley adjusted his eyeglasses on his nose.

"Your girlfriend," Meehan replied.

"Sara?" Fred asked incredulously. "How did she get it?"

Meehan shrugged. "Luck. The details aren't important. We need our property back."

Utley laughed caustically. "From Sara? I doubt it."

"She'll cooperate."

"You don't know Sara," Fred rebutted.

Meehan sighed and walked back to the table. "I have all the information I need to encourage her to cooperate."

"Like what?"

"Leave that to me. It won't be difficult." He patted Utley on the cheek, his hard gaze locked on Fred's face. "I need your help."

Utley shook off Meehan's touch, his eyes fearful. "I want no part of it."

Meehan held his thumb and forefinger an inch apart. "We're that close to millions of dollars, Fred. Do you want to see it go down the drain simply because we didn't even try to meet our obligation to DeLeon?"

Utley's defenses started to collapse. He wanted the money a lot more than he cared about Sara. "I can't face her," he said weakly, sinking into a chair.

"You don't have to," Meehan reassured him. He sat down, stretched out his legs, and gave Utley a friendly smile.

"You won't hurt her?"

Meehan chuckled. "Of course not. I'll have her detained until we're safely out of the country. By the time she's released you'll have a new identity and a passport that will take you anywhere you want to go. With enough money to last a lifetime."

"What do you want me to do?"

"Call her," Meehan responded. "Get her to come over here on a pretext. Tell her it's important and you don't want to talk about it on the phone." Meehan stood up and looked at his watch. "She should be home by now."

"What do I say?"

"Keep it simple. A personal crisis. A death in your family." Meehan touched Utley's arm and walked him to the patio door. Utley took the cue and followed. "Something like that would do nicely," Meehan added.

"I don't know if I can do it."

"We have no other option," Meehan said gently,

as he slid the door open. "Come on, let's get it over with. We'll get through this, Fred. It's just a little bump in the road."

"I hope so," Utley replied.

Meehan waited for Fred to go first, closed the patio door behind him, and followed him into the living room. He stood close with an encouraging smile and watched Fred dial the number with a shaking hand. Fred's nervousness should help encourage Sara to agree to come, he thought happily.

Utley used the death-in-the-family ploy. His voice cracked nicely, and he sounded persuasively distraught. He hung up and breathed a sigh of relief. "She's coming over in half an hour. That was hard for me to do."

"I know it was," Meehan said, patting him on the shoulder. He grabbed Fred's lower jaw with his left hand and yanked down as he jammed a pistol into the now-gaping mouth with his right hand. Utley didn't have time to scream as the bullet exploded in his brain. Meehan relaxed his grip and Fred collapsed on the floor, the pistol protruding from his mouth.

Meehan smiled, bent over the body, wiped the pistol grip clean, wrapped Utley's fingers around the weapon, and got busy tidying up. The suicide angle might just hold up indefinitely, but it wasn't essential. It was Friday night and Utley wouldn't be missed over the weekend. That gave him more than enough time.

Meehan checked his watch, his hands sweating inside the latex gloves he wore as he removed all traces of his presence. Sara would arrive soon, and

Benton should call shortly after that to report on his meeting with DeLeon.

He hoped Sara wouldn't crack too easily.

Sara had half a notion to call Fred back and tell him she wasn't coming over, but the sudden death of his mother had obviously shaken him up.

Fred wasn't one to ask for unnecessary attention, and the demands of her job often forced her to neglect the few good friends she had. In spite of Fred's unwelcome romantic interest in her, he was still a friend.

With no word from Kerney or Eddie Tapia in the last twenty-four hours, she was more than a little worried about them. She recorded a short message and Fred's phone number on her answering machine for Kerney, and suddenly realized that she missed him. The question was, how long would the feeling last? So far, it felt very authentic. In her Jeep Cherokee, she checked her hair in the visor mirror. Her smile amused her; it was blatantly lascivious. Chalk another one up for Kerney, she said to herself.

Fred's car was in the driveway when she arrived, and the drapes to the large picture windows on either side of the front door were closed. She walked up the brick path to the house and rang the bell. When it opened, Jim Meehan stood in front of her, a friendly smile on his face.

"Hi, Sara," he said amiably.

"What are you doing here?" she asked.

"I've been waiting for you," he replied, as he raised a sap from behind his back.

She saw the blow coming, tried to sidestep it, and

drove the palm of her hand at Meehan's nose. He turned his head and the blow caught him on the cheek. She clawed for his eyes with her fingers as he hit her hard with the sap above her ear. She was unconscious before the side of her head bounced against the doorjamb.

Meehan grabbed her as she fell and carried her inside.

She woke up handcuffed, tied to a straight-backed chair, with her feet bound. Fred Utley, sprawled on his side, his cheek pressed against the carpet, stared at her with a dead, startled eye. A gun stuck out of his mouth and his lips were seared black with powder burns. Sara felt her stomach turn over. She swallowed, held her breath until the sensation passed, and looked for Meehan. He sat on the couch at the far side of the room with a boyish, pleased smile. The back of her head hurt like hell.

She raised her wrists away from the small of her back, and handcuffs bit into the bone. "Why did you kill Fred?" she asked, concentrating on Meehan to avoid the grotesqueness on the floor.

"He killed himself," Meehan answered casually. "The strain of becoming a rich man was just too much for him. What kind of funeral do you think he'd like?"

"Didn't you ask?"

"I didn't have the time," Meehan said. "I think something original would suit him. A Tibetan ritual, perhaps. By ancient tradition they put bodies on a mountainside for the vultures to pick clean. Do you think Fred would like that?"

Sara shrugged.

"How about you? What kind of funeral would you like?"

"Full military honors," Sara answered. "Something you'll never get."

Meehan laughed. "You're so spunky." He got up from the couch and stood over her, rubbing his hands. "A spunky, meddlesome cunt in uniform."

"Fuck off, Jim."

He slapped her. "Pissing me off isn't smart." He smiled and walked behind the chair. Sara froze when she felt his fingers on her shoulders. Gently, he rubbed her neck. "You're all tensed up."

"Take your hands off me."

He tightened his fingers around her neck. "I want the coins and letters."

"I don't have them."

Meehan laughed. "That's what Kerney said before he died in Juárez." He felt her stiffen. He twisted her face upward, forcing her to look at him. "You must be bad luck, Sara. Both of the men you were fucking are dead."

He could feel Sara's jaw tighten as she clamped her mouth shut. He released her face and patted her cheek. "We'll keep Fred company for a while," he informed her cheerfully. "It will give you time to think about your options." Humming to himself, he turned out the lights and returned to the couch.

Eddie stopped the car in a parking lot on the El Paso side of the bridge. The stink from Kerney's vomit had dissipated enough to make breathing bearable. He could hardly believe all the stuff the lieutenant had told him about a secret cave with hidden treasure. It sounded like something out of the movies.

"Your turn," Kerney prompted.

Eddie told him what he knew about Benton and DeLeon.

The main problem, Kerney mused, was putting the final pieces together before they ran out of time. "Did Benton mention any names when he was talking with DeLeon?" he asked.

"No."

"We need to find out more about him," Kerney proposed as he opened the car door.

"I'll backtrack on Benton," Eddie volunteered. "Maybe I can find out where he was staying, where he hung out—that sort of stuff."

"You need to get that arm looked after," Kerney countered.

"I will. You're not in great shape yourself," Eddie reminded him.

"I'll survive," Kerney said. "Okay, see what you can dig up. I'll let Sara know what you're doing." Kerney pulled himself out of the car, his hand gripping the door to keep his balance.

"Thanks."

Kerney shut the door and looked at Eddie through the open window. "Don't thank me. I owe you a lot. I'm too old to be brawling in dark alleys with guys like Benton. Leave a message with Sara Brannon if you find anything."

Eddie nodded. "You're heading back to the base?"

"Yeah. Be careful, Eddie."

"You got it, Lieutenant," Eddie said, shifting the car into gear.

He watched Kerney hobble to his truck. The vehicle lurched and stalled as Kerney tried to drive away. He cranked the truck engine again, eased the clutch out, and rolled slowly through the parking lot.

Kerney was some piece of work, Eddie decided. With the odds totally against him, Kerney had stood his ground and done a lot of damage before Benton had him down. Eddie wondered if he could do as well under the same circumstances.

The living room was dark except for the weak light that spilled into the room from the kitchen and illuminated Fred's body. Meehan was behind her, and all Sara could hear was the sound of his breathing. The handcuffs were killing her, and she had lost most of the sensation in her fingers. She tried moving her hands to restore the circulation and bit her lip to keep from gasping with pain. She heard the rustling of clothing as Meehan paced behind her chair. Was Kerney really dead? She didn't want to believe it, but the possibility plagued her. She needed to stop dwelling on it and stay focused on Meehan—stay angry. He planned to kill her, she was sure of it, but he was waiting for something to happen first. It gave her time.

She made another attempt to force her finger into the back pocket of her jeans. She'd stopped for gas in town and out of habit had stuck the charge slip in her pocket. She brought her hands as high as she could and wiggled a finger into the pocket.

Meehan heard the sound. "Are the handcuffs too tight?"

She froze. "Yes. Please loosen them."

"I don't think so," he said after a long pause.

He started pacing again, and she dug her finger back into the pocket. The receipt was crumpled and wedged in a corner. She inched it slowly along the seam and checked her movement when Meehan stopped pacing. In the mirror above Fred's body she could see his silhouette. His back to her, he gazed out the patio door. Slowly she wiggled the receipt free, and it fell out. She probed for it on the chair cushion but couldn't find it, so she shifted her fanny to the back of the chair, hoping to conceal it.

"Restless?" Meehan asked, turning toward her. His thoughts were on Benton. The phone call was way overdue. Each minute added to the chance of discovery. He needed to move on.

"Bored," Sara replied. Her class ring was almost over the knuckle of her finger. She kept pressing against it with her thumb.

"You've been very patient. I appreciate that." He came around the chair and stood directly in front of her, his groin inches from her face. She pulled back her head and closed her eyes, waiting for him to touch her again. He stroked her face with the back of his hand. "It's time to go," he announced.

"I'm fine right where I am," Sara snapped. The ring came off her finger, and she palmed it.

"Why are you always so bitchy?" Meehan inquired, as he slipped on the latex gloves. "Nothing seems to please you."

He untied the rope from around the chair and pulled her to him so she could feel his erection. She tensed up nicely. He released her, turned on a table lamp, and put the chair back in its original position.

Meehan didn't notice the credit card receipt on the cushion; he was busy rubbing the chair's indentations from the carpet with the heel of his shoe. Satisfied, he turned off the lamp, grabbed her around the waist, and dragged her out of the house.

At the Cherokee, he bent her facedown over the hood and fished the car keys from her pocket. She dug her heels in the gravel as he yanked her to the passenger door. When he reached to open it, Sara dropped the ring. Meehan pushed her inside the Jeep, walked to the driver's side, and got behind the wheel.

Two clues, she thought gratefully. Enough to raise suspicion, if found. Much better than nothing.

The night was warm and still. A million stars sparkled in a clear sky. Meehan smiled affectionately at her as he started the engine and drove away. She smiled back through thin lips, wondering if she would get a chance to kill the bastard.

Kerney made it back to Las Cruces in just over a half hour, driving at top speed. At a gas station off the interstate the attendant kept a wary eye on him. Dried blood covered his suit jacket, shirt, and face, his right eye was half closed, his lip was puffy, and his pants were crusted with dirt. Kerney smiled at the kid as he dialed Sara's number at the pay phone. The kid probably figured him for an ax murderer, he thought.

The message on Sara's answering machine gave him Fred Utley's number to call. He hung up in exasperation and dialed the number. He let it ring for a long time before disconnecting. He had a peevish thought that maybe Sara and Utley didn't want to be disturbed; if that was true, he had become a one-night stand for the first time in many years.

Business is business, he decided, looking up Utley's address in the phone book. If he interrupted something, so be it.

The attendant seemed ready to dive under the counter when Kerney approached him and asked directions to Utley's house. He stammered a lot but finally gave Kerney the information he needed. Kerney left a ten-dollar tip on the counter.

Utley lived in a trendy rural subdivision in the foothills outside the city limits. Scrub-covered, waterless hills good only for rabbit hunting now had hundred-thousand-dollar homes tucked into knolls, banked against outcroppings, and standing monolithic on scoured plots. City lights winked in the valley below, fading into darkness where the rich bottomland and the irrigated farms near the river met the urban sprawl.

Utley's house, some distance from the others, was dark when Kerney arrived. Only one car was in the driveway, a Japanese sport coupe. The thought that Sara had gone home pleased him.

Ringing the doorbell brought no response. Maybe they were out somewhere in Sara's Jeep. He went back to the truck, got a flashlight, and inspected the coupe. It had a civilian employee pass to the missile range on the bumper and was unlocked. He found Utley's registration in the glove box. He swept the driveway with the beam of the flashlight. Two grooves in the gravel, deep and closely spaced marks, caught his attention. There was a glitter of gold in the gravel. Kerney picked it up. It was a West Point ring with Sara's initials engraved inside the band. He got his pistol from the truck and tried the front door. It was locked.

At the side of the house was a high wall with a locked, wooden gate. He climbed the wall and walked around the house to a covered patio. Charcoal in the barbecue pit was still warm. He stood to one side of a sliding patio door and gave it a push. The door slid open. He made a quick scan, saw nothing, and stepped into a large combination kitchen and dining area. He moved quietly to the living room. He saw a body, dropped to a prone position, and killed the flashlight.

There were no sounds in the house, but he waited several minutes before shining the flashlight at the body again. It was Fred Utley and he was very dead.

Kerney did a fast room search of the house before returning to the living room and turning on the lights. From the color of his skin, Utley hadn't been dead for very long. For some reason a chair had been moved in front of Utley's body and then replaced in its original position. The carpet fibers had been partially fluffed up to erase the imprint of chair legs. There were slight signs of abrasions on the wood finish, and a wadded-up piece of paper on the cushion. He picked it up and smoothed it out. It was a gasoline credit card receipt charged to Sara's account.

Utley's death was no suicide, and Sara had been here, tied up, and then taken forcibly away from house. She was alive when she left but could be dead and lying in a ditch by now. His pulse quickened. He used the telephone in the bedroom to call Andy Baca.

The doctor at Fort Bliss looked Eddie up and down and asked him suspiciously where in the hell he had been. Eddie told him Juárez, and the doctor made him strip and wash with a disinfectant while he called to verify that Eddie was really an investigator assigned to White Sands Missile Range. Flat on his stomach, covered with a hospital gown, Eddie watched while the doctor worked on him. The nerve blocker dulled the pain but not enough to keep the surgery from hurting. After Eddie was sewed up, the doctor bandaged his arm while a haggard-looking nurse gave him a tetanus shot and a sheet of written instructions on how to care for his wound.

Eddie had left his personal car at Fort Bliss after dropping Isabel and the baby at the bus station, and an MP sent to fetch his travel bag stood by the door watching him dress, holding Eddie's gear.

"You want me to take you to your car?" the MP asked.

"Not yet," Eddie said, reclaiming his handgun, wallet, and badge case from the bag. He stuck the holstered weapon into his belt, put the wallet and case in his back pockets, and motioned for the MP to follow him.

Outside the hospital, Eddie searched Benton's car while the MP waited. It didn't take long to find out where Benton had stayed in El Paso. The ashtray contained a room key and a bunch of motel receipts. A workout bag in the backseat held a smelly sweat suit, a towel, a jockstrap, and a very choice 9mm handgun, with three extra clips. Eddie turned the gun and clips over to the MP and asked him to have the vehicle impounded and the weapon checked. The MP called for a tow truck and gave him a ride to his car.

The motel, in a barrio bordering an industrial section of the city, was a fleabag. A row of smokestacks from a nearby smelter dwarfed the houses and the businesses along the strip. Three hookers waved to him as he drove into the parking lot.

Eddie let himself into Benton's room. It was a box with a bathroom and closet jutting out of one corner. It smelled of years of cigarettes and cheap booze. He started his search and quickly found out that Benton liked guns. Under the pillow on the bed was a Colt .38 revolver, and in the bathroom a toiletry kit contained a .22 Saturday-night special. The single dresser held a Gideon Bible and nothing else. Benton kept his clothes in two large canvas duffel bags, clean clothes in one and dirty clothes in the other. He probably didn't like the cockroaches getting into his wearing apparel, Eddie thought, as he watched one dart out of the wastebasket. The only thing in the trash can was a greasy brown paper bag containing food wrappers and a cash register receipt from the Caballito Bar.

He took another tour through the room before leaving and found a laptop computer and printer in a carrying case on the floor by a phone jack.

Next door a hooker cooed and moaned in time with the squeaking bedsprings. He grabbed the computer case, locked the room, and stood in the parking lot. Just down the street, on the opposite corner, the neon outline of a rearing pony flashed on and off above the entrance to a bar. Eddie smiled to himself, put the computer in his car, and walked to the Caballito Bar.

The bar, filled with workers from the factories, bustled with activity. Eddie found room at the bar and ordered a *cerveza*. When the bartender brought it, he gave him a twenty-dollar bill and asked if he knew a gringo named Benton.

The bartender, a man with a hook nose and dark circles under his eyes, took the bill, made change, and said he didn't know anybody by that name. He walked away to serve another customer before Eddie could ask another question.

The wall over the bar held a velveteen painting of a conquistador and another painting of a señorita wearing a lace mantilla. A hand-printed lunch menu was tacked between the two pictures. Eddie called the bartender back and asked if a gringo had been coming in recently to buy take-out lunches.

"Oh, that guy," the bartender answered, taking another twenty-dollar bill from Eddie's hand, plus the eighteen dollars in change on the counter. He stuffed the money into a tip jar and lowered his voice. "I don't know his name."

The Freddy Fender song on the jukebox ended and the bartender stopped talking. A man at the pool table dropped more quarters in the slot and started punching buttons. The music blared; a mariachi song. Two female shift workers at the end of the bar started singing along. "If it's the guy I'm thinking about," the bartender continued, "he comes in to buy take-out. Always orders a hamburger and fries. He doesn't like Mexican food."

Eddie described Benton to the bartender.

"That's him." The bartender walked away to fill an order. Along the rear wall, a small audience watched the pool game. Behind them was a mural of wild mustangs galloping across a mesa. When the bartender finished pouring drinks, Eddie motioned for him to come back.

"Did you ever see this guy on the streets?" Eddie inquired.

The bartender plucked another twenty-dollar bill from Eddie's fingers. "Once. I saw him over by the self-storage units."

"Where is that?"

"Down by the factories. You can't miss it."

"What was he doing when you saw him?" Eddie asked.

The bartender smiled. "He was driving through the gate. Probably checking on his property. Everybody who rents space there keeps a close eye on their merchandise. The city can tear down Smeltertown, but they can't stop the *contrabandistas*."

Eddie thanked the man, finished his beer, and went to the telephone next to the jukebox. It was time to call Kerney.

Andy Baca watched his officers work. They had cordoned off the driveway and brought in high-intensity lights to help with evidence collection. An officer photographed the heel marks and tire imprints, while another searched Utley's car. Inside, the crime scene unit lifted prints, vacuumed rugs for fibers and trace evidence, and photographed the body. On the patio a deputy sifted through the ashes in the barbecue pit.

Kerney was inside with Andy's captain of detectives, giving a statement. The medical examiner arrived with two paramedics in a county ambulance and started unloading a gurney. The sound of another motor came up the road. The driver parked behind a patrol unit, got out, and walked over to him.

Andy nodded when Major Curry drew near. "Tom," he said. "Thanks for coming."

"No problem," Curry replied. "Are you sure this cop of yours has his story straight?"

"I believe him," Andy replied, "and the evidence backs him up."

"He thinks Sara was abducted?"

"It looks that way. I've got a statewide APB out on her vehicle, plus El Paso and west Texas. Kerney's worried that she may have been taken somewhere and killed."

"Jesus," Tom Curry snorted. "I've got a patrol covering her quarters in case she turns up. Do we have a suspect?"

"No, but another wise guy surfaced in Juárez," Andy said.

"Who is it?"

"Kerney didn't tell me, but he's probably on ice in the Juárez morgue."

"Did Kerney take him out?"

"No, one of your people did. A Corporal Eddie Tapia. Kerney says the corporal saved his life."

"Where is Tapia?" Curry asked.

"In El Paso. He took a knife cut on his arm. Nothing serious. He's probably finished getting sewed up and is backtracking on the perp."

"Where's Kerney?"

Andy nodded at the front door as Kerney stepped outside the house. "Be gentle, Tom," he advised. "The man has had a shitty night, and his attitude stinks right now."

Curry watched Kerney limp down the walk to a pickup truck and open the door. His suit was dirty and spattered with dried blood.

Curry and Andy walked to him.

"You're Curry?" Kerney asked, looking at the uniform and the insignia of rank. He opened his bag, searched for a clean shirt, and pulled one out.

"I am."

"Good. I need to talk to you. Eddie Tapia just called. He found where Benton was staying, and he has a lead on a rented storage unit. I'm going down to hook up with him."

"Greg Benton?" Curry asked.

"That's right." He slipped out of the suit jacket, undid the tie, unbuttoned the shirt, and stripped it off. The scar on Kerney's stomach was nasty, as bad as any combat wound Curry had seen. Kerney threw the dirty clothes into the cab of the truck and put on the fresh shirt. "You know who he is?"

"I know who he's supposed to be," Curry replied.

"Is he CIA? Defense Intelligence? NSA?" Kerney asked, stuffing his shirttail into his pants.

"I don't know," Curry answered.

"He belongs to somebody," Kerney said. "Check it out."

"Of course. Are you assuming Utley was part of it?"

Kerney got in the truck and slammed the door.

"He had to be." He smiled at Andy. "I'll be in touch."

"Let me send somebody with you," Andy pleaded.

"I can handle it," Kerney retorted. He drove away.

"I need to make a phone call to Washington," Curry said, frowning at the receding taillights.

"Be my guest," Andy replied.

DeLeon's meeting with Francisco Posada was short and to the point. Posada promised him all the required facts about Kevin Kerney, and he would see what could be learned about Eddie the *jorobado*. Most certainly Don Enrique would know by morning where Kerney lived, so he could be found and killed quickly.

Carlos was due to return with a progress report on the search. DeLeon waited patiently at his table, watching the action on the floor. Luisa, his diversion for the weekend, still occupied her time gambling with his money at the monte tables. He looked forward to his weekend with her. She hoped for marriage and eagerly demonstrated her talents, but he saw no future in marrying any woman. Eventually, all of them grew tiresome.

Dominguez waddled in through the back door, looking very pleased with himself. His belly heaved in exertion as he stopped in front of DeLeon.

"Señor?" He was out of breath.

"What is it, Dominguez?" DeLeon replied.

Dominguez opened his hand. "I thought you might like to have this." He held out a wallet. "I took it from the dead man."

"Put it on the table," DeLeon said, without interest.

Dominguez did as he was told. "Señor?"

"What is it now, Dominguez?" DeLeon said testily. *Mother Mary help me if I ever need a real policeman,* DeLeon thought to himself.

Dominguez unbuttoned his shirt pocket, took out a plastic card and a key, and handed them to DeLeon. "I also found these on the body."

DeLeon's indifference faded as he looked at the card. It was a keyless entry card to a storage compound in El Paso. He turned over the metal locker key. A number was stamped on it.

DeLeon smiled. "How much money was in the wallet?"

Dominguez's grin faded. "Four hundred dollars, *patrón,"* Dominguez admitted.

"Is it securely in your pocket?"

"Yes, Don Enrique."

"I will double it. You have done me a service."

Dominguez's grin returned, filled with gratitude. "I am glad you are pleased."

"I am. Now go and wait for Carlos. Send him to me as soon as he arrives."

Dominguez left, almost running. DeLeon turned the card over in his hand. Truly, could it be so easy? Was he holding the key to a fortune that did not have to be bought and paid for? When Carlos arrived he would be sent to investigate. Perhaps Eddie, the charlatan *jorobado,* had brought him luck after all. If true, it would make an amusing story; one he would enjoy telling.

DeLeon's laugh was loud enough to make some

nearby customers pause and look in his direction.

Benton's car was not in the motel parking lot, and there was no response when Meehan knocked at the door of the room. Sara was on the floor of the backseat of the Cherokee, gagged and covered with a blanket. The heavy traffic of hookers with their customers made sticking around unwise. Meehan decided to cross the border into Mexico, tuck Sara safely away, and come back to look for Benton.

Meehan bypassed the direct route to Juárez and crossed the border at Santa Teresa. The road to Casas Grandes, a dirt washboard that intersected a main highway, was lightly traveled. He turned east toward Juárez before reaching the highway, staying on farm roads and skirting the few little settlements south of the city. To the north, the runway lights of the Juárez airport came into view, shimmering in geometric rows. When he was parallel to the Rio Grande, Meehan cut over to a paved highway that passed through several small villages. He turned off at two barren ridges that loomed up to a plateau above the river bottom. The road dwindled to a set of ruts in the dirt and dropped suddenly toward the river. His headlights lit up crumbling walls, old foundations, and deteriorated stone fences. Across the river, low-lying west Texas mountains showed a wrinkled, windswept face to the night sky.

The ruins of the hacienda, protected in a hollow against the ridge, surveyed a narrow strip of bosque at the banks of the Rio Grande. Meehan stopped in front of a rock stable that encircled a stone granary.

He found a flashlight in the glove box, pulled Sara out of the vehicle, and removed the gag.

Sara looked at the granary. Chiseled stone steps twisted around the outside of the tower. At the base, an entrance wide enough for a horse and wagon stood like an open black mouth. The house, an old hacienda undergoing restoration, was roofless. Scaffolding surrounded the walls, and a parapet had been rebuilt with new bricks. Freshly peeled vigas—beams for the ceiling—were secured to the walls, and rough wood framing defined new openings for doors and windows.

"This is interesting," Sara said. "Is it a new theme park?"

Meehan smiled. "It's more like a nature center. Let me show you around. There's one attraction I think you'll really like." Sara looked pale and dispirited, in spite of the attempt at humor. She had softened up nicely, Meehan thought.

He turned her by the shoulders, pushed her against the hood of the car, and cut the rope around her ankles. She spun, kicked for his groin, and missed, catching him on the shin instead. He slapped her in the mouth with the butt end of the flashlight. She fell against the Cherokee, stunned but conscious.

Meehan grabbed her by the hair and wrenched her neck. "You think you're a tough little bitch, don't you?" he snarled.

"No," Sara answered. She could feel the blood in her mouth. "I'm not a bitch at all."

"Move, cunt." He pushed her along in front of him, through the remnants of a kitchen, past a crumbling adobe fireplace, to a stone staircase that descended to an underground room. Sara balked at the top step, and he jabbed her in the kidney with the flashlight. She stumbled forward, Meehan holding her by the handcuffs to keep her from falling. Bags of concrete on pallets, milled lumber, and construction equipment filled the underground room. DeLeon's restoration project was further along than Meehan had realized. It meant he would need to deal quickly with Sara to avoid any chance encounters with the construction crew.

He prodded her through the large room, past a pile of tarpaulins and rags, to a massive wooden door anchored in the bedrock by thick iron hinges. He raised the heavy latch and pulled the door open. The air, cool and stale-smelling, rushed out. Sara recoiled, so he jabbed her again in a kidney to force her to move.

"Get in," he ordered, pointing the beam of the flashlight into the pitch-black room. He pushed her to her knees and lit a kerosene lamp that hung from the low ceiling. "Stand up and turn around," he said when the lamp was burning.

Sara did as she was told. The rock walls of the tiny room were uneven and black with soot. The jagged ceiling was inches above her head. The lamp cast a pale glow. "Is this what you wanted to show me?" she asked.

Meehan nodded and poked at some rotting boards with the toe of his shoe. A dozen insects scurried into view.

"Scorpions?" Sara asked.

"Big ones," Meehan confirmed, lifting the lamp off the hook and setting it on the ground. "Heat attracts them. Especially body heat. Some of them drop from the ceiling. Keep your chin up."

She stared at Meehan with loathing.

He stepped back, swung the door shut, and threw the latch. "I'll try to get back before the lamp runs out of fuel," he called to her. "If not, keep yourself entertained."

"Screw you," Sara replied.

She barely heard Meehan's receding laughter as he walked away, her attention riveted on the ceiling. The thought of scorpions falling on her made her shudder. She saw an insect dart from under a board and squashed it with her boot. She killed several more before she realized that she was crying.

Eddie sat in his car feeling frustrated. Bordertown Storage Company was a series of long, rectangular concrete buildings surrounded by a high chain-link fence topped off with concertina wire. Finding it was no sweat, but locating the locker Benton had rented would be an entirely different matter.

He coasted to the motorized gate and stopped at the curb. The manager's office inside the fence was closed for the night. The sign on the door advertised twenty-four-hour access, but there was no way in unless he climbed the fence and crawled over the concertina wire. He drove slowly past the gate and looked down the long rows of buildings, hoping somebody was inside who would let him in. The aisles, wide enough for semitrailers to maneuver in, were empty.

He went back to the front gate and wrote down the phone number on the company sign. Back at the bar he would call, get somebody to come out to open up, and wait for Kerney. He turned the car around and headed back toward the barrio.

Leaving the Little Turtle, Carlos was in fine spirits. Instead of having him beaten, as he'd expected, DeLeon had given him an entry card and a locker key and ordered him to go to El Paso to search a storage unit. A careful man by nature, Carlos took his customary precautions. He drove past the business without stopping, and circled behind two large warehouses opposite the storage units. He parked in the darkness, took out his binoculars, and trained them on the fenced compound. He studied each aisle thoroughly. All seemed quiet. He would wait ten minutes before entering, just as a precaution. He put his thumb in his mouth and adjusted his upper plate.

Headlights appeared on the pavement, and a car came into view, traveling slowly. It stopped in front of storage compound, motor running. He picked up the binoculars, but the glare of the lights by the gate blocked his view into the car. After a few minutes, the car moved away. Soon the car came back, and Carlos picked up the driver in his glasses. He grinned to himself when he recognized Eddie, the phony *jorobado*.

He put aside the binoculars and reached for his gun. It would be interesting to talk to Eddie again, Carlos thought.

Eddie's car made a U-turn, and Carlos started his engine, headlights off. He let Eddie travel a short distance away from the bright lights before he made his move. He accelerated, jumped the curb, and rammed into the rear of Eddie's vehicle. The collision was harder than Carlos anticipated. Both cars recoiled, tires skidding, as Eddie responded to the sudden impact by hitting the brakes. Carlos was thrown forward, the seat belt tightening across his chest. He only had seconds in which to act. He got out, ran to Eddie's car, pulled open the door, and stuck his pistol in Eddie's face.

"My little *jorobado* friend," Carlos growled. "It is very nice to see you again." He brought the barrel of his weapon down on the front of Eddie's head. As Eddie slumped forward, he caught him, then pulled him from the car and carried him into the darkness between two buildings. He dumped Eddie next to a propane gas tank and went back to the automobiles stalled in the middle of the street. He kicked the pieces of broken glass toward the gutter and moved the cars to the curb, parking them close together to hide the damage.

Eddie was still unconscious when he returned. He rifled his pockets, found a wallet and a small leather case, and used his cigarette lighter to inspect the contents. The case contained a military police badge and an identification card with Eddie's picture. The hunchback was a United States Army criminal investigator. Carlos grunted. Don Enrique would be very pleased to have Eddie back. And pleased with Carlos, also.

The wallet was less interesting, except for the money. Carlos extracted and counted the bills: over seven hundred dollars. Masquerading as a beggar was profitable. He put the money into his coat pocket.

He lit a cigarette and nudged Eddie with the toe of his shoe to see if he was awake. Eddie did not move. Using his lighter, he inspected Eddie's face. He was still unconscious. The blow to the head had sliced the scalp. A flap of skin dangled at the hairline on Eddie's forehead, and blood trickled down his face.

As soon as Eddie stirred, Carlos sat him upright against the propane tank. He wanted Eddie to see what was going to happen to him. He placed Eddie's hands palm down on the pavement of the parking lot and waited for his eyes to open. When they did, Carlos stomped on each hand with the heel of his shoe.

Kerney stopped in front of the bar. Before he could get out of the truck, a fat hooker with a round, cherubic face leaned inside the open window. She wore a sleeveless dress that showed tattoos on both of her substantial arms.

"No thanks," Kerney said, pushing against the door to move her out of the way. Her bulk made it impossible for him to budge her.

"Are you Kerney?" the hooker asked.

"Yes," Kerney answered, puzzled.

"Eddie asked me to give you a message."

"What is it?"

"He said you'd pay me."

Kerney didn't believe her but decided not to quibble. "How much?"

"Fifty dollars," the hooker announced.

Kerney dug out his wallet and handed over the money. It was the last of his emergency cash. "What's the message?" he demanded.

The hooker pulled down the top of her dress and stuck the bills inside her push-up brassiere. There was a tattoo of the Virgin Mary above her left breast. "He went to the self-storage units. He said if he wasn't back when you got here, you could find him there."

"What self-storage units?" Kerney asked.

The hooker pointed down the street. The fat underside of her arm jiggled. "Bordertown Storage. You can't miss it. Look for the lights."

Kerney nodded, clutched, and put the truck in gear. His right foot missed the accelerator and the engine stalled. He was having a hell of a time with the leg.

"Want me to drive you there for another fifty dollars?" the hooker asked with a grin.

Kerney glared at her. "No thanks." He restarted the engine and drove down the street behind a slow string of low-riders. He was annoyed at Eddie. Déjà vu all over again, he thought. Another cop who couldn't stay put.

Away from the clip joints and motels, rows of assembly plants, sweatshops, and warehouses lined the street. Beacons from the smelter stacks across a field blinked warnings to aircraft in the night sky. The glow of a bank of mercury vapor lights announced the presence of Borderland Storage. Kerney drove past two parked cars and stopped at the locked front gate. There was no sign of Eddie. He cruised for a block before swinging back for another pass. His headlights picked up fresh skid marks and small bits of reflective plastic in the middle of the street near the cars. One car had a Chihuahua license plate. He couldn't see the other license plate, but there was damage to both vehicles. That was enough for Kerney.

He turned onto a side street, killed the engine, and got his pistol from the glove box. His knee barely tolerated the shock as he trotted to the cars. He was halfway there when he heard Eddie scream.

CHAPTER

12

There was something wet and sticky in Eddie's left eye. He blinked, squinted, looked up, and saw Carlos standing over him. Before he could move, he felt a horrible pain in his right hand. He screamed, and screamed again as Carlos stomped on his other hand.

Gasping, he shook his head, trying to stay conscious. "You bastard." It was all he could manage. His hands felt cemented to the asphalt.

"You speak pretty good English for a *jorobado*," Carlos said, lighting another cigarette, waiting for Eddie to pull himself together. "What are you doing here, Eddie?"

"Fuck off," Eddie answered, trying to move his right hand.

Carlos hit him in the mouth. Eddie's head bounced off the tank. He sucked in a deep breath and waited for the throbbing to stop.

"Are you working with that gringo Kerney?" Carlos asked.

Eddie shook his head. "No."

"You're a lying piece of shit," Carlos retorted, balling his hand to a beefy fist.

Eddie turned his head so Carlos wouldn't hit him in the mouth again. The punch caught him high on the cheek. Eddie winced and sucked in more air. Blood made it impossible to see out of his left eye. "Finished?" he asked through clenched teeth.

"Just starting, you *puta*. Tell me why you're here."

"I'll tell you," Eddie replied. "Just don't hit me again, all right?"

Carlos relaxed and nodded approvingly. Kerney stood behind Carlos, at the corner of the warehouse, with a finger at his lips.

"Give me a minute, will you?" Eddie asked.

"Sure, but make it fast. I don't have time to play with you."

Eddie coughed and mumbled something under his breath.

"What?" Carlos asked.

"I said fuck you," Eddie replied as Kerney brought the pistol butt down on Carlos's head.

Eddie liked it a lot when Kerney hit Carlos again. *"Madre de Dios,* I'm glad to see you," he said, staring at Carlos's prone body.

Kerney reached for his hand to help him to his feet. "Not the hands," Eddie barked. "He broke all my fingers."

Kerney knelt down and looked. It was too dark to

see the extent of the damage. Kerney grabbed Eddie under the arms, lifted him to his feet, and propped him against the propane tank.

"I think I'm going to faint," Eddie said.

"Hold on." Kerney took out a handkerchief, pushed the flap of loose skin back into place against Eddie's forehead, and dabbed the blood from his eye.

"Thanks," Eddie said weakly.

Kerney kept his hand on Eddie's chest to hold him upright. He could feel Eddie's rapid heartbeat. "How's your head?"

"Spinning."

"Can you stand without falling?"

Eddie, eyes closed, waited for the sensation to subside before he answered. "Of course I can."

"Are you sure?"

Eddie opened his eyes and made a face. His teeth hurt. "Just don't ask me to walk yet."

Kerney let go, retrieved Eddie's wallet and badge case from the asphalt, and searched Carlos. He found a key, a card, and some money in a coat pocket. He used Carlos's cigarette lighter to inspect the stuff.

"What have you got?" Eddie asked.

"A way into the storage compound." He held up the folded bills. "Your money?"

"Army funds," Eddie said. "Keep it for me."

Kerney nodded, used his belt to tie Carlos's hands behind his back, flipped him over, and positioned him within kicking distance of Eddie's foot. "I'll be back in a minute. If Carlos wakes up while I'm gone, kick him in the nuts."

"Gladly," Eddie replied.

It took only a few minutes for Kerney to return, cuff Carlos, and dump him in the bed of the truck. Under the glare of the headlights he sat Eddie down and inspected his hands. The knuckles were fractured. He bandaged them with tape from his first-aid kit while Eddie winced and refused to look.

"How are they?" he asked when Kerney finished.

"Broken," Kerney answered, cleaning Eddie's head wound and covering it with a Band-Aid.

"I know that. How bad?" Eddie demanded.

Kerney considered what to say as he pulled Eddie to his feet. "You'll be fine after the doctors work on you," he promised. "I've seen a lot worse."

"You're not lying to me?"

"No, I'm not. Let's get you to a hospital."

"No way," Eddie said gamely. "First I want to see what's in that storage unit."

"You need a doctor."

"So do you, for chrissake," Eddie retorted.

"Are you sure you're up to it?"

"Yeah. Let's go look. I want to see if all the shit you told me is real."

"So do I," Kerney agreed. He left Eddie alone in the glare of the headlights, got behind the wheel of the truck, and opened the passenger door. If Eddie couldn't walk under his own steam, he would take him directly to the hospital. Eddie stood with a disgusted look on his face, his bandaged hands cradled at his chest. He wobbled to the truck and climbed in. Kerney reached over and closed the door.

Kerney opened the overhead garage door to the storage unit, turned on the lights, and drove his truck inside. Scattered around the room were sealed crates, packing boxes, and wardrobe trunks. He got a tire iron from the truck, walked to a large wooden crate, and pried it open while Eddie stood next to him.

"Madre de Dios," Eddie said. The crate was filled with dozens of antique Army rifles, all in mint condition.

"Isn't that something?" Kerney asked with amazement.

They moved on and found military uniforms by the dozen, boxes filled with spurs, saddle blankets, and headgear, and crates brimming with sabers, pistols, and scabbards. One large box held cavalry saddles by the score. Reading Gutierrez's list was one thing, but actually seeing the cache was mind-boggling.

The urge to open everything was almost irresistible. Kerney forced himself to stop, checked on Carlos, who hadn't stirred, and dragged him out of the bed of the truck. "Have you seen enough?" he asked Eddie as he propped Carlos against a packing crate.

"Amazing," Eddie replied. "It's like something from a movie."

Carlos started to come around. He groaned and looked at Kerney with hate-filled eyes. "You hit me pretty hard, gringo," he said.

"You'll live," Kerney said.

"You won't," Carlos replied, glancing at Eddie.

Kerney lifted Carlos's chin with the point of the tire iron. "Pay attention to me, Carlos. No threats. Cooperate and I won't fuck you up. Give me the names of Benton's partners."

"Eat shit," he answered.

Kerney poked the tire iron into Carlos's Adam's apple, cutting the skin. Blood trickled from the wound. "I'll make a deal with you, Carlos. Talk and I won't rip out your larynx." He dug the tip in farther, and Carlos started choking.

Unable to speak, Carlos nodded his head.

"Who were Benton's partners?"

"I know only one other," Carlos answered. "A gringo, like you."

"His name?" Kerney increased the pressure slightly.

"I don't know. Señor DeLeon did business with him privately."

"What kind of business?" Kerney demanded, pressing a bit harder at Carlos's Adam's apple.

"I don't know," Carlos gurgled.

A voice behind Kerney spoke. "He's telling you the truth, Lieutenant."

Kerney pivoted to find James Meehan looking at him over the barrel of a pistol. For some reason, Kerney wasn't surprised. "Captain Meehan."

"Drop the tire iron," Meehan ordered.

Kerney did as he was told.

Meehan's eyes found Eddie; another unexpected factor in the equation. He glanced at the bandages on Tapia's hands. "It seems you've hurt yourself, Corporal."

"I'm just fine, Captain," Eddie replied, trying not to look stunned.

Meehan scanned the room for any more surprises. "Where's Benton?" he demanded.

Eddie and Kerney said nothing.

"Dead," Carlos finally replied.

The information stung Meehan. The complications never seemed to end. He'd have to adjust again, but he could do it. "Who killed him?" he asked.

"I did," Kerney answered, before Eddie could reply.

"I'm impressed. Benton was very proficient."

"Where is Sara?" Kerney demanded, changing the subject.

"Safely tucked away," Meehan answered. "You have something of mine."

"I can't help you."

Meehan cocked his weapon. "Don't tempt me. You've caused me enough problems. The coins and letters. Where are they?"

"I'll trade for them."

"Is Sara worth that much to you?"

"Whatever it takes."

"It's possible," Meehan allowed. "Let me think about it. Stand up, Carlos." He watched him struggle to his feet. "Why are you here?"

"Señor DeLeon sent me," Carlos replied, trying to buy time and think things through. The *patrón* would not want him to say too much.

"Meaning?"

Carlos hesitated. "We found a key on Benton's body. I came to take a look."

Meehan chuckled. "Such a den of thieves." Sara's creative ploy had almost worked. One more score to settle with the bitch. "I'll sort that out with Enrique later. Remove his handcuffs," he told Kerney.

Hands free, Carlos rubbed his wrists.

"Walk to me," Meehan ordered. Carlos approached. "I need your help."

"What do you want me to do?"

"I want you to keep Kerney company."

Carlos nodded.

"Good," Meehan said. "You've got your deal, Kerney. I'll exchange Sara for the coins and letters. Carlos will go with you."

"Agreed," Kerney replied.

"What about Eddie?" Carlos asked.

"He stays here."

"DeLeon wants him," Carlos said. "Alive."

"That can be arranged."

"Where do I meet you?" Carlos asked.

"DeLeon's hacienda. Be there in three hours," Meehan ordered. It would give him time to dispose of Sara. Then he would kill Kerney, if Carlos was too stupid not to do it himself, and turn Eddie over to DeLeon. Everything would be tidied up and there would be nothing left to investigate.

"I'll be there," Carlos said.

"You can't drive worth a shit," Carlos said. He sat next to Kerney, a handgun stuck in the gringo's rib cage, watching him trying to work the brake pedal with his right foot. The truck lurched to a stop at a red light.

Ramming Eddie's car had damaged the radiator of his vehicle, which forced Carlos to ride with the gringo in the truck.

Carlos was not in a good mood. His neck and head hurt, Kerney's piss-poor driving made him nervous, and he wasn't sure if he had done the right thing in agreeing to help Meehan. The only happy thought was that he would kill the gringo as soon as he turned over the coins and letters.

The traffic light turned green, and Kerney deliberately stalled the truck. The street was completely empty. He restarted the engine and let it idle. "Think about it, Carlos. DeLeon doesn't need Meehan anymore. You can give him the whole package, free and clear."

"And all you want is the woman?"

"That's all I want."

"She must be some piece of ass," Carlos suggested.

"Call DeLeon," Kerney replied, nodding at the pay phone next to a bus stop shelter. He coasted to the curb and stopped. "Let him decide."

"Keep driving," Carlos said.

"Don't be bullheaded. Meehan is just using you."

"I don't know," Carlos said, unsure.

"Let DeLeon decide," Kerney repeated.

He should call Don Enrique and get further orders, Carlos thought, looking at the pay phone. Things were getting confusing. Probably the *patrón* will want all of them killed, he speculated. That was okay with Carlos. "Get out of the truck."

Kerney opened his door.

"My side," Carlos told him, his pistol pointed at Kerney's right ear.

Kerney gave him an apologetic smile. "I can't. My leg. Sorry."

Carlos hesitated. "Benton fucked you up a little, no? Okay. I'll follow you out. Keep your hands where I can see them."

"No problem." He turned toward the door, hands above the steering wheel, and watched Carlos's reflection in the windshield. As Carlos jockeyed around the gearshift, he shifted his concentration for an instant. Kerney spun back and slammed his elbow into Carlos's nose. Carlos's head bounced off the back of the seat, and Kerney hit him again with his elbow, this time in the mouth. As his head rebounded a second time, Kerney pounded his face into the dashboard. Carlos's false teeth flew out of his mouth and landed on the floorboard.

Kerney took the pistol from Carlos's hand, pushed him back against the seat, and raised an eyelid. Carlos was out cold, with a smashed nose and his bottom front teeth embedded in his lip. He removed the ignition key and went to the pay phone.

The military police dispatcher at Fort Bliss didn't want to believe a cockeyed story about lost treasure and a wounded Army corporal, so Kerney demanded the man talk to Major Curry while he stayed on the line. Within two minutes the dispatcher was back, asking for instructions. Kerney gave him directions, told him to send troops, medics, and an ambulance for Eddie on the double, and hung up.

Carlos was still unconscious. Kerney needed a way to make him spill his guts quickly. There was no time for a drawn-out interrogation.

Sara shook her head furiously to dislodge the scorpion that fell into her hair. It crawled down her cheek and stung her before she could grind her face against the wall and mash it. The sting was painful. The flame of the kerosene lamp flickered as the fuel burned low, making it hard to see the insects. She had stopped counting how many she had killed. She could feel the remains of the squashed bug on her face. The blood in her mouth from Meehan's blow felt like dried paste. Cold, she couldn't stop shivering as she continued to lose body heat. She hovered over the lamp and crunched another scorpion into oblivion. Staying alert was the key to survival.

She started pacing the length of the cell. It was an old wine cellar that had been used as a jail cell many years ago. There were Spanish names, dates, and inscriptions scratched into the walls. She kept searching for something to use as a weapon. She wanted Meehan to come back, but not until she could find a way to kill him.

At the end of the Southern Pacific railroad yard where lines of old boxcars sat on spurs, Kerney rolled Carlos out of the truck and got busy. Down the line was an old brick engine barn built like a horseshoe with a series of huge bay doorways that yawned at the night.

Carlos, stripped naked, hog-tied, and lying face-down on the railroad ties, looked ridiculous. A rope ran from around Carlos's chest to the rear truck bumper. Kerney had a clear run of several hundred feet before the spur dead-ended.

He bent over Carlos and listened to his curses. The broken nose and missing false teeth made Carlos sound like Bullwinkle with a Mexican accent.

"You son of a whore," Carlos said. "Your mother eats sheep shit." Carlos couldn't breathe very well, so he stopped for air.

"Finished?" Kerney asked.

"You better kill me, gringo."

"I'm going to do that, Carlos. But you won't have any nuts left before you die. That I promise you." He gave Carlos a friendly pat on the head and walked toward the truck.

"Wait a minute," Carlos said, suddenly worried.

"No time," Kerney said.

"Wait," Carlos said, starting to feel panicked.

Kerney got in the truck and slammed the door. He cranked the engine and drove fifty feet down the tracks. Even at a snail's pace, the undercarriage pitched and rolled over the railroad ties. Through the rearview mirror he could see Carlos bouncing along. He stopped before any serious amount of skin could be stripped off and went to check the damage. Carlos had his head pulled up to keep his face from smashing into the ties.

"Anything broken yet?" Kerney asked.

Carlos grunted. His chest hurt. There were cinders embedded in his flesh from his knees to his shoulders. His testicles were burning. It felt as if a grinder were scouring off his skin.

"I'll pick up the pace a bit." Again, Kerney patted Carlos on the head.

Carlos decided Kerney would turn him into a deballed vegetable. "Wait," he pleaded.

"I'm waiting for the directions to the hacienda," Kerney replied.

"Okay," Carlos said, and the directions tumbled out.

When Carlos finished talking, Kerney cut him loose from the bumper, rolled him off the tracks into a pile of cinders, and told him to be patient, help was on the way.

Lying in the cinders, Carlos renewed his insults. Kerney stuffed Carlos's shorts into his mouth to shut him up.

On the way to the border, Kerney called the military police again. This time, Kerney didn't have to wait to be taken seriously. He told the duty officer where to find Carlos, asked about Eddie, learned Tapia was en route to the hospital, a squad of military policemen were at the storage unit, and Tom Curry had arrived from Las Cruces by helicopter.

The major wanted to talk to him right away. Kerney hung up before Curry could get on the line.

Sara's shaking intensified, and she kept moving, trying to stay warm. She felt woozy and disoriented—all the classic signs of shock and hypothermia. It had taken a long time to maneuver a board against the wall and break an end piece with the heel of her boot. A hand-forged iron nail protruded from the wood. The board kept slipping from her fingers as she tried to pick it up with her hands cuffed at her back. She crouched down again, got a firm grip, and stood up, clenching the board in a hand.

She began pacing again to fight off the shivers, stopping to scrape the rotting wood against the wall to loosen the nail. Finally, it broke free and clattered to the floor. She searched blindly behind her back to retrieve it, her fingers stiff and cold. When she had it she could tell it was a good size, four or five inches long. If she could keep it out of sight and strike at the right time, it would do some damage. All she needed was the opportunity.

She heard footsteps approaching. The latch squeaked and the door swung open.

"It's time, Sara," Meehan said. He pulled her roughly out of the cell into the room.

A kerosene lamp by the pile of tarps lit up the

room. He walked her over and pushed her down on the pile. She got quickly to her feet and tried to rush him. He knocked her down with a swipe across the face.

He walked up to her. "I always thought you liked your sex rough. Is that the way you want to play it?"

She glared at him. "Is that the only way you can get it up, Jim?"

He reached down and slapped her. "Don't ever say that to me."

Kerney crawled as silently as possible, unable to avoid dislodging pebbles and loose earth as he moved up the hill. Each sound made him flinch in fear of discovery. He inched along and stopped behind a melted adobe wall. The terrain made it impossible for him to approach from any other direction. The ridge behind the hacienda, a steep embankment, would have been too difficult to climb down. He skirted the ridge on foot and started crawling when he reached the ruins of the settlement along the riverbank. With the moon up it was the only way to stay undetected.

Fifty yards above him was the hacienda. Adjacent to it, hard against the ridge, were the remains of a small village chapel, and a granary tower that looked like a fortress turret. The site, an excellent defensive position, commanded a clear field of fire down the hillside. The rock corral and the thick walls of the hacienda hid any sign of movement.

Sara's Cherokee was in front of the hacienda.

Kerney pulled himself away from the protection of a low wall and crawled on. He heard no sounds from above. He closed the distance cautiously, fighting the urge to get to his feet and run.

Scrambling to her feet, Sara watched Meehan unzip his trousers and show her his erection. He moved between her and the stairs to keep her from bolting. Behind him she saw moonlight and stars in the night sky. He aimed the pistol at her belly.

"Turn around, Sara," he ordered. Her face was puffy, her lips and her eyes were red. Meehan liked what he saw.

"No," Sara said.

He waved the barrel of the gun. "Turn around or I'll pistolwhip you."

She turned and tightened her fingers around the nail, hoping that he wouldn't see it. He was breathing rapidly as he came near. He kicked her legs apart and pulled her blouse out of her jeans.

"Loosen the cuffs," Sara pleaded, as Meehan undid the button of her jeans and opened the zipper with his free hand. The muzzle of the gun dug into her side.

He laughed in reply, slipped his hand under her panties, and pulled her jeans and panties down to her knees. She waited until he put the gun away, grabbed her hips with both hands, and rubbed himself against her fanny. Twisting suddenly, she drove the nail into his groin and felt it penetrate.

Meehan yelled and pulled away. She spun, kicked, and caught him on the thigh. It threw him off balance, but he didn't fall. Sara smashed her forehead into his face. He went down, reaching for his pistol.

"Bitch!" Meehan snarled. He held his crotch where the nail had gashed him.

"Fuck you, Meehan," she said. Her foot was next to the lantern. She kicked it, and liquid flames spread across the floor, lapping at his feet. Pulling her jeans up as much as she could, she stumbled toward the steps. Meehan would have to shoot her in the back to stop her now.

"Stop!" Meehan shouted.

She kept going, waiting for the impact of the bullets. She wanted to see the night sky one more time. Halfway up the steps, a figure appeared and a hand knocked her down.

"Roll!" Kerney commanded as he dropped into a prone position.

She heard the sound of Kerney's weapon the instant she recognized his voice. He wasn't dead! Meehan was on his feet, his pistol aimed at her chest. She pitched down the steps as Meehan staggered and returned fire. Two rounds ricocheted above her head.

Kerney fired again and again, and Sara watched Meehan fall.

The tarps were burning, and flames lit up the room. Sara stared into the fire without moving until Kerney's hand brushed her cheek.

"Don't touch me," she said, pressing her face to the floor.

"Okay. Okay," he said gently, taking his hand away. Her face was cold to the touch, and her body was racked with shivering spasms.

"Don't look at me," she demanded.

"I won't. Relax. It'll be all right." Meehan

moaned, and Kerney went to check him out. He picked up Meehan's handgun and looked at his wounds; he had taken two rounds in the belly and another in the hip.

Sara rolled herself into a ball, knees pulled up to her chest, and stared at Meehan. She wanted him to burn in the fire that closed in on his body. She felt Kerney unlock the handcuffs. Painfully, she brought her arms from behind her back.

"Did you kill him?" she asked.

"He's still alive," Kerney answered. "Stay put." He returned to Meehan and dragged him by the feet up the stone steps. He got a blanket from the Cherokee, covered Sara, walked her outside, and gave her Meehan's pistol. "Are you okay?" he asked.

"I'm fine," she answered flatly. The weapon felt good in her hand.

"Did he . . . ?"

"No. Almost."

"Can you use the pistol?"

Her laugh was lifeless. "You bet I can."

"I'll get my truck and take you to the hospital."

She shook her head violently. "I don't want anyone to see me this way."

"Whatever you say."

Meehan didn't move while Kerney went for his truck. Sara gripped the pistol with both hands, hoping he would, so she could shoot him. The flames had spread to the lumber in the cellar, and waves of heat rose up from the underground room. The warmth felt wonderful.

Meehan was dead when Kerney returned. He took Sara to the truck, where the heater was going full blast. She sat directly in front of the vent, her teeth chattering, thinking that she never wanted to be cold again.

She said nothing until she noticed something strange on the floorboard. "What's that?" she asked.

Kerney turned on the interior light. Sara's face was pale and drawn. Still clutching Meehan's weapon, she looked at him intensely. There were bruises under her eye, on her cheek, and next to her mouth.

"What?" Kerney asked back.

She pointed the pistol at the floorboard. Carlos's upper plate was on the mat. "That."

"False teeth. They belong to a guy called Carlos. He told me how to find you."

"So that's how you did it."

"Yes, ma'am."

"My name is Sara, not ma'am."

"Can I ask you a favor, Sara?"

"What is it?"

"Could you point the pistol somewhere else?"

Sara looked at the gun in her hand, nodded, and put it on the seat between them. She bit her lip, and Kerney could see tears in the corners of her eyes. She turned her face away and said nothing more. She didn't protest when he turned her over to the doctors at a hospital in El Paso. He watched the ER team wheel her into an examining room before he called Major Curry.

Finished with Curry, he hung up and turned to find a place to sit down. The leg gave out and he fell to his knees in the corridor.

When Kerney awoke, he was in a hospital bed. Andy Baca stood over him, a worried look on his face.

"How's Eddie?" Kerney asked.

"Out of surgery and doing well," Andy answered. "The doctors said he should have full use of his fingers."

"Good. And Sara?"

"They're discharging her today. She's been asking about you."

"She's okay?" Kerney demanded.

"Fine. She's a pistol," Andy responded.

"I know it." He rolled over and went back to sleep.

CHAPTER

13

---- · ---- · ----

Two weeks passed before the Army sent Sammy's body home. Terry called Kerney as soon as the casket arrived. The family had gathered by the time Kerney got to Maria's home. Rows of shoes lined the front step and the path to the door. Kerney pulled off his boots and went inside. The living-room furniture had been removed, and a casket in the center of the room was surrounded by two circles of mourners sitting on the floor. Kerney squeezed in next to an old man, who gave him a somber nod and returned to his silent prayers. Terry caught his eye and smiled.

A trio of women entered from the kitchen and placed trays of food at the foot of the casket. An elder, dressed in soft deerskin and velvet, rose and began offering food to the guests. After serving everyone, he put the remaining food in a woven basket.

A second, identical basket was circulated for the collection of mementos of Sammy's life. Terry contributed his son's Army service ribbons. Maria added Sammy's paintbrushes. Hoping it was acceptable, Kerney put a snapshot of Soldier, the mustang named in honor of Sammy, in the container. The old man next to him grunted his approval. The casket was opened and both baskets were placed inside. Then the silence ended and the meal began.

The family ate and told stories of Sammy's life; anecdotes, filled with detail, that lifted the somber mood. The wake continued until dawn, when Kerney went home to change for the burial service at the Santa Fe National Cemetery.

He got to the cemetery as the funeral procession was coming slowly down Tesuque Hill, led by tribal police cars. The honor guard assembled in front of the covered pallet as Sammy's coffin was carried up the hill.

Kerney hung back at the fringe of the crowd that surrounded the canopy and searched for a glimpse of Sara. Some military brass had arrived in a missile range staff car, a bird colonel and a young lieutenant. Sara, Eddie Tapia, and Major Curry were not with them.

The ceremony was brief. With the coffin on the pallet, Maria, Terry, and Sammy's grandparents stood at one side under the awning. Taps, played by two buglers spaced widely apart, created a mournful echo. The traditional rifle salute was fired by National Guardsmen in dress blues. The ritual finished with the slow, precise folding of the American flag from the coffin and the deliberate hand salutes as the flag passed to the colonel, who made the final presentation of the colors to Maria. The detail retired, and Sammy's casket was placed on a wagon pulled by a tractor to an open grave.

At the grave, Maria clutched the flag, tears flowing freely, with Terry close by her side. The tribal elder waited until the casket was in the ground, then, kneeling, placed a small pottery water jug in the grave and broke it with a stick. He sprinkled corn pollen on the coffin and nodded at the assembly.

Sammy was now ready to start his journey. The services were over.

During the next four days, Kerney went daily to the pueblo. Maria and Terry stayed together at her house, sleeping in blankets on the floor of the empty living room. She could not be alone in the house until Sammy's spirit was gone. On the last night the elder returned and purged the house of Sammy's spirit so he would have no reason to return.

Kerney waited outside with people he now knew by name. When Maria and Terry finally emerged, both looked tired but less troubled. He hugged each of them. Maria kissed him gently on the cheek and patted him with affection.

"You must come back to visit," she said. "Often."

"I will."

"Promise?"

"Yes."

Terry's hug was bearlike. "I need to talk to you," Terry said in his ear.

"If it's about the money, forget it," Kerney replied.

"It is. I want you to take it back."

He shook his head firmly. "I've been paid. I'll explain later."

Terry released him, and they shook hands.

The leaves in the tall cottonwood trees rustled in the night air. Terry and Maria were saying goodbye to the last of their guests. From the edge of the plaza, Kerney turned back to look and saw Terry hug Maria and walk off into the darkness of the night, Maria left alone under the porch light. It gave him a sad feeling.

Back home, Kerney sat on the corral rail and studied the night sky. The stars were pinpoints of soft, quivering light. Quinn, his landlord, had decided to sell the ranch. It wouldn't take long for it to be gobbled up, probably to be subdivided into ranchettes by a developer.

Except for two pieces of mail, there had been no contact with anybody involved in the investigation. Andy sent him a check for a month's pay and a note that said he liked the idea of using him on special cases and wanted to talk about it. The second envelope was from the Department of the Army. It contained a government warrant for twenty thousand dollars. The accompanying letter explained that it was for professional services provided to the provost marshal at White Sands Missile Range. Kerney put the money in the bank.

Soldier nudged Kerney's hand, looking for another treat. He scratched the horse's muzzle and looked across the volcanic rift at the clouds parked over Santa Fe. City lights created a rosy glow in the underbelly of the fluffy cumulus clouds.

Since returning home, Kerney had taught Soldier

how to turn and guide with the touch of a rein against his neck. Now he responded easily to a one-handed cue. Soldier's gait had smoothed out and he wasn't skittish anymore. It was time to take him to his new home.

"So what are you going to do?" Dale Jennings asked, watching as Kerney opened the door to the horse trailer.

"Hell if I know," Kerney replied. He walked Soldier out of the trailer and put him in the corral. Soldier trotted over to the bay.

"Move down here," Dale suggested. "I still need a partner. You can have the foreman's cottage."

Kerney gave Dale a sidelong glance.

"I guess not," Dale noted. "So what do you want to do?"

"Right now? How about a trail ride? Are you up for it?"

Dale rolled his tongue over his teeth. "Anyplace particular in mind?"

Kerney tilted his chin toward the mountains on the missile range.

"You're kidding."

"Why not?"

Dale put both arms on the top railing of the corral and studied the two horses. After a long pause he swung around, leaned against the corral, and grinned at Kerney. "The bay could stand to shed a few pounds."

Using an old horse trail, Dale and Kerney reached the 7-Bar-K in short order, even with Dale's frequent stops to reminisce. Kerney had to break him away from the sight of the space harbor and the test facilities dotting the basin; Dale was shaking his head in incredulity as he remounted.

"Looks smaller than I remember," Dale said, as his eyes moved over the ranch house. He looked at the alkali flats to the north. "Hard country," he commented. He glanced at Big Mesa. "And to think your folks had a fortune hidden up there, just waiting to be found."

"Luck of the Irish," Kerney said.

"Why did you want to come back?"

"I forgot something." He left Dale holding the reins to the horses and went inside. When he came out he was holding the horseshoe from his first pony that he had nailed over his bedroom door when he was eight years old.

"How are you feeling, Sergeant?" Sara Brannon asked. She was in Eddie Tapia's new quarters on the base. His promotion, along with some string-pulling on Sara's part, qualified the Tapia family for a single-family dwelling.

The house, a typical military box arrangement, had been transformed by Eddie's wife, Isabel, into a warm, comfortable home. Handmade curtains covered the windows and houseplants filled the living room with splashes of color.

"I don't know how to thank you for all this," Eddie replied with a grin.

"The plants are lovely," Sara commented. "It looks very nice."

"Isabel keeps bringing stuff home from the nursery. She wants me to dig flower beds for her in the backyard as soon as I can use my hands again."

Sara nodded. The fingers on Eddie's hands were

braced with splints, held in place by rubber bands attached to metal braces around his wrists. Pins were inserted in each broken knuckle to immobilize the joints. The appliances looked like weird pincers.

"Don't rush it," Sara cautioned.

Eddie grimaced. "I don't have any choice."

"Isabel tells me you're getting cranky."

Eddie nodded. "Yeah, I guess I am. Sitting around the house is getting old. I asked for a desk job—anything—but the doctor won't even talk to me about light duty."

"I've got a detail for you. We've been ordered to appear before the commanding general at fourteen hundred hours, in uniform."

Eddie immediately became worried. "What's up, Captain?"

Sara shrugged. "I haven't the faintest idea."

Eddie looked chagrined. "I can't dress myself, ma'am, and Isabel went to town with the baby. She won't be back in time to help me."

"I have an MP standing by to assist you," Sara said, looking at her wristwatch.

"Ma'am?" Eddie ventured.

"What is it, Sergeant?"

"Have you heard from Lieutenant Kerney?"

"No, I haven't," Sara said flatly. "Let's get you ready to see the general. We don't have much time."

Sara left Eddie with the MP and drove to the headquarters building. Tom Curry was waiting with Isabel and the baby. Both mother and child were dressed in new outfits. Excitement danced in Isabel's eyes. The general's aide, the public information officer, and the post photographer were assembled in the reception room. A few minutes before fourteen hundred hours, Major General William Cunningham Tyson entered the room, greeted his guests, and looked at the two presentation cases arranged precisely in the center of a long conference table. At exactly two o'clock, Sergeant Eduardo Jesus Tapia was ushered into the room, escorted by a spit-and-polish military policeman. The distress on his face vanished when he saw Isabel standing, with tear-filled eyes and a proud smile, next to the commanding general.

"Sergeant Tapia," General Tyson said, "on behalf of the Secretary of the Army, it gives me great pleasure to award you the following decorations for exceptional service and meritorious achievement."

The aide read each citation, and Tyson pinned the medals on Eddie's chest. Eddie stood rigidly at attention, in a state of total disbelief. Captain Brannon smiled. Major Curry smiled. The general smiled. Isabel dabbed her eyes with a handkerchief and smiled.

"Thank you, sir," Eddie said huskily, grinning from ear to ear.

"I'd shake your hand, Sergeant," Tyson replied, "but I don't think that's a good idea. If I had my way, you'd be wearing a Purple Heart along with those decorations."

"I didn't expect this, sir," Eddie replied.

"There's more, son," Tyson said. "If you can stand it, the provost marshal has arranged a small party for you tonight. Several dozen of your closest friends will be at the NCO club."

Tyson motioned to the photographer. "Let's get a

few more pictures over here, Specialist. And make sure you give prints to Mrs. Tapia."

The day after Eddie Tapia's party, Sara met for a briefing with a bird colonel from West Point, a military historian who had been sent to research the Big Mesa treasure. A portly, energetic man in his early fifties, the colonel had commandeered a warehouse inside a secure compound and was working out of a small office in the building. Military police were on twenty-four-hour guard duty to protect the treasure that was being sorted, catalogued, and examined by the colonel's team.

Colonel Alverson sorted through some notes at his desk. "It's really an accumulation of three distinct Apache raids. The documents and the coins, as you know, are from the O.O. Howard expedition to treat with Cochise in the Dragoon Mountains of Arizona in 1872. It was Howard's greatest achievement. He was so eager to return east and publish his story, he left for Washington with a small party, leaving the main detachment to follow. A band of Apaches camped at Canada Alamosa, led by a warrior named Loco, skirmished with the detachment near Orogrande and ran off wagons carrying mail, Howard's war chest, and his personal papers."

The colonel set the note aside. "The Apache had no interest in the white man's money or his writings, and were probably after horses and weapons."

"Then why was everything saved?" Sara asked.

"No reason other than expediency, I would imagine. Apache warriors traveled light and fast. They would raid and store caches of what they didn't need or couldn't carry for future use."

"What about the weapons?" Sara inquired. "Surely they would arm themselves immediately."

"Good point," the colonel replied, picking up another note. "I'll get to that shortly. All the uniforms, saddles, and equipment in the cave were part of a resupply shipment to the forts south of Santa Fe. It left Fort Marcy and traveled down the Camino Real to Fort McRae, where one contingent went south and another went east, heading for Fort Stanton. The convoy heading to Fort Stanton was ambushed by an Apache leader named Victorio in a pitched battle that lasted all day. Victorio mauled the troopers badly and escaped with six wagons. The lading records show that one wagon carried weapons. Victorio obviously put the guns to use—none of the makes or models from that shipment match the weapons found in the cave.

"Now, as for the weapons that were in the cave," Alverson continued, "in the 1870s, the Army convened a board of officers to study and make recommendations for new armaments to replace the Civil War weapons still in use in the field. Like any good bureacrats, the board tried to save money by having manufacturers modify existing weapons. They ordered changes in the caliber, rifling, hammer design, cartridge specifications, and the like.

"The pistols and rifles in the cave were sent west for field trials as part of a testing program. One of Victorio's lieutenants in the Warm Springs tribe was a warrior named Nana. In fact, Loco, Victorio, and Nana were all part of the same band. Nana had an uncanny ability to find ammunition trains. The Apaches believed that the ammunition spoke to him. Nana intercepted the experimental weapons, but didn't get the ammunition. Without the bullets the guns were useless. I can only assume that Victorio stored the weapons with the hope Nana would supply the bullets at a later date. It never happened, and when Victorio and his band were wiped out in Mexico in 1880, the cache passed from living memory."

Colonel Alverson looked out the open door of the office at the racks and tables in the warehouse that were filled with so many wonderful treasures. "It's almost priceless," he said, his eyes sparkling. "And you, Captain, deserve more than praise for your efforts."

After leaving the colonel, Sara rode in a small caravan to Juárez accompanied by a State Department official and a Mexican consul general. Two MPs and Carlos followed behind, with Carlos sporting new false teeth and a rebuilt nose, courtesy of the Medical Services Corps. He would be part of an exchange with DeLeon. The Army would get back the 9th Cavalry letters that had been given to DeLeon to authenticate the cache, and DeLeon would get Carlos, two hundred thousand dollars' worth of diamonds, and a valuable cavalry officer's sword and scabbard that Colonel Alverson had been reluctant to give up. A Fort Knox officer with an MP escort carried the ransom in a third vehicle.

On the drive, Sara listened briefly to the tedious conversation of the two bureaucrats as they talked about the delicate negotiations leading up to the exchange. It made DeLeon sound like an upstanding citizen and not the scumbag he really was. Sara tuned them out.

In Juárez, the convoy was joined by a motorized

contingent of Juárez police, who cleared traffic along busy streets and hurried them into the empty Juárez bullring. Sara got her first look at Enrique DeLeon. He stood between two high-ranking Mexican army officers next to a black limousine. He was chatting casually to the men, with an animated, pleased expression on his face.

Sara got out of the car with the diplomats and watched the exchange. DeLeon seemed uninterested when Carlos walked toward him with the Fort Knox officer. He accepted the package of diamonds from the officer, passed them wordlessly to Carlos, and jerked his head in the direction of the limousine. Carlos scrambled inside. Then DeLeon took the sword and scabbard from the officer, unsheathed the blade, inspected it, and smiled at Sara before passing it to one of the Mexican officers.

DeLeon's arrogance made Sara steaming mad. She thought of a perfect place to put DeLeon's new sword. Failing that, she would lock him up and throw away the key.

As the chargé d'affaires and consul general started to reenter the limousine, Sara broke away and walked briskly to DeLeon. The man from the State Department tried to call her back. The two Mexican army officers closed ranks next to DeLeon.

"I'd like a word with you," Sara said.

Enrique DeLeon smiled. It reminded Sara of Jim Meehan.

"Of course," DeLeon replied.

"Alone," Sara snapped.

DeLeon nodded and disengaged himself from the officers.

Sara led him a few yards away.

"What is it, Captain?" Enrique asked.

Sara looked him coldly in the eyes. "If any harm comes to Eddie Tapia or Kevin Kerney, I'll see you dead."

"Aren't you being a bit melodramatic?" DeLeon suggested. His eyes were hard, estimating her.

"No, DeLeon, I'm not. I know how you operate. Interpol supplied me with a wealth of information about you."

"Pure speculation," DeLeon retorted, raising his hands in a gesture of repudiation. "Unfounded falsehoods."

"You've been warned," Sara said, cutting him off. "If anything happens to Kevin Kerney or Eddie Tapia, I will kill you myself."

He laughed condescendingly, and she waited calmly, eyes locked on his, until the laugh died out. Then she turned on her heel and walked away.

On the ride back to the base, Sara thought about Kerney. He had been a fixture in her mind since the night at the hacienda. She had a premonition that he was thinking about her, in spite of the fact that he'd made no attempt to contact her. Maybe it was time to test the hypothesis and find out if what she felt about him was true, or only wishful thinking. She'd do it right after Tom Curry's retirement party.

Having money was convenient, if you wanted to get things done quickly. Quinn's affluence proved that beyond a shadow of a doubt. He was already moved out, lock, stock, and barrel. The household goods and furniture were in storage, and Quinn was in Heidelberg, Germany, preparing to start a two-year appointment as a professor of psychiatry at a medical school. House hunting and touring the German countryside on the weekends, he sent notes to Kerney with instructions on what needed doing at the ranch.

After leaving Dale at the Rocking J, Kerney kept his promise to visit Erma Fergurson. It was time well spent, and he ended the visit feeling that some of the bad memories of his family's hardships, losses, and tragedies had been smoothed out.

So much for the past, Kerney thought, wondering about the future. He still had no idea where he was going, and only Dale Jennings knew he was leaving Santa Fe.

For the last week, Kerney had played tour guide to cowboy-clad real estate salesmen, trailing rich Californians looking for the perfect Santa Fe hideaway. One salesman, who wore a Stetson and talked in a thick eastern accent, brought out a Hollywood couple five days in a row. They just loved the place. It was so rustic and western. An offer was in the hopper.

His arrangement with Quinn to stay on as caretaker expired that very afternoon. It was none too soon, according to Kerney's way of thinking. He was packed and ready to go. His furniture would stay behind. None of it was worth hauling around. Except for some changes of clothes, everything else was boxed, in the truck and covered with a tarp.

He sat on the front step of the cabin and looked out over the Galisteo Basin. He would miss the valley. Wherever he landed, Kerney decided he would need to be in a place just as beautiful. Doing what, God only knew.

A trail of dust blew off the ranch road, signaling

the arrival of the listing agent coming to get the keys. But it wasn't the vehicle Kerney was expecting. He stood up and waited on the porch step until the Jeep Cherokee stopped and the driver got out.

"Hello, Captain Brannon," he said, pleasure in his voice, as Sara walked toward him. She wore boots, jeans, and a tank top.

"It's Major Brannon," she corrected, smiling at him with her green eyes.

"Congratulations," Kerney replied.

"Don't be so quick with the applause," Sara replied. "The promotion came with a two-year assignment in Korea."

"You'll do just fine," Kerney predicted.

"If I don't freeze my butt off when I get there," Sara agreed, studying him for any evidence of a more personal reaction. "You look well," she added.

"I'm doing okay," Kerney admitted. "How is Eddie?"

"He's coming along. The doctors took the pins out of his fingers. He's started physical therapy."

"That's good to hear," he answered. There was a brief silence.

"I got to meet Enrique DeLeon," Sara declared. Clearly, the conversation wasn't going anywhere.

"Did you give him my regards?" he inquired.

"As a matter of fact, I did."

Kerney felt clumsy. He was killing the conversation deader than a doornail. "I looked for you at Sammy's funeral. I thought you might be there."

Sara took one step toward him and stopped. "I wanted to go, but I couldn't get away." She waited for more. He just stared at her.

"Passing through Santa Fe?" Kerney asked awkwardly, looking at her vehicle. The back of the four-by-four was filled with gear.

Sara shook her head. "I came to see you."

"Really?" Surprise made Kerney's voice sound thin. He concealed it by clearing his throat.

Sara took her time before replying. She decided to trust the instinct that had brought her to Santa Fe. "I am not a one-night stand, Kerney," she said.

The corners of his eyes crinkled into a smile. "I'm not either."

She laughed and tossed her head. "So why didn't you call?"

He shook his head. "I guess I was too much of a coward to find out how you really felt."

"I've been feeling rejected."

"Don't do that."

"I have another option to suggest."

"Which is?"

"A one-time offer. You've never been to Montana, have you?"

"No. Never." A smile broke across his face.

"I make a pretty good tour guide."

"I could use a vacation."

"There are certain conditions attached to this offer," Sara said, taking his hand and walking him toward the cabin.

"What are they?"

"I'll show you."

In the bedroom, astride Kerney, Sara arched her back and smiled down at him.

"How did you know I was leaving Santa Fe?" he asked.

"Dale told me."

"You saw Dale?"

"Yes." Sara moved her hips. "Stop talking. I'm not finished with you."

"Do I get to meet your parents?"

"You may not get any further than this."

Visit
❖ **Pocket Books** ❖
online at

www.SimonSays.com

Keep up on the latest new
releases from your favorite
authors, as well as author
appearances, news, chats,
special offers and more.

SPECIAL PREVIEW

MEXICAN HAT

Michael McGarrity

**Available in Paperback
from Pocket Books**

**The following is a preview of
Mexican Hat. . . .**

1

A thick cloud broke and rolled toward the distant hogback. Sunlight pierced the narrow canyon, casting long shadows and soft morning colors into the ravine. Pale green cotton-woods, shimmering in a gentle breeze, bordered a dry, rocky streambed. Driving into the sun, Kevin Kerney dropped the visor to block the glare, slowed the truck, and grunted in frustration. He was lost. In front of him juniper and piñon trees climbed steep slopes to a ridgeline that slashed abruptly above the canyon and pointed directly at a serrated peak. From the lay of the land and the piss-poor condition of the forest road, it was unlikely the route would take him to the Slash Z summer pasture.

He stopped and consulted the quadrangle map. Three private ranches straddled Dry Creek Canyon, deep in the foothills of the Gila Wilderness. He'd passed the first two at the wide mouth of the canyon where rangeland and cactus flats spread to the breaks and dipped down to the San Francisco River. Kerney was a good mile beyond where the third ranch should be.

He glanced at the radio and rejected calling the Glenwood ranger station to ask for directions. He might be new to the job and a seasonal employee to boot, but he was capable of getting oriented without any help. He backed the truck down the road to the cutoff, got out, and found a Forest Service sign that had been ripped off a post and tossed in some underbrush. The spur he'd taken was closed to vehicles. That solved the problem. Kerney backed farther down to the fork and rattled over an equally primitive route that traveled away from the hogback.

After a steep rocky climb, the road leveled as he entered a thick stand of old-growth ponderosa pines that peppered the north face of the mountain. Deep shade made it feel like dawn instead of full morning. He topped out at the crest and stopped the truck, letting the engine idle. A saucer-shaped park, sprinkled with oak and pine, stretched for several miles in three directions. Smack in the center a cabin sat in a small grove of pine trees. A windmill and stock tank were nearby. A barbed-wire fence encircled the cabin to keep away the grazing cattle that moved slowly through the tufts of long grass.

Kerney took in the view, his thoughts turning over the ways he could restore the abandoned homestead and revive it into a year-round cattle operation. There was a perfect cove at the far end of the field where a house, horse barn, and feed shed could be sheltered. The old cabin could easily be converted into a repair shop, to be used when winter came and all the things that needed fixing could be attended to when the weather made outside work impossible. The road to the cabin was in sorry shape and needed to be graded and packed with base course so it could be used year-round. New fences would have to be thrown up to segregate the land into pastures to prevent overgrazing, and a new corral and loading chute were necessary, but all in all, one man could handle it, if he was willing to work sixteen-hour days and forgo time off for a couple of years. With federal grazing rights, he could run several hundred head of cattle and maybe make a small profit, once the operation was up and running.

Kerney shook off the daydream. It was foolish to think that he could ever raise enough cash to buy such prime land,

and the owner would be an idiot to sell. He would have to settle for a lot less when the time came to put his money down and get back to the business of ranching. He popped the clutch and drove over the rutted tracks that led to the cabin.

From horseback on the ridge, Phil Cox watched the lime-green Forest Service pickup as it traveled across the field, bouncing in the deep furrows of the ranch road. The driver slowed several times to keep from spooking the cattle that wandered into his path. That was enough to tell Phil that Charlie Perry wasn't driving. Whenever possible, Charlie used his horn with perverse pleasure to run a few pounds off Phil's beef. Charlie believed cattle grazing was destroying the national forest. He wanted the Gila pristine and pure from boundary to boundary; no cattle, no private land, and no ranchers to mess up the wilderness.

Phil didn't recognize the man who parked next to his horse trailer and limped to the cabin fence. After a dozen or so steps his gait smoothed out a bit. Phil hollered, got the ranger's attention, and nudged his horse down the trail, leading a saddled gelding. He wondered who in the hell the Glenwood station had sent to meet him. The ranger waved a greeting as Phil approached.

Phil dismounted, hitched the horses to the back of the trailer, and walked to the ranger. "I don't believe we've met. I'm Phil Cox."

"Kevin Kerney," the man replied, grasping Cox's hand. "You're a hell of a way off the beaten path."

Phil nodded. "True enough. The Forest Service would love to buy me out and retire my grazing rights." He judged Kerney to be in his early forties. His features were strong and his skin was weathered, with fine lines at the corner of deep blue eyes. "I won't do it."

"Neither would I," Kerney replied, as he looked around. With no evidence of a holding pen or a loading chute in the shallow valley, there was only one way to get the cattle in and out. "Do you move your stock on the hoof?" he asked.

Phil smiled. Maybe the ranger wasn't a complete idiot. "That's right. I use the Triple H pens down on the flats for loading. It takes a couple of days to herd them out, but it's fenced most of the way, so we don't have to chase a lot of strays."

"About two hundred head?" Kerney guessed. Phil Cox, a slender man with bushy eyebrows and light brown hair, matched Kerney's six-one frame, minus about ten pounds. His eyes were slate-gray and he had a dimple in his square chin. He was in his late thirties, but his voice sounded younger.

"Give or take a few, with the new calves," Cox agreed. "I could run more on land higher up, if I had a mind to, but when the Forest Service raised the grazing fees, I cut back. I was expecting Charlie Perry to show up."

"He's supervising a prescribed burn in the Blue Range, so you're stuck with me."

"New to the district?" Cox asked.

Kerney nodded. "They sent me down from the Luna station to fill in until Charlie gets back."

"I thought I knew all the Luna rangers."

"I'm temporary help."

Phil nodded to encourage more of an explanation. With the cutbacks in funding, hiring seasonal help was now standard operating procedure for the Forest Service, but commissioned rangers were usually career employees.

Kerney didn't volunteer any additional information. "What can I do for you, Mr. Cox?" he asked instead.

"I'm not sure you can do anything at all," Phil replied. "I found a bear carcass I thought Charlie Perry would like to take a look at."

"Poachers?" Kerney asked.

"Maybe," Phil allowed.

Kerney nodded. He limped to his truck, opened the door, took out a small day pack and a hand-held radio, and returned to where Phil waited. "Let's go take a look."

Phil Cox gestured at the gelding as he swung into the saddle. "We have to ride in. Climb aboard."

He watched Kerney lengthen the stirrup straps, tie down the day pack, and eye the size of the saddle before swinging himself onto the gelding. "Who's riding with you?" he asked with a slight smile.

Cox smiled back. "PJ, my oldest son. He's thirteen. I've got him posted at the carcass to keep the coyotes away."

Kerney adjusted his rump in the undersized saddle. Riding with a saddle that didn't fit jarred the back and jolted the tailbone. "How far do we have to go?" he asked.

Phil looked a bit sheepish. If Charlie had been sitting on the gelding he never would have known why his tailbone was sore at the end of the ride. Charlie preferred helicopters to horses.

"Not far," Phil replied.

Kerney nodded. "That's good."

Phil took the lead across the grasslands. There was something familiar about Kerney that he couldn't pin down. He was left with the feeling that he knew the man.

PJ Cox had his father's eyes and the same dimple on his chin. He cradled a varmint rifle in his arms. Lean and deeply tanned, the boy wore a battered cowboy hat pulled down tight on his head. Phil introduced Kerney, and PJ stuck out his hand.

"Glad to meet you, sir," he said politely.

"Same here," Kerney replied, shaking PJ's hand. "Thanks for looking after things while your dad went to fetch me."

PJ glanced up at Kerney, pleased with the expression of gratitude. "No problem," he said.

The carcass was twenty feet away. Kerney took a long look at it. "When do you think the bear was killed?" he asked PJ.

"Yesterday," PJ answered promptly. "It hasn't even started to smell bad yet."

Kerney nodded in agreement. "Did you take a close look at it?"

"No, sir." PJ glanced at his father. "My dad said to leave it just the way we found it."

"That was good advice," Kerney replied with a smile.

He gathered up some twigs and walked an ever-tightening circle around the bear, staking each track and sign that he saw. He could feel Phil and PJ watching him as he worked. Ten feet from the body he found the discarded, eviscerated bowels of the animal. Close by were tracks of bear cub prints and the imprint of a boot heel in soft sand. He finished the circle, returned to the horses, got two cameras from the day pack, and started taking pictures. Phil Cox and PJ remained quiet as he shot Polaroid and thirty-five-millimeter photographs of everything he had staked as evidence. Finished with the perimeter search, he walked to the carcass.

The black bear, a female, had been skinned and beheaded, and all four paws had been cut off. Coyotes had been at her, ripping into the soft underbelly, but the animal had not been fully gutted. The ground, swept clean with the branch of a cedar tree to remove footprints, was stained with the juices and blood from the coyote feeding. Kerney took more pictures, gathered some hair samples, and scraped dried blood out of the cavity into a plastic bag before returning to Phil and PJ, who were perched on a boulder. Both stood up when he walked over.

"What do you think?" Phil asked.

"Trophy hunter," Kerney speculated. "Knew what he was doing, from the looks of it. Took out the bladder and bowel before he started skinning. One clean entry hole through the chest from a high-powered rifle. Minimum damage to the pelt. Have you seen anything like this before?"

"Heard about it," Phil replied. "It happens every now and then. A royal elk or a buck deer with a good set of antlers gets taken, or a cougar or a bear like this. Charlie can tell you more about it."

"What would Charlie tell me?" Kerney prodded.

"That some people pay big money to hang a bear skin on their wall," Phil answered.

"Like who?"

"Nobody I know," Phil replied shortly. "There isn't a rancher in the county who would kill a bear that's mothering cubs unless it was marauding."

"You saw the cubs?"

Phil shook his head. "Just the tracks. That's my boot print you took a picture of."

"How long have you and PJ been up here?"

"We camped down at the old cabin last night and came up before dawn looking for strays. When we found the bear I called for Charlie on my cellular phone."

"Have you lost any stock?"

"Not that I know of," Phil replied. "I wouldn't shoot the damn bear and call the Forest Service to come and fetch it, if that's what you're getting at. That would be pretty stupid."

"That would be stupid," Kerney agreed. "Have you seen anyone in the area?"

Phil answered with a tight shake of his head.

"Did you hear any shooting?"

"No."

"Did you pass anyone on the road when you came in?"

"No." Phil stiffened and his eyes narrowed. "I already told you I didn't shoot the bear."

"I'm not accusing you, Mr. Cox," Kerney replied.

"It sounds that way to me."

"Maybe we should back up and start this conversation over again," Kerney proposed.

Phil gave Kerney a slight shrug of his shoulders. "Hell, I'm sorry I sound so gruff. It's not you. I guess I've got a knee-jerk reaction to anything that smacks of criticism. Nowadays it seems like us ranchers get blamed for everything that goes wrong in the national forest. At least you're not giving me a Charlie Perry lecture about how my cattle are destroying the forest."

"Is Charlie a hard-core environmentalist?" Kerney asked.

"And then some. He's one of those back-east, urban conservationists. A big-city fellah who wants to save us from ourselves. I take it you haven't met him."

"I haven't had the pleasure."

"Well, you're in for a treat," Phil said sourly.

Kerney nodded vaguely, his eyes studying the mesa. From what he could see, the tabletop mesa fell off sharply on all sides. It was a rock-strewn piece of ground, no more than half a mile long and a quarter mile wide, with wide beaches of shale broken by clearings of grass, wildflowers, and clumps of piñon and cedar trees.

"Is the trail the only way in?" he asked.

"Unless you're a mountain goat," Phil answered.

Kerney smiled in agreement, took the hand-held radio from his pack, made contact with the Glenwood office, and gave a brief report. He was told to stand by until relieved.

"Charlie's on his way," Phil predicted.

"You think so?"

"Bet on it."

"While we're waiting for Charlie, would you and PJ like to lend a hand and help me look for the cubs?"

Phil found himself liking the ranger's manner. "Might as well," he replied with a smile.

They searched the mesa in sectors. Phil and PJ were good trackers. The boy found recent claw marks on a piñon tree near a cow path, and Phil found fresh bear scat by a rotten log. They fanned out, working between the trees, and Kerney discovered a shooter's nest behind a cedar tree. In the spongy, needle-covered soil a small blind had been constructed of branches and dirt, just large enough to conceal a prone rifleman. There were tracks of a four-wheel all-terrain vehicle in a sandy hollow off to one side.

PJ called out in an excited voice just as Kerney finished photographing the tire tracks. Kerney jogged to catch up with the boy and his father, who stood looking down into a rock crevice. A bear cub, huddled behind the dead body of a sibling, whimpered as PJ bent over with his hands on his knees for a closer look.

Phil turned to Kerney and said something that was lost in the sound of an arriving helicopter.

"What did you say?" Kerney shouted.

"I said it's a damn shame," Phil Cox shouted, as they walked to where the chopper landed.

The pilot shut down the engine as a man disembarked and ran, head lowered, through the dust cloud kicked up by the rotor wash. He nodded at Phil Cox and turned his attention immediately to Kerney.

"You're Kerney," he snapped. He was a man in his early thirties, with a serious face and sharp brown eyes. Sand-colored hair flapped over his forehead. He wore a yellow firefighter's jumpsuit and hiking boots.

"That's right," Kerney replied.

"Charlie Perry," he said, brushing his hair back into place. A strand fluttered back down his forehead. "I sure hope you haven't fucked everything up."

The helicopter blades slowed to a dull thudding sound. "That would be embarrassing," Kerney replied.

Charlie's eyes narrowed at the sarcasm. "What have you done so far?" he demanded.

"Staked evidence. Took photographs. Did a field search."

"Show me the carcass," Charlie ordered, as he started walking away from Kerney.

Kerney didn't move. After a few steps Perry turned to face him.

"There are two cubs over where PJ is standing," Kerney said, motioning toward the boy. "One is dead. The other one looks sickly."

Charlie walked back to Kerney and gave him a sour look. "Why didn't you call it in, for chrissake?" he demanded. "I would have brought my wildlife manager with me."

"We just found those cubs," Phil interjected. "Get off your high horse, Charlie."

Charlie gave Phil a tight smile and looked at Kerney. "Wait here," he ordered, as he turned on his heel and went to the chopper.

As he talked to the pilot, Phil nodded his head in Charlie's direction. "Now, isn't he a piece of work?"

"I like his warmth," Kerney replied.

Phil chuckled. "He sure puts a man at ease, doesn't he?"

Charlie returned carrying a canvas duffel bag. "I'm sending the chopper back for my wildlife manager after you've shown me what you've done," he said to Kerney. "The pilot will drop you off at your vehicle. I'll take it from here."

Kerney gave Perry a tour, while Charlie fired questions at him, each one more terse than the last, his tone peevish. When Charlie finished grilling him, Kerney turned over the Polaroids, exposed film, and evidence and stepped back to take another look at the man. Perry had close-set eyes and a pinched nose. His fingers were long and nervous. Almost skinny, Perry stood under six feet tall. His shoulders sloped a bit.

Charlie flipped through the Polaroids without comment and stuck them in the breast pocket of his jumpsuit. He looked up at Kerney without any change in expression. "You can take off. Get back on patrol."

Dismissed, Kerney nodded wordlessly, gathered up his gear, and headed for the helicopter.

Phil Cox walked along with him. "It seems to me you did a damn good job out there."

"Thanks. This was my first case where the victim was a bear," Kerney admitted.

"What other kind of cases have you had?"

"The two-legged variety," Kerney said as he climbed into the helicopter. "But that was some time ago."

The pilot cranked up the engine. Phil stuck his head through the open door into the cockpit as Kerney strapped on the seat belt. "I didn't mean to sound so pissed off at you." He finished the apology with a shrug of his shoulders.

"You didn't. Thanks for your help. And thank PJ for me."

"I'll do that. Stop by for a visit when you have the time."

"Be glad to," Kerney answered.

Phil waited for Kerney to ask for directions. "I'm over by Old Horse Springs," he finally added, when Kerney remained silent. "Turn off at the Slash Z sign on the highway."

Kerney smiled. "I know where it is."

There was no answer to Kerney's knock at the door of the Triple H ranch house. A station wagon with an Albuquerque car dealer decal on the tailgate was parked in front of a double garage. He knocked harder and waited. The limbs of an old cottonwood at the back of the house overhung the roof. The home, a contemporary single-story ranch-style, was neat as a pin on the outside. The landscaping, apple trees bordered by a moss rock planting bed filled with flowers, was carefully tended. Against a small hill within hailing distance stood a weathered horse barn with a corral and a loading chute built out of old railroad ties nearby.

Kerney knocked again, got no answer, and gave up. On his way to the truck, he heard a woman's voice calling from the backyard.

"Cody, you get in here right this minute! I mean it, young man!"

He turned the corner of the house in time to see a shirtless, shoeless boy scoot up some steps and fly through the open door of a screened porch into an old stone house set back against a ridgeline. The screen door slammed closed behind him. It must be the original ranch house, Kerney thought. Square and chunky, it had a big stone chimney at one end, a rock foundation, and old-fashioned casement windows.

Kerney knocked at the screen door. The porch floor was stacked with moving boxes in various stages of being emptied. From inside the house he heard two children, a boy and a girl, arguing over who had been given permission to feed a puppy. The animal, a short-haired mongrel no more than twelve weeks old, answered Kerney's knock with a wag of its tail, pushed the screen door open with its nose, sniffed Kerney's boots, and wandered down the steps into the yard.

"Hello," Kerney called out.

The children's chattering stopped, followed by their rapid arrival at the porch door. They were attractive kids with brown hair, fair skin, and bright, inquisitive faces.

The girl, about eight years old, had long braids that she twisted absentmindedly with her finger. She gave Kerney a shy smile. "Hi," she said.

"Hello. Are your parents home?"

"My father doesn't live here."

"Can I speak to your mother?"

"We're very busy right now," the girl replied.

"I won't take much of her time."

"I'll ask her." The girl retreated into the darkness of the front room.

The boy, about five, dressed in cutoff jeans, stood directly in front of Kerney, squinting up at him. He peeled an orange with his fingers, stuffed a wedge into his mouth, and dropped the rind on the floor.

"What kind of policeman are you?" the boy asked as he inspected Kerney's holstered handgun and the badge pinned on his uniform shirt.

"I'm a ranger with the Forest Service."

The boy swallowed the orange slice. "I'd like to be a policeman when I grow up," he said. "Or a rancher like my grandfather."

Kerney hunkered down to get on eye level with the boy. "Which job do you think you'd like best?"

"Ranching," the boy replied. "You get to ride horses and drive trucks. I like driving the tractor best. My grandfather lets me sit on his lap and steer. That's fun."

"I bet it is."

The boy held out his orange. "Want some?"

Kerney pulled off a portion and thanked the boy.

A woman wearing shorts and a peach-colored sleeveless

jersey stepped through a side door that led from the kitchen to the porch. She glanced at Kerney, who rose to greet her, and paused to look into some open boxes. "That's where my saucepan is," she said to herself, taking it out of the carton. "Cody, pick up that orange peel and go help your sister. I see Cody has been feeding you," she said to Kerney as she approached.

"He gave me a piece of his orange," Kerney answered.

Cody gathered up his litter, stuffed it into a pocket, and refused to budge. He wrapped his arm around his mother's leg as soon as she moved into striking range. Her hand dropped gently to his bare shoulder. "Your fingers are sticky," she said.

Cody smiled up at her.

"My parents are in Silver City for the day," the woman said. "Is there something I can do for you?" She didn't wait for an answer. "It's not a forest fire, I hope. That damn helicopter flew over twice this morning."

Kerney shook his head. "No." With creamy skin, cobalt-blue eyes, and black hair that spilled against her shoulders, the woman was very good-looking. The bones of her face, fine and delicate, were set off by a strong mouth that hinted at toughness. Late thirties, Kerney guessed. He looked down at the boy, who still had his arm firmly wrapped around his mother's thigh. Slightly above average height, the lady had long, well-formed legs.

"Somebody killed a black bear on the mesa," Kerney explained. "I'm looking into it. Have you seen any unfamiliar vehicles go by recently? Or any strangers?"

"Why do people do that?" she demanded, stomping her foot. "That makes me so mad." She shook her head in disgust. "Just a minute." She pried Cody's arm from her leg. "Go," she ordered, in an even tone of voice.

Cody didn't move.

"Right now, young man," she added, with the hint of a threat in her voice.

Cody groaned, gave her a dirty look, and shuffled off to the kitchen.

"I've been so busy moving in, I haven't noticed anything except this mess," she answered, gesturing at the boxes.

"Besides, that damn house my parents built blocks my view of the road. I swear I'm going to tear it down after they die. I just hate it. If they want to live in a house like that, they should move to Albuquerque."

"It looks well cared for," Kerney noted, trying to remain neutral.

"My father prides himself on keeping things in perfect order. But the house belongs in a subdivision, as far as I'm concerned."

"It does seem a bit out of place." Kerney took out a business card and wrote his name on the back. "Could you have your father call me?" he asked, handing her the card.

The woman studied the card. "Kevin Kerney," she said, looking over his shoulder. "Bubba, get over here!"

Kerney turned. The puppy was busily digging up a flower bed. It took one short leap, then wheeled and trotted off toward the house the woman hated.

"Cody. Elizabeth. Go get Bubba before he destroys all of Grandmother's flowers."

The children tumbled down the porch steps and started chasing Bubba.

"I named him Bubba because he's so damn stupid," the woman explained.

She looked at the card again, then back at Kerney and caught him staring at her legs. Her eyes measured him directly. He was tall, with square shoulders, brown hair with a hint of gray at the sideburns, and calm blue eyes that looked back at her without flinching. His features, angular and strong, were offset by a mouth that seemed on the verge of a smile.

"I'll give Dad your card."

"Thank you," Kerney said, smiling in earnest now.

She watched him walk down the flagstone path with a limp that threw him slightly off-center. She switched her attention to her children, who had chased Bubba back into the yard and were trying to tackle the puppy as he barked and ran between their legs. She smiled as the chase turned into a game. She tapped the business card against the back of her hand and looked at it once more. Kevin Kerney. She liked the name.

She stuck the card in the frame of the screen door where she wouldn't forget it and went inside. There was an incredible amount of unpacking still left to do.